Of Men and Their Mothers

Also by Mameve Medwed

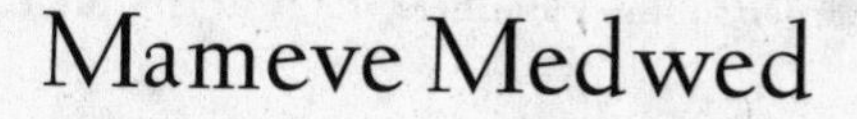

AVON

An Imprint of HarperCollins*Publishers*

A hardcover edition of this book was published in May 2008 by William Morrow.

This book is a work of fiction. The characters, incidents, and dialogue are drawn from the author's imagination and are not to be construed as real. Any resemblance to actual events or persons, living or dead, is entirely coincidental.

HarperCollins books may be purchased for educational, business, or sales promotional use. For information please write: Special Markets Department, HarperCollins Publishers, 10 East 53rd Street, New York, NY 10022.

FIRST AVON PAPERBACK EDITION PUBLISHED 2009.

Interior text designed by Rnea Braunstein

The Library of Congress has catalogued the hardcover edition as follows:
Medwed, Mameve.
Men and their mothers / Mameve Medwed.—1st ed.
p. cm.
ISBN 978-0-06-083121-9
1. Divorced women—Fiction 2. Massachusetts—Fiction 3. Domestic fiction I. Title.
PS3563.E275M46 2008
813'.54—dc22 2007025947

ISBN 978-0-06-083122-6

09 10 11 12 OV/RRD 10 9 8 7 6 5 4 3 2

For two remarkable men,

Daniel and Jono,

from their proud and lucky mother

Of Men
and Their Mothers

ONE

If you look inside my refrigerator, here's what you'll see: one shriveled lemon, one kiwi-banana yogurt a week past its sell-by date, a bottle of Don Cossack vodka, a five-year-old bag of coffee beans from Brazil. If you pull open the freezer compartment, you'll find two All-White Deluxe Pollock's Potpies so old they qualify for archeological excavation, three ice-encrusted Popsicles, and breast milk in a mayonnaise jar, the Hellmann's label still intact.

No, it's not my breast milk. It's Jack's, or, rather, the property of Jack's client at Somerville Legal Services. Jack is my on-the-way-out boyfriend. The milk belongs to Darlene Lattanzio, whose mother-in-law has custody of Baby Anthony Vincent Lattanzio while the courts and the Department of Social Services decide whether Darlene's an unfit parent. Darlene hates her mother-in-law.

I can empathize. Mine was worse, I told her when she telephoned a few months ago about sending Jack to make a deposit in my breast-milk bank.

"No way," she said.

"You'd better believe it," I said.

"Not so," she said.

"Yes, so," I said.

On and on we went like toddlers in the sandbox until I declared a truce. "We'll agree that we *both* have horrible mothers-in-law," I mediated.

Actually, mine is an ex-mother-in-law. Mother of the unlamented ex, Rex Pollock, heir to those freezer-burned Pollock's Potpies still in my fridge. I don't get it, all those women friendly with their former spouses, yakking to them on the telephone, meeting for an old-times'-sake dinner. The previous and current husbands and wives even vacation together, their babies siblinged up with halves and steps. One big happy blended family, all the lumps and odd ingredients filtered through a sieve and smashed smooth.

Not my situation. To take a page from the tree-falling-in-the-forest book—can you count a mother alone in her kitchen as part of a family if you can't see anyone else there? My son is at his father's for his court-mandated summer visit. He's one hour away, though he might as well be on another continent.

I guess I should introduce myself. Maisie, birth certificate Margaret, Grey, formerly Maisie Grey-Pollock. Though I usually reply, "Cambridge," when people ask me where I live, my official residence is actually Somerville, Massachusetts, on Forest Street. Outside my window, I can see the green signpost that announces CAMBRIDGE/SOMERVILLE LINE. Half of my toilet seat and all of my washbasin are in Cambridge; the rest of my apartment is in Somerville. My parking sticker bears the Somerville city seal and I'm registered to vote in the firehouse on Lowell Avenue. When I get up to flush, I sometimes have one foot in each city, a symbol of my divided, sliced-down-the-middle life. This worries me.

I've got a lot to worry about. In due course you'll hear the complete catalog. My immediate focus, however, is the breast milk. It's been there longer than the glaciered Popsicles. At first, Jack swore that Darlene Lattanzio's landlord was supposed to fetch it. He didn't. Next there was talk about a boyfriend showing up with an insulated tote bag. No one rang my bell. This really annoyed me as I waited out the eight A.M. to six P.M. sentence of household imprisonment customarily set by deliverymen. Meanwhile, things went bad between Jack and me, and in the process of deciding whether we were going to survive as a couple, the breast milk got forgotten. I didn't accuse Jack of not giving his pro bono client (his law firm insists on a certain number of hours of public service) the same attention he would have allotted one of his corporate bigwigs. But I certainly thought about it.

Now I wonder how long I can freeze the breast milk. I take out the jar; the milk is the color that the stationer who engraved my wedding invitations called ecru. I wanted to make my own invitations—my own silk screens on handmade 100 percent recycled paper—but Mrs. Pollock, the MIL-in-waiting, wouldn't hear of it. No class, she said, a phrase she repeated almost as often as the words *the* and *it*. Once, from the other side of the room, I heard her stage-whisper to her son, "I must say I have doubts about your fiancée's"—ominous pause—"background. Her taste. And intelligence."

She was wrong. My family—the Greys, my father's Episcopalian side—had the background. Or at least what passes for class among certain near-extinct American dinosaurs—good lineage, good bones, good if shabby antiques, good schools, fish forks and dessert spoons. My mother, the daughter of CCNY college professors descended from Talmudic scholars, provided the intelligence. We just had no money. The life of the mind doesn't fill the pocketbook; trust funds depleted by black-sheep heirs don't pass through the generations to cushion earnest but clueless businessmen like my dad.

But my mother-in-law will require a whole separate section, if not a doctoral dissertation, all her own. For the moment, let's keep to the subject at hand: this jar of milk *in* my hand.

I shake the jar. It's frozen solid. What did I expect? The slurping liquid of a Magic 8 Ball? I suppose Darlene Lattanzio was in love with the father of her baby, too. But when things go sour and the milk of marital kindness curdles (if you will), look where love gets you. The fallout can flatten hearts and minds like a category-five hurricane. Until nothing is left in its wake except the baby, the prize in the Cracker Jack box of a cracking marriage.

I know it's a cliché, but still . . . can there ever be a greater love than that between a mother and her child? All you have to do is sign up for an introductory art history course and study all those Madonnas. The blissful look on the face of the mother. The adoration passing between her and her child, the way she clutches him to her breast. As if she'll never let go.

When your child is a newborn, you can't begin to imagine the letting go. During the first halcyon years of marriage, could you predict that your husband would ever be other than your heart's desire? Cradling your infant, can you conceive of never again cuddling a sweet-smelling soft-cheeked baby? No matter what comes later—overactive sweat glands, a scratchy jaw—the maternal, if not the marital, bond remains. And even though, these days, there seems to be a war zone in the hall between Tommy's room and my own, such a tie is a consolation.

I look at the photo stuck to the refrigerator. Tommy scowls from the back row of his soccer team. How can Darlene not feel about Anthony Vincent the way I feel about Tommy? It's in the blood. It's in the hormones. It's an artifact of the umbilical cord.

I'm not naive. I understand that some crazy rotten people abuse children, neglect them, or worse. But I'm pretty sure Darlene isn't one of them. Did she really leave Anthony Vincent alone to go to a bar? Jack didn't think so. He confided that, contrary to most of his pro bono clients, this particular accused was innocent of the accusation. He swears that the father was at home slumped in front of the TV. His sleep apnea caused him to snore so loudly, one of the neighbors offered to testify as to those thunderous stops and starts. Then the neighbor moved away, with no forwarding address. As a result, it's the baby's father's word against the baby's mother's. And it's the baby's father's mother—the MIL—swooping in and laying a claim on what's not hers.

If you ask me, I know Darlene's innocent the way I knew O.J. was guilty. When you experience such visceral certainty, gloves that don't fit, or snores that rattle walls hardly matter. Only a loving mother would go to the trouble of pumping her breasts and messengering jars of breast milk over to a neutral party's refrigerator.

Now I scrape some ice off the Hellmann's glass and slide the jar into two doubled-up Ziploc bags. I throw away the Popsicles. I dump the Pollock's Potpies in the trash. And even though I need to rid my life of emotionally charged artifacts, I stick the milk back in the freezer. How can I toss it out knowing I might be depriving a child?

It's been sixteen years since I had breast milk. I never needed to pump it or freeze it or refrigerate it. For all those months until Tommy's serious teeth came in, I was an endless on-site, on-the-spot, on-demand fount of nourishment. "I'm here. I'm right here," I used to call to him. "I'm at your beck and call."

"You're not here for me," was Rex's parting salute.

"And I suppose your mother is?"

"I won't even grace that with a reply." Rex opened his car trunk and hoisted into it his suitcase, his box of books, and the basket of dirty underwear his mother was dying to export to her own Tide-and-Clorox-stocked laundry room to wash. *And* iron. Do I dare mention she ironed his BVDs?

These days Tommy's the one who's hardly ever here, either hanging out in the Square with his friends or tethered to his iPod, so inaccessible he might as well be at that boarding school for children from broken homes his grandmother wanted to send him to.

I sigh a few mother-of-a-teenager sighs. There are some things I can't do anything about. And others I can. I find Darlene Lattanzio's telephone number stuck to the refrigerator with a grinning chicken magnet. I dial.

"Yeah? Who is it?" a man answers.

"Mr. . . . Mr. Lattanzio?"

"You jokin' or what?"

"Whom am I speaking to?"

"Not that nutcase of a husband, that's for sure. Lady, I'm not buying anything. What do you want?"

"Are you the . . ." I pause. ". . . the *gentleman* who was supposed to pick up . . ." I pause again. Somehow the words *breast milk* seem too sexually charged to voice to a perfect stranger—and a hostile one at that—over the phone. ". . . a package in Somerville?"

"What the hell do you take me for? The UPS guy? Who is this? Some kind of hoity-toity anchorwoman?"

"Could I speak to Darlene, please?"

"Why?"

"I have a question for her."

"Yeah? Well, get in line. Like where did she put the keys to my car? Like when will she get her ass home? Like why's there nothing in the fucking fridge? Like . . ." He stops. I hear a bottle cap pop off, then the slam of the phone.

Well, it's pretty obvious that Darlene is still making bad choices in men. We've got more in common than we thought: not just lousy mothers-in-law, but boyfriends as iffy as the husbands who preceded them, and nothing in our fucking fridge.

What does it mean that the only nourishing item in my refrigerator is the property—close personal property—of somebody else? What does it mean that I'm only incubating it? I might as well be the holding tank for chickens waiting to be baked into a Pollock's Potpie. Or the rented womb of a surrogate mother. This dilemma is all Jack's fault.

Jack. In spite of our mutually-agreed-to cooling-off period, in spite of our planned meeting two weeks hence to hash things out in the demilitarized war zone of Redbones's bar, I think about breaking our pact and calling him. Jack's been my boyfriend for nearly a year, that is, if an on-the-cusp-of-forty woman can have a "boyfriend." A boyfriend is what Tommy is to those girls who leave the vampirish red marks all over his adorable neck and who instant-message him half the night, keeping him from history papers and algebra. What's Jack to me? You'd need a

Shakespeare to come up with the right term and a Freud to deconstruct the emotional symbols behind the word.

Well, whatever he is, I dial the number of his Boston law firm—the chances that he'll be occupying his cubicle at Somerville Legal Services are slim.

"Maisie," exhales his secretary, Judy Pareti, the second she picks up the phone.

Oh, how I hate caller ID. "Hi, Judy," I answer. I hold off from my once habitual *how's the husband, the kids, seen any good movies lately?* attempt to bond with the (platonic) women in Jack's life. "Is he in?" I ask. "This is a business call," I clarify, as if I'm a client needing an estate plan.

"Haven't heard from you in a while," she says. "Let me check."

I wonder what women she *has* heard from. Perhaps a whole catalog of female names was lining up on the caller ID waiting to be put through to Jack. At least with my ex-husband, there was only his mother and me. Not much of a comfort. Jack, on the other hand, is what one of Tommy's Jessicas or Sophies or Zoes or Chloes or the current (though one hopes equally temporary) September Silva would call a babe magnet. Like Tommy. "I can't help it," my son would say with his bad-boy grin. "Women just fall all over me."

"They're *girls,*" I said. "At your age, they're *girls.*"

"Maisie," Judy says now, "I can put you through. But just for a minute. He's up to his *ears.*"

"Maisie," Jack snaps. "I thought we called a moratorium." He taps a pencil against the receiver, a Morse code whose dots and dashes signal *Don't waste my time.*

"I'm fine, thank you. How are you?"

"Do you have a *legal* problem?" He sighs. "I assume if

there were a problem, I'd hear about it." He hesitates. "Right. I guess I *am* hearing about it. What's up?"

"It's Darlene Lattanzio's breast milk. I want to get rid of it."

"That's why you called me at work?"

"Is that a crime?" I ask. Maybe it is a crime to call an on-the-outs boyfriend at work; a boyfriend who was never that much in; a boyfriend who never met your son; a boyfriend who, during that son's summers away, never placed his running shoes under your bed, stuck his toenail clippers in your bureau drawer; a man who never left an extra set of clean underwear behind.

But he is a man who left his client's breast milk in my refrigerator. Which when you look at it—the way I see it—does connote a kind of intimacy.

"If I remember correctly, your refrigerator was never so full that storing a client's property meant an encroachment on your space," he points out.

"Not my *physical* space." I wait. "But certainly my personal space, my psychic space. Besides, Darlene Lattanzio isn't my client; she's yours." I stop. "And you do have a freezer compartment of your own." A fact that, for some reason, has never before occurred to me.

Nor to Jack either, obviously, since he shuts up. Maybe he feels that storing a client's breast milk in your bachelor flat is like keeping somebody's box of Tampax on your night table. Maybe the utilitarian purpose of breasts threatens a guy for whom milky mounds connote only all things erotic. I shake my head. I don't want to get into this.

Neither does Jack. "Look, I'll call Darlene and ask. Maybe the milk's no longer any good—hasn't it been a few weeks?"

"Indeed. *Longer.* Besides, when Tommy comes home from his father's, I'm going to have to fill my fridge with all the healthy food a growing boy needs."

"I understand." In the background, I hear Judy's voice pose a question. "Overnight it," Jack orders. "Actually, Maisie, I'm glad you called."

"You are?"

"Yes, I was meaning to telephone you. In fact, I put a notation in my daily planner for this afternoon."

I could just picture it: *File Supreme Court appeal, Meet with presidential committee, Set up multinational corporation, Sign trust documents for Saudi royalty, Call Maisie.* I am not thrilled. "In spite of our moratorium?"

"This is business. I have an idea. It's about Darlene."

"Oh." I try not to sound too disappointed. "A new batch of breast milk traveling on the Underground Railroad to Somerville?" I ask.

"She needs a job, some stability. But she's not trained for much of anything, though she picks up a little money, off the books, cleaning houses. It's not enough. Plus she'll have to have flexible hours when she gets Anthony Vincent back from Mrs. Lattanzio."

"Are you suggesting I hire her to clean my house?"

"Of course not." Somehow his tone of voice does not imply my apartment is so spick-and-span I don't need extra cleaning help. "I thought you might take her on in your business. Let her work for you at . . . oh, what's it called? . . . yes, Factotum, Inc."

What's it called? The nerve, I fume, Factotum, Inc., being not only part of our pillow talk for almost one solid year but also the topic sentence in the contracts he helped draw up for me.

Oblivious, he goes on. "I think it would be great for both of you if you hire her."

I am too proud to say I can barely scrape by myself, let alone hire a second person; besides, if I were to hire a second person, Darlene Lattanzio would not be the person I'd have in mind. "As you know, my company is a company of one," I lecture.

He reads my mind. "You don't have to *pay* her. That was not my intention. I thought she might work out as an intern. I thought she could learn"—he pauses—"a trade?"

I ignore the question mark on the end of *trade*. "Really?"

"I figured she could start with you."

"You're kidding."

"Come on. You could use some help. Let's face it, your life is a bit of a mess."

"There's nothing wrong with my life that getting rid of Darlene Lattanzio's breast milk won't cure."

"Think about it. It will be good training for her. It'll be a help to you."

"Will it?"

"And you'll be making a contribution to closing the gap between the haves and the have-nots. Look at it as your own pro bono work." In the background a buzzer goes off. Voices rise. Someone calls, *Jack*. "Gotta run," he says.

"I'll think about it," I reply, but he has already hung up the phone.

TWO

About my job.

But, first, let me backtrack to high school.

Though I was a good listener, good at offering advice, good at keeping confidences, good at making and holding on to friends, I was not a good student. My report cards stressed my plays-well-with-others qualities, my sturdiness, my reliability, over my academic promise and intellectual curiosity. When it came to college, I was not a top-twenty candidate. My SATs were merely passable. The only high school extracurricular activities listed on my college applications were the French and Latin clubs where I held no office higher than recording secretary. Prom coordinator, I was warned, didn't qualify. My volunteer work in soup kitchens and nursing homes was neither dramatic nor original. I did not organize food drives for the victims of catastrophes or rock abandoned babies in the corridors of county hospitals. I did not spend my summers in Haiti. I did not dig latrines in Nepal. Instead, I scooped ice cream at Ben & Jerry's.

While I was voted second runner-up to Miss Garland Street Middle School in eighth grade and Miss Congeniality at Lincoln High, I was smart enough not to list these under Honors (however tempted by the unsullied white space of that section). In my northern New England high school, from which most of my classmates went into the army, juvenile detention, early marriages, or shoemaking assembly lines, higher education usually meant the state university.

Nevertheless, I went to Wellesley. I was a legacy. *All* the women in my father's family—my grandmother, aunts and great-aunts, first cousins and cousins many times removed—had rolled their hoops around Lake Waban and along Wellesley's green and pleasant lawns. Back when there was Grey money, a Greek Revival Grey Hall capped the building campaign. There was a Grey reading room in the library, a Grey scholarship for an underprivileged student from a New England mill town, and a targeted Grey progeny fund. How could they not accept Margaret Grey? Hoop rolling coursed through her blood.

I met Rex the summer after my freshman year. I was living in my temporarily roommate-free dorm room on campus, retaking the science-for-poets survey course I had flunked. The rest of the time, I performed my community service for bad scholars by shelving books in the library. I kept myself in coffee and tuna-fish sandwiches by serving pizza in the town pizzeria. I was unhappy. The shouts of happy children attending the ecology day camp on the quad surrounded me. Their labs, unlike mine, were fun. They, unlike me, had playmates. The only semi-grown women scattered about the dormitories that summer were either the grinds doubling up on extra classes to get through in three years or the Olympians in training. I could hear the jocks through my window in the early mornings and summer evenings. *Go Go Go,* they'd yell. *Get that ball, hit that puck, bash that birdie. Yay, Wellesley!*

I wasn't feeling very Yay, Wellesley. My New Hampshire high school boyfriend had married two weeks before, a girl he'd met in the Electrolux training program the day after I'd left for my freshman year. I'd been planning to break up with him anyway at Thanksgiving, but *I* wanted to be the one to give the old heave-ho. My ego was being vacuumed away like so many dust bunnies sucked up by a top-of-the-line Electrolux.

I missed men. I missed those casual male/female friendships, the jabs and jokes and opportunities to flirt. While it may seem inappropriate to blame a monastic women's college existence for my failure to find a boyfriend, and though I was not open to *absolutely* anyone with two arms, two legs, Y chromosomes, and male genitalia, I was an easy mark. Rex was sitting by himself in the corner booth of the pizza parlor where I worked. I saw a broad back, a collar hidden by a mass of glossy hair. He turned and there was that profile: pyramided cheekbones, jutting chin, the Roman nose that countered the prettiness in such a way as to transform a conventionally handsome face into something thrilling and sexy. I gaped. He grinned.

By sophomore year I was wearing a one-carat emerald-cut engagement ring from Shreve, Crump & Low. Thus cosseted, I majored in art history, a concentration that, when I went to Wellesley, was rumored to be the easiest. When I confessed to my adviser my embarrassment over ancestral privilege and my undistinguished academic record, she shook her head. Academic glory has little to do with professional success, she declared. Social skills and people smarts can often achieve more than the straight As, she promised. "I have great faith in you, Maisie," she added. Though I didn't believe her, her words comforted me.

Needless to say, I did not graduate with distinction. I was not called up to the podium on Prize Day. Most of my professors couldn't put a name to my unscholarly face. And while I wasn't the one to win the hoop-rolling contest, which meant being the first either to marry or to make CEO, I was still the first to marry. Then, before I could contemplate a career and fill out a W-2 form, I had Tommy.

I did not go to my tenth reunion, which coincided with both my tenth wedding anniversary *and* the day my divorce papers were signed. I wouldn't have attended even if those two life-shattering, *me*-shattering events hadn't occurred. What did I have to show for my ten-year distance from my elite women's education? Had I made the most of my subsidized eight semesters? With shame I pored over my class notes: the travels, the professions, doctorates, publications, the many little genius prodigies, the philanthropy, the good works, the work. Every month when the alumnae magazine arrived, I wanted to roll that hoop down to the lake and jump right in after it.

But I had a child—not a violin prodigy, not a trilingual genius, not an American Ballet Theater ingénue or a playwright in training or a mathematical whiz or the cute redhead advertising cereal on mainstream television. But a child, nonetheless. And I needed a job.

Art history was out. I could no longer separate the Manet from the Monet on a lecture-room slide. In fact, predivorce, I had applied for a volunteer docent position at the Boston Museum of Fine Arts and wasn't called back. The ex (that is, the ex's mother) paid for Tommy's tuition at his Cambridge day school; for obvious reasons, my argument that public school was good enough for me didn't hold water with his father and paternal grandmother.

The apartment was put in my name; the alimony was generous. But I couldn't sit around all day reading British mysteries to distract myself or watching *Oprah* to get empowered. The ranks of my stay-at-home-mom friends were thinning as, their kids in school, they joined the workforce to fulfill their college dreams.

What was my college dream? Getting through. What was I good at? No one thing in particular. But I was a little bit good at a selective bit of everything. And, perhaps, I figured, I might as well claim the people smarts attributed to a Miss Congeniality.

Thus was born Factotum, Inc.

Rather than explain what I do, why don't I just check through my computer files and give you a sample of my client base. Don't worry. Professional ethics forbid my releasing private information—addresses, e-mails, phone numbers—without official authorization.

In no particular order:

Professor Alistair Livingston (two hours every weekday morning plus emergencies) Emeritus in philosophy at Tufts. As a result of surgery, he has a fused spine.

Needs: I tie his shoes, take books from low shelves, pick up newspapers from the front yard, perform any task that requires bending. I hire carpenters to lay ramps over stairs, install safety bars in the shower. I clip his toenails. (My job is to do what my clients won't or can't do for themselves.)

Note: We talk philosophy. At least *he* talks philosophy. I'm learning about Kant and Kierkegaard.

Subnote: He's a bit of a groper. Fortunately, I can just scoot out of his way, as his lechery is severely limited by his disability.

The Misses Amelia and Emily Elderberry (three hours, four days a week, from three to six P.M.) Two octogenarian spinster sisters who share the family manse. Arthritic and frail, they employ an even older, more arthritic live-in housekeeper.

Needs: grocery shopping, goldfish maintenance, a good listener. Their ancient cat, Ralph Waldo, must be transported to frequent appointments at the vet. Their bureau drawers overflow with embroidered lace handkerchiefs (does anyone use handkerchiefs anymore?), which they expect me to fold and neaten.

Note: Every afternoon at four, they offer me tea. They've stockpiled tins of biscuits from S.S. Pierce, left over from decades ago when the store went out of business. They interrupt each other; they repeat the same stories, usually ones about "Mummy" and "Papa" and which handkerchief they bought when on what world tour.

Professor Seamus O'Toole (five days a month) Renowned James Joyce expert at Harvard. He's married to a young wife, Georgette, who works 24/7. He seems a little scared of her. He has a bad back, which, while not so handicapping as Professor Livingston's fused one, is still limiting.

Needs: I type and enter some of his lectures into the computer, collate material, keep him supplied with Guinness and single malt. I consult with the department secretary to make sure his appointments are up-to-date.

Note: I love his voice, its musical lilt, its dramatic pitch, his astounding vocabulary.

Subnote: Like a lot of academic superstars, though, he can be annoyingly pretentious and self-involved.

Jeremy Marshall (flexible hours, depending on his schedule) A chemist who works in a huge biotech firm near MIT. Since he travels all the time, I haven't even met him. He pins instructions for me on his bulletin board.

Needs: I sort his letters, put out his trash on Sunday nights, water the plants, cancel and restart his papers, stock the refrigerator. I'm there to let in the cleaning service since he doesn't trust them with a key. At the first sign of silverfish, I call the exterminator. Though I keep away from the piles of scientific journals and the shelves of his chemistry texts, they always look pristine.

Note: I can blast his CDs when I'm working in his empty house. And he tells me to help myself to his cache of Smuttynose Old Brown Dog Ale.

Genevieve Rochester (twelve hours a week) Food columnist.

Needs: alphabetizing and cataloging her cookbook library. When that is done—will it ever be done? (she has three rooms jammed to the rafters with helter-skelter books)—I'm going to sort her spatulas, set up her address book on the computer. I'm also helping her to organize her recipe files. Sometimes I take on sous-chef duties, mincing, dicing, peeling, scrubbing.

Note: She's writing a treatise on Victorian ices. I'm the taster. By the way, I hate the curry and the fish ice cream. The cucumber's only so-so. Love the Nesselrode.

Robert Levin (four hours every other day) He's a lawyer suffering from obsessive-compulsive disorder. He saves newspapers; he saves paper bags, plastic bags, Styrofoam food containers, string, jelly jars, rubber bands, toothpicks, matchboxes, *National Geographics*, the *Times* crossword puzzles even though he never pencils in one word. He prints out articles from the computer on odd things—the history of tartan plaids, cricket scores in Pakistan, population charts in India, the names of counties in California, the rivers of Nebraska, champion high school debating teams across the country—and saves those.

Needs: My Sisyphean challenge is to throw stuff away. The more I chuck, the more he adds.

The list goes on, but I'll stop here. My client base expands and changes due to varying needs at any given moment and the lovely word of mouth spread by grateful customers. "What would we do without you, Maisie?" they cry. These people really appreciate me. Unlike certain others. Unlike the exes of times past and those exes yet to be.

Now I re-create my conversation with Jack. I analyze each sentence, his tone of voice. Why does he always sound as if he's doing me a favor? As if his favors are as crucial to Maisie Grey's survival as mother's milk is to Anthony Vincent Lattanzio? Speaking of which—milk, that is . . . How will Darlene Lattanzio fit into my very personalized, very targeted service industry? I suppose I *could* use an extra pair of hands, especially if no money passes hands. In fact, it could be a godsend to have a substitute available when I'm scheduled for a parent-teacher conference or a haircut or a root canal. Or . . . *Or* in case a romantic tryst looms anytime soon. Fat chance! I reach for a pad of paper. Of course, I'll need to set up some standards of admission.

Standards at least as high as those of the Boston Museum of Fine Arts, which didn't return the call of an art-history-major Wellesley graduate when I applied to work for free.

Just so you know—alumnae-note ambitions notwithstanding—Factotum, Inc., suits me just fine. It gets me out of the house. I like my clients. I help others. I keep my own hours. I'm my own boss. I don't have to dress for success. A volunteer opportunity with me and my sole proprietorship would be a feather in Darlene Lattanzio's lactating-mother's/cleaning-woman's cap. Darlene Lattanzio would be lucky to be awarded the privilege to intern for me.

Am I protesting too much? you wonder. Maybe. But what would you do if you had a mother-in-law who sneered at you, who shook her head and clucked, "You call *that* a job!"

THREE

Because every time I think of my mother-in-law I want to take to my bed, I'll try to give you the twenty-four-hour-bug version rather than the lingering chronic illness any mention of her induces in me. At present, my mother-in-law lives in Wellesley—two miles from the campus that awarded me my B.A. Her faux Tudor manor is where my son and his father turn up for Sunday dinner so she can stuff artery-clogging food into her grandchild and wield her bad influence. Tommy's got just enough ADD-induced energy to stay pretty wiry. Still, the last time I left our son at the border crossing between our two cars, his father looked as if he'd put on weight. My fear, among many, is that his mother will turn them into Tweedledee and Tweedledum, replicas of her own zaftig amplitude. Not that I care about the ex's waistline, but I'd like to save Tommy from the trauma of an untimely parental death due to carb and trans-fat overload. I also worry about the contagiousness of her rotten personality and lousy values. Not to mention the possible contamination from her terrible taste. Taste that includes plastic flower arrangements, chandeliers fit for a bordello, white-and-gold "French provincial" furniture made in North Carolina, cellophane left crinkling on oversized lampshades, and white wall-to-wall everywhere, even on the toilet seat.

Maybe you think I'm being petty. I know that white shag carpeting is no indication of a mean spirit. Ordinarily I'd chalk up such decor to a matter of individual preference. But when every single beat of a person's heart emits vibes of ill will to one's fellow man, a son's wife in particular, then I think it's okay to use white shag as a metaphor for the blackness within.

Let's start at the beginning of the saga of the MIL and me, of our forced-upon-each-other relationship. I tried. I promise I tried. I won't even attempt to enumerate the charm I poured on, the flowers I brought, the compliments I squeezed out between my gritted teeth, my wasted perfect manners, my thank-you notes for nothing. How could she not like me? I longed to lay out the evidence: my circle of friends, some who went all the way back to kindergarten; the letters of appreciation—totally unsolicited—sent by grateful babysitting clients and volunteer organizations; my Miss Congeniality award; my plays-well-with-others reports; my high college grades in people smarts and social skills; my nice family—not a mass murderer among them—and the fact that her adored son adored me.

I redoubled my efforts. There had to be good in her, I was sure, I just needed to tap the right vein. She had, after all, given birth to the man I loved. I brought chicken soup—homemade—when she had the flu; and though I ended up in bed for three days, I never confessed the source of those germs. After her pedicurist retired, I offered to varnish her toenails. She refused with such horror you'd have thought my scissors dangled from the murderous hands of Sweeney Todd. Jettisoning all self-respect, I commiserated with her about the psychological difficulties a mother might have in relinquishing her son to another woman; her despair almost brought me to tears until I remembered that the woman she was weeping over was me. The situation was hopeless. Even the most determined Pollyanna would throw in the towel. You'll understand when you study the following list of the earliest indignities:

1. The first time we met, I stuck out my hand; she whipped hers behind her back. "I thought my son would bring home a *pretty* girl," she snarled at me. Not only was this rude, but, if you'll pardon immodesty in the cause of truth, I was more than acceptable looking, proved, as I've previously noted, by my designation as "Miss Garland Street Middle School" second runner-up.
2. When Rex called to announce we were engaged, she hung up the phone. When my mother called to congratulate her, mother to mother, she slammed it down even harder. Later, to his credit, Mr. Pollock telephoned from the drugstore's public booth to wish us both all the best, adding in a whisper to Rex, even though he was blocks from home, "Don't tell your mother I called."
3. She refused to come to the party I threw for Rex's business school graduation. "I know I'll have a bad time," she stated, mouth turned down in her trademark jack-o'-lantern grimace that terrified small children and cowed domestic animals.
4. Even though I was the granddaughter, on my

mother's side, of Talmudic scholars and, as the child of a Jewish mother, officially Jewish, she pronounced me a shiksa, then declared she expected me to keep kosher despite the fact that her own cabinets held complete sets of dishes for lobster and roast pork. What's more, the chunks in her bestselling Pollock's Chunky Potpie were cubes of ham.

5. She complained that I was not only not pretty, but also not rich.

I could go on, a list of grievances that will spread across my kitchen floor and down my front hall like an unfurled super-sized roll of paper towels. I'll spare you. I'll spare my own stomach. Instead, I'll try to offer a semicohesive, selected-highlights account of the wedding and its aftermath.

When she realized her crying and moaning, her threats to disinherit her son, her slanderous attacks on my looks, on my bipartisan religion, on my partisan (Democratic) politics, her intimations of meal-ticket plots and golden-egg digging, and her suspicions of a greedy eye on the Pollock's Potpie prize were no obstacle to a joining of our two, however unequal, houses, she started to worry.

That we were envisioning city hall, crepe-paper streamers, jug wine and lasagna contributed by our friends made her even more frantic. What would everyone think? The neighbors? The employees? The sisters in Florida? The down-on-their-luck envious extenuated family members? The customers? For hours she wailed, sending her husband into the garage to put on earplugs and chainsaw birdhouses. Then, at last, heavy-footed and ham-fisted, she stepped in.

Rex had adored my sample invitation—a silhouette of

the two of us framed in a wreath of entwined hearts. Or at least he had said he loved it. "You came up with that all by yourself?" he'd exclaimed.

"So homemade," Mrs. Pollock dismissed.

What could I do? They were paying for the entire wedding. The venue, the flowers, the canapés, the ecru invitations. The dress that I made myself from a couple of yards of Mexican lace, the dress I hand-embroidered with little forget-me-nots around its scooped neck, was rejected for a hooped Bridezilla fantasy that kept my new groom two feet away when we had our first dance.

"Wedding-wise, it's kind of after the fact, but in the future, can't you stand up for me?" I, emboldened by champagne, asked Rex, who was waltzing me around the garish mini-Versailles, holding me, because of my skirt, at arm's length like a junior high school kid with an embarrassing erection. The band was playing "Blue Skies," though, in retrospect, it should have been "Stormy Weather." I waved a gloved arm toward the chopped-liver pyramids and the ice-sculpture swans and the cake modeled on Tara.

"I've defended you all along, Maisie," he said. "Right from the start I told her that, to me, you were beautiful."

"You did? You told her that?"

"Of course."

"And?"

"And . . . ," he began. He stopped. "Never mind," he said. He pulled me closer. "I'm on your side. Naturally, I'm on your side. But we have to pick our battles, and this means so much to Mother . . ."

I should have figured out before the wedding that you can't pick battles with a battle-ax.

An old boyfriend once told me he always checked out a potential date's mother to see what the daughter would be like at fifty. Why didn't I do the same? Would things have been better if I'd checked out the mother before the fact, before body parts got inserted into the usual places, before toothbrushes claimed space in each other's medicine cabinets? Would Rex turn into his mother when he hit the halfway mark? I should have done the due diligence.

Why did I put up with this absolute dictator, this tsarina, you might ask? The usual—I was in love. Blinded, deafened, crippled by it. No Prince Charles's whatever-love-is waffling for me. I was sure.

And pregnant, though I didn't know it at the time.

What I *did* know about was Oedipal complexes. Intro to Psych was required freshman year. Why didn't I apply what I'd learned in school to how I lived my life? I certainly recognized the only-son syndrome. Three big sisters, older than Rex by a decade and more, all now lived in Florida with husbands forcibly retired from the chicken potpie business because of incompetence. When Mrs. P. perimenopausally produced the male heir, she finally caught up to the carrot that had dangled in front of her through four pregnancies. "A boy earns you a fur coat," her other half had promised. "My mink! My mink!" was rumored to have sailed out among the ecstatic *My son! My daughter!* screams of delight heard along the birthing ward of the Newton-Wellesley Hospital. And true to form, she named her prince regent Rex, the pint-sized king of his domain, the infant dispenser of mink.

Soon enough Rex ascended not just to the Pollock's Potpie throne but also to man-of-the-house, albeit *out* of the house, status when his father died the day after our wedding. Keeled over from a heart attack, this unassuming picture of health boasted of regular checkups and a low-fat/low-carb diet based on the leanest skinless white-meat breasts exclusive to the Heart-Friendly Thin-Is-In pie. Mrs. Pollock should have been the one to keel over—her lousy diet, her negative point of view, plus the shock of the wedding she didn't want, the effort of holding her mouth in a thin downturned line through horahs and toasts, the utter stress of the newly minted daughter-in-law that drunken cousins were hoisting up in a rented gilded ballroom chair.

Slim and fit, Arnie Pollock was fond of buttonholing strangers to declare he sported the same size belt he wore when he was twenty-one. "Touch me here," he commanded the first time we met. Then he placed my palm flat against the concave depression under his lime green golf shirt. "Can you believe it?" he marveled. "And at my age."

In between his morning and evening constitutionals and his supermodel meals, he made a lot of money in the chicken potpie business. He started as a plucker at a wholesale poultry-produce warehouse, a place, in his description, so rank it'd need an Upton Sinclair to do it justice. Penniless, crowded into a Dorchester tenement, practically a character out of Dickens, he counted on the perks of his profession—those yucky chicken necks and gizzards and hearts, the discarded bits and pieces everyone shunned—for basic nourishment. These he brought home to the MIL, who cooked them into one of her keep-to-your-budget pies. Okay. Okay. To give her credit, she was a pretty decent baker. That is, if you didn't care about your cholesterol and your arteries, and if your body-mass index didn't mind the lard she denied using however incontrovertible its major-ingredient evidence. Besides, let's face it, when your daily fare is something Oliver Twist might decline, then a chicken potpie can taste like Michelin five stars. But it was Arnie Pollock whose idea it was to sell the pies on a bridge table set up with a folding chair and a homemade sign in a sawdusted, feather-floored, underutilized corner of the warehouse. And it was Arnie Pollock who parlayed his tenth-grade street-smarts education into becoming the chicken potpie Frank Perdue of the greater Boston area.

Even now, long after his death, you can still find Pollock's Potpie ads on late-night cable. These little dramas star Ina and Arnie Pollock as the Pollock Pie-Perfect Persuaders, a tongue twister from the Peter Pepper school. First you see a long shot of the Pollock commercial kitchen, so spruced up with vases of flowers and platters of fruit, gleaming copper pots, two clucking chicks in a beribboned cage that it could be a *House & Garden* centerfold.

Then some cloying music plays. The camera cuts to Ina and Arnie at a brocade-swathed dinner table, candles lit, plastic hydrangeas hiding their faces from each other. *Ina and Arnie, the Pollock Pie-Perfect Persuaders* unreels along the bottom of the screen, like a CNN news caption. "Here's what we've got cookin'," Ina says. She dips a silver spoon into a piecrust as gold as King Tut. Instead of four and twenty blackbirds, a plume of steam rises, widens, and hovers, mushroom-cloud-like, over the plate. She passes the spoon to Arnie. He tastes. He smacks his lips. The frame freezes. The music gets louder. They both smile the rictus of the dead. "Pollock's perfect chicken potpies," they croak. "Put a Pollock's Potpie in your freezer."

Who are the people who buy this stuff after watching such an ad? I wonder. A horde obviously, consumers throwing their salaries at Pollock's Potpies, the Hearty, the All-White Deluxe, the Heavy Veggie, the Wings à la King (with cheese), the Chunky (with ham). They put

Pollock's Potpies in their freezers and, in the process, stick rings on Mrs. Pollock's fingers and china dogs on her Wellesley mantelpiece. The American dream. The Pollocks had been poor and then became rich, unlike us Greys, who'd been rich generations back and became progressively poorer.

We got the call about Mr. Pollock on our Bermuda honeymoon, just as we were easing into some early morning, post-wedding-night marital sex (though, unbeknownst to Mrs. P., we'd been having steady premarital sex for a good four years and inside my uterus a tadpole Tommy was already developing body parts).

Of course I was sad, of course I felt awful for Rex. Mr. Pollock, in his own cipherish, chicken-obsessed fashion, had been nice to me. Way before I was family, he told his truckers to deliver me assorted potpies every month. I could order an expensive, free-range, top-of-the-line asparagus and artichoke deluxe anytime I wanted. Mr. Pollock always asked after my work and my parents and the state of my health. At the wedding, he handed me an envelope. Inside was a check for ten thousand dollars. "Please don't tell the wife, dear," he begged. "Give me your word." And waited, trembling, until I shook my head collusively.

As soon as that morning call came, I rushed to pick up the extension in the bathroom. I couldn't help detect, between the sobbing and the what-is-to-become-of-me, a hint of relish that our honeymoon was cut short.

Eight months later, little Tommy was born, a bruiser weighing nine and a half pounds who Grand-Ina (the name she picked despite Rex's warnings of phonic similarities to *vagina* and which Tommy shortened to Grina—long *i*—as soon as he could talk) insisted arrived a month premature.

Rex was/is a good son, I'll give him that. But shouldn't the object of one's devotion be worthy of it? It may be a hormonal, evolutionary, instinctive necessity that a mother love her child, but does there have to be the same degree of reciprocity on the part of the child himself? *Mom* isn't a Pavlovian word that should generate an automatic heart-brimming response. "It's awful being an only son," Rex once said to me.

"But think of all that love you don't have to share."

"Love like that can be a burden."

Yet here, despite such acknowledgments, and as a result of one of life's cruelly ironic twists, we ended up with an only son ourselves. Not for lack of trying. And with no mink coat incentive either. We'd had a false sense of confidence; after all, I was so fertile even my diaphragm and Rex's backup condom didn't stop Rex's go-get-'em sperm from making the obstructed journey to my come-hither eggs. How could we not have been convinced we'd be able to produce a sibling for Tommy the moment we wanted to?

We gave up after the fertility drugs and before the IVF. By then, we were barely talking. The nights not designated for perfunctory sex found Rex over at his mother's mowing the lawn, repairing the screens, staying for supper because he was tired of what was now, in the at-home procreation lab, strictly microwave fare. And because, by some fluke, she'd roasted too-big a chicken whose scent, wafting up the pungent Pollock's garlic and rosemary plus seven-secret-spices blend, brought back especially poignant Proust-like memories of Mr. Pollock. Carting Tupperware containers of chicken tetrazzini and noodle-pudding leftovers, he'd skulk back home to watch sports long after I'd gone to bed.

He turned to his mother. I turned to Tommy. And maybe for a while, even with my superior insight and Seven-Sister freshman survey course in psychology, I was depending, Mrs. Pollock style, too much on my child to fill the widening hole in my life. A temporary and aberrant situation, which didn't mean I developed any sympathy or understanding for the MIL. It's one thing to love someone. And believe me, I do realize that certain people's hearts export outsiders into emotional tent cities for foreign refugees. Still, it's another thing to be mean to someone your beloved loves, the mother of your one grandchild within a one-thousand-mile radius. I would never treat Tommy's girlfriends the way my mother-in-law treated me. Putting aside personal preferences, I always smile and offer tea and a chat to September Silva, Tommy's current heartthrob, she of the pierced nose and the black fingernails and the "like" bracketing every other word.

And yet, on insomniac, introspective, darkness-of-the-soul, what-went-wrong nights, I wonder if, deep down, maybe the MIL wasn't totally responsible for our breaking apart. Granted, she was an impediment to two people joined in holy matrimony. Granted, she has a lot to answer for. Perhaps, however, my forsaking-all-others love for Tommy was, to Rex, a discordant echo of his own Oedipal history.

FOUR

I'm at my kitchen table pounding the keys on my laptop. Across the screen stretch the spreadsheets for Factotum, Inc. I'm trying to get my accounts in order, hoping to figure out my bills. In half an hour, Darlene Lattanzio is coming for an interview. "What's the point of an interview," I'd asked Jack, "since I've already agreed? Since it's a done deal?"

"Not for you. For *her.* So she feels like she's gone through regular channels to earn the job. So she doesn't have to think her lawyer is arranging things."

But you *are,* I wanted to point out. I shut my mouth. Looming in nine days and seven hours is Jack's and my meeting to discuss our "relationship." I'm not optimistic. The very act of penciling in a state-of-our-union summit shows that it's something that can be contained in one square of a daily planner—the opposite of the big spilling-out mess of highs and lows, of push and pull, and, especially, of the yearning to spend time together that might constitute your average, more promising romance. What did I expect of a man of forty-five, never married, a classic commitment-phobe? "I'm not interested in marriage," Jack warned me from the start. "My mother has had four husbands. The institution is full of rot."

I didn't want marriage either. After all, men come with mothers. Jack's commitment aversion meant one more mother I didn't have to deal with. For those reasons, our relationship worked. For a while. But maybe I was rationalizing. Maybe it's in the nature of a woman to move closer, and in the nature of a man to move back. Don't ever expect to change your guy, we women remind ourselves while continuing not to follow our own wise advice.

Wasted energy. I've been wrong about men more than I've been right. It's time to concentrate on something I can control. I separate my bills. I type in my list of expenses, including the literary atlas of Ireland I'd picked up from Porter Square Books for Seamus O'Toole and the hours spent carting Ralph Waldo to the vet for the Misses Elderberry. I file the receipts. I add in credits and subtract debits. I adjust the reading glasses I bought at CVS. I chose the vintage harlequin style with rhinestones in the corners rather than the serviceable owl-shaped faux tortoiseshell. But even though the frames don't scream Executive of the Month, I still feel highly professional. Look at me! I want to yell, wearing reading glasses, doing my accounts, the compleat businessperson.

A situation I was neither born to, bred for, nor trained in. Married right out of school, I went from my parents' house to my husband's with no gap year to find myself. Rex, M.B.A. in the making, did all the accounts, paid all the bills, figured out our taxes, even balanced my own scribbled mess of a checkbook. Until I was twenty, my parents provided food and shelter. *Gentlemen and ladies do not discuss money,* they admonished me. Since my doted-on-only-child needs were met, I assumed money was as abundant as the snow outside our porch and the maple syrup on the top shelf of the middle kitchen cabinet.

But even thus protected, *over*protected, I still remember many nights wandering into the kitchen to spy my mother and father at the envelope-stacked table sorting bills into *pay now/pay later* piles, my mother's voice lowered to a whisper so as not to worry the child. She, whose forebears fled pogroms on foot across the steppes with only the clothes *on* their backs, Cossacks *at* their backs, wanted her daughter to have everything the New World could offer its lucky citizens. My father, rich in ancestry, family portraits, and family silver, couldn't accept that the buck had stopped a generation before it could reach his progeny.

My parents kept the facts of their financial life from me. It was only when it came time to apply to college that I learned about the birds and bees of our economic balance sheet. My first choice was the University of Vermont, a three-hour drive from home. My high school had attended a model UN on its campus, which overlooked Lake Champlain. Ferryboats chugged across the lake. Montreal was close enough for a weekend date. Everywhere I looked, boys and girls strolled hand in hand, music poured out of open windows, and parties seemed to erupt all over, even on school nights. What's more, the boys were cute, red cheeked, athletic, plentiful. When one plaid-scarved, fleece-clad Adonis smiled at me, then asked, "Hey, how's it going?" those words, that face, clinched my higher-education plans.

Or so I thought.

"It will have to be Wellesley," my mother said. "You can get the Grey scholarship."

"Not an all-girls' school!" I'd exclaimed. "I may as well

commit social suicide! There goes my whole life!" The perfect brat, I flung myself against the sofa and sobbed.

My parents looked at each other. "Tell her," my mother commanded.

"Must we?" my father asked.

My mother set her mouth in a firm let's-face-the-music line. She dipped her chin. *Your turn*, her gesture said.

"You know, Maisie," my father began, "how we used to explain to you that we *chose* not to have mod cons . . ."

I nodded. I was a fully complicit partner in the Grey-family-values code of ethics. We were too good for dishwashers and dryers and color TV and stereos and thick carpeting and air conditioners and current-model cars. To us such things represented the detritus of a modern and lesser civilization. We were Brahmins. We were Greys. We disdained the useful, the convenient; we held on to our clouded mercury-blackened mirrors, our faucets that separated the water into the scalding and the freezing, our toilets that flushed with chains. We were convinced garbage disposals ate your silverware, a roaring furnace gave you colds, and baths soothed our bodies better than showers.

"Let me set you straight," my father said in the saddest whisper I'd ever bent close to hear. "The truth is, it really wasn't because we *chose* not to have them." He paused. "It was because we couldn't *afford* them."

It was one of those shocking, significant moments. Like finding out your parents had sex, that your leaders could lie, that true love might not last. We didn't have a shower not because we disdained it but because we couldn't afford it. Oh, the irony, I thought once I was old enough to appreciate irony.

Still later—to add irony to irony—came the realization

that, with Rex, I could have afforded every modern convenience beckoning from every aisle of a big-box appliance store. And though Mrs. Pollock was convinced I married Rex to get my greedy hands on power showerheads and convection ovens, I am my parents' child, a woman who never coveted the latest dazzling example of cutting-edge technology let alone an Hermès pocketbook or a mink coat.

Now I check the time in the upper-right-hand corner of my computer screen. Two minutes before my appointment with Darlene Lattanzio. I tuck my papers and receipts back into their neat folders. I turn off the laptop. I fluff a couple of sofa pillows and run a comb through my hair.

At the exact dot of four—extra credit for promptness—my buzzer rings.

Whatever I am expecting Darlene Lattanzio to look like and to act like—a preconceived notion based on the name, the DSS involvement, the loutish boyfriend, the copious yellowing milk, the legal-aid connection, the custody dispute—the woman who rings my bell in one timid buzz, who tiptoes up my three flights of stairs so soundlessly that when she appears on my landing it's as if she alit there like a hummingbird is the opposite of what I had imagined.

Obviously I am guilty of the worst kind of before-the-fact profiling because what do I see? Not a lick of makeup. No gold chains, no sequined tank tops, no door-knocker earrings, no nail extensions with sparkles set into them. No attitude. In fact, she is so colorless, such a mouse, that she practically disappears into the sand-toned walls of my building's communal corridor. She's wearing an oversized beige turtleneck, faded jeans ironed into knife-edge pleats, pristine sneakers that look like they'd traveled through the heaviest cycle of the washing machine. Her beige/brown hair is pulled back into a no-nonsense ponytail. Her eyes are pinned to her feet, or rather, to my in-need-of-a-scouring welcome mat.

"Mrs. Miss . . . ," she mutters to the floor.

"Maisie." I hold out my hand.

She offers hers tentatively. All bird bones and chapped skin. "Maisie?" she repeats, a question mark on the end. She shakes her head. Her fingers inside mine tremble. "I couldn't."

"Well, if we're going to work together"—I smile—"you'll have to find a way."

"I'm not sure . . ."

I give her my sternest schoolmarm look. "*I'm* calling *you* Darlene," I point out. "Please make the effort. *Please?*"

"Maisie," she tries, then covers her mouth as if she's just uttered forbidden syllables.

"With practice, you'll get used to it." Though Darlene looks my age, I know she is a lot younger—a hard life, custody problems, a horrid mother-in-law can furrow the brow and blotch the skin. Not to mention, I stop to consider, how the wrong mother-in-law can turn a Maisie Grey into a Dorian.

Darlene clears her throat. A small fluttering.

"What is the matter with me?" I say. "Leaving you standing here. Come on in."

Keeping two paces behind, Darlene follows me down the hall and into the living room. She pauses in the doorway. Her eyes swivel around my four walls, the sunny bay with the thriving though neglected plants, the cheerful prints, plain but comfortable sofas and chairs, the hand-me-down rugs, the shelves of books. "Nice," she whispers.

I look at it through Darlene's eyes. Two small bedrooms off a long hall. An old-fashioned kitchen at the end. A large sunny living room; one bathroom, its tub holding a curtained-off shower, turquoise and pink tiles from the fifties, a washbasin with a single spigot that mixes hot and cold, and the toilet centered on the Cambridge/Somerville line.

I start to feel guilty. I have a roof. I have food or at least the money to buy it. I have checks coming in for services rendered. I have child support. I have an education to fall back on. I watch Darlene, frozen at my threshold, and feel even guiltier.

"Please sit down," I say. "Can I get you some tea? Coffee?" I try in vain to discern the plump ovals of lactating breasts under her shapeless turtleneck. "Milk?"

Darlene perches on the edge of the sofa as if snakes lie ready to uncoil from its tied-spring upholstery. "No, thank you." She twists her fingers on a nonexistent wedding band. "It's too much trouble."

I jump up. "No trouble at all."

"I wouldn't want to . . ."

"I insist. What would you like?"

"I don't . . ." She considers. "Do you have a Coke?"

"I'm afraid not," I apologize. I'm tempted to defend the benefits of the water flowing through my own Cambridge/Somerville faucets against the detriments of caffeinated cavity-promoting carbonated beverages when I catch myself. I'm not her sponsor in the La Leche League. "I'm trying to keep the fridge full of healthy food for my sixteen-year-old," I explain instead. What I don't tell her is that the only healthy food now in my fridge is her own breast milk.

"I would never give my Anthony Vincent a Coke . . . ,"

she begins. "Even when he's old enough." Tears start to form at the corners of her eyes.

"I'm sure you wouldn't," I soothe, good mothers united.

"Just so you know." She plucks at a thread on her jeans. "No matter what anyone else would say," she adds. Her hands fold into fists.

I think of the ex, of the not-nice man who answered the phone, of the custodial mother-in-law. "Jack told me about the problems you are having with your son." I use my gentlest social worker's voice.

She wipes at her eyes. She unearths a wad of Kleenex from her pocket. She blows her nose.

"How old is Anthony Vincent?"

"Fifteen months, three weeks, five days." She reaches back into her pocket. She pulls out a photograph encased in a pink plastic heart. She hands it over. "See," she says.

I take it. A little boy in a navy suit with slicked-down hair; he has big blue eyes and clutches a miniature baseball bat. "Adorable," I pronounce. "What a darling."

"Isn't he?" For a second Darlene's whole body becomes animated, then, just as fast, it deflates like an unknotted balloon. She blows her nose again.

Now that she's sitting right across from me, I want to ask her what I should do with her breast milk, how long I should keep her abandoned personal property that nobody bothered to collect. I want to ask if she's still pumping her breasts and giving the milk to Jack. *Jack.* I stop. Where *is* he storing those Ziploc'd bags? What *othe*r women are harboring them?

I force my attention back to the woman here in my living room. I have so many questions: Has her mother-in-law managed to get hold of the farmed-out frozen packages?

And who, exactly, is the milkman making that particular delivery? I wonder if Anthony Vincent has been weaned. Can I ask a perfect stranger something quite so intimate?

I return the photograph. I try again. "About those problems with your son . . ."

She dabs at her eyes. The Kleenex has now disintegrated into shreds. "I don't want to . . ." She looks at the photograph. She caresses it. She actually gives it a little kiss, then puts it back in her pocket. "I mean, now's not the time . . . I mean, I'm here about a job . . ."

"I understand."

"He said you would. He said you had trouble with your own son. With your own mother-in-law."

"He said that? He told you that?"

My voice must be unduly harsh because she flinches. "I'm sorry," she whispers. "I didn't mean . . ."

"It's okay. I'm sure neither of us wants to talk about unpleasant things when we've just met."

She nods. She twists her ringless ring finger some more.

I adjust a pillow on my chair. She is now twisting her finger so hard she must be rubbing off skin. I wait.

"Mr. Gordon," she begins at last.

"Yes?" I encourage.

"Mr. Gordon, when I was down at the legal aid, said you wanted to hire someone to help out in your business."

"Not exactly hire. Your lawyer suggested an internship. You do know, don't you, that you wouldn't be paid?"

She shrugs her shoulders, as if not being paid was all anyone in her position would expect. "I suppose . . ."

"Jack thinks it's a great idea. You'd get some experience. It would be something to put on your résumé."

"I don't have a résumé."

"Well, of course you don't. Not yet."

"I've only held these nothing jobs. On account of having Anthony Vincent so young."

"Then this will be a start. This will help you build a résumé." I wince at my own how-are-we-doing-today cheeriness. "You'll need one for any future employment."

"I guess . . ."

"No guesses. I know. For a fact. And the job will certainly count as a plus for any future disputes over your baby, over Anthony Vincent."

She blinks fast. In seconds those tears will start to spill.

I talk even faster. As if my words can dam their inevitable flow. "You'll see. Working for Factotum, Inc., will help you. You'll help me, and together . . . well, we'll help each other." I explain how jointly we can accomplish so much, the satisfactions of a job well done, the benefits of doing for others, the rewards of hard work and contented customers, the opportunities for learning new skills . . .

She leans forward. "Excuse me?" she begins.

I stop. "Yes?"

"If you don't mind me asking . . ."

"Ask away."

"What are the new skills?"

I describe my clients. I recite the list. I itemize the chores required for each customer. I catalog the challenges each person presents.

A half smile forms on her bloodless lips. "It sounds kind of like the job I do now. Cleaning people's houses and stuff."

"Hmmm," I reflect. "Well, I imagine you could look at it like that. But it's so much more." I picture the dry cleaning now in my car. The plant food for Mr. Marshall's African violets. The cookbooks to be dusted and alphabetized. Not that any second-grader wouldn't be able to figure out that

Julia Child belongs at the opposite end of the shelf from Patricia Wells. Are such chores that different from scrubbing a sink?

"Mr. Gordon says you graduated from college. Wellesley College. I've heard the name. I know it's a pretty famous school."

If you want to be stuck in a convent. "I suppose so. It's one of the Seven Sisters."

"Seven sisters?"

"Never mind. Go on."

"My question is . . ." She pauses. For the first time she looks straight at me. "Do you have to go to college to do what you do?"

Of course is poised on my tongue—propaganda promoting a good education as the basis of everything. I hesitate. Try as I might, I don't think I can make any kind of rocket-science case for Factotum, Inc. Have I put my art history to use? My study of the great philosophers? Edith Wharton and Henry James? Meteors and planets? "Not absolutely," I allow. "Not technically."

"I didn't even finish high school," she confides. "Besides, anyone can clean a toilet."

"Factotum, Inc., isn't a cleaning service," I protest. "Let's consider what our goals are here," I add. "You'll take this job, this *internship*, and develop skills, especially interpersonal ones. Also you'll gain business-management expertise. Why, in time, you might even go back to school, set an example for Anthony Vincent." I smile.

Her own smile back now seems a little forced.

I've got her life figured out, all right. While I'm at it, why not give her a new man, another child, let her earn her Ph.D. What the hell, I'll award her a Fulbright. Who knows, after these triumphs on her behalf, perhaps I'll be ready to take on myself.

We make a plan for her to start next week. She looks disappointed when I tell her jeans and sneakers will be more than appropriate. What did she expect? A briefcase, navy blazer, stacked heels, and panty hose? "It's all going to work out just fine," I state with a conviction that's mostly an act.

Which she must sense because she sighs, then says, "I've changed my mind."

I sit up. So much for doing favors for legal aid. For an on-the-way-out boyfriend. So much for helping a fellow mother, a fellow ex-husband-plagued, boyfriend-plagued, mother-in-law-plagued sister in distress. "Really?" I ask.

"If it's not too much trouble, I'd like a glass of water, please."

I look at my watch. It's five o'clock. Maybe it's a little early here on the Cambridge/Somerville line, but somewhere in the world—Australia, China, France—the sun has already passed over the yardarm. "I've got a better idea," I say. "Let's open some wine."

FIVE

I'm getting ready for work. A quick shower, clean underwear, and yesterday's jeans and turtleneck. Dingy sneakers. Silver hoops in my ears. I've got the routine down to seventeen and a half minutes flat. The coffee's made. The whole-wheat toast pops up; I have just enough orange marmalade to coat one slice. I fetch the *Globe* from outside my door along with Chinese food menus and an exhortation to support John Aherne for city councillor. I glance at his sweet, open Irish face, his good-Democrat credentials, his B.A. in English literature and long list of volunteer activities. *A man who'll make a difference* is his slogan.

It's a lovely August day with none of last week's enervating humidity. My hair won't puff up to double its size. I'm meeting Darlene Lattanzio at Seamus O'Toole's house in an hour. Her first day. Her first project. I'm going to be a harsh taskmaster, a demanding employer. That she's not technically my employee is irrelevant. As her mentor, I've got my own volunteer activity here. And I'm going to make a difference.

I pour the coffee. I open the paper. I flip fast through the depressing news about Iraq, the religious right, cronyism in the White House, the disintegration of the rule of law. I turn to the obituaries—what does that say about me: a cusp-of-forty obsession with mortality, trying to comfort myself with a lack of this morning's untimely—that is, my age—deaths?

I look across my room to my humming, grunting refrigerator polka-dotted with snapshots of Tommy as a baby and notes to myself almost as old as the long-lived decedents. Messages reminding me to get items we no longer eat, though the penciled scribbles are so faded you probably can't tell whether I was out of canned peaches or stewed apricots. I'm afraid I haven't written a grocery list for this particular Westinghouse since dinosaurs roamed the earth.

I carry my dishes to the sink. I have my pocketbook slung over my shoulder and my car keys in my hand when the phone rings. I think about letting the machine pick up. But it could be Tommy.

It is Tommy. My heart lifts.

"Hi, Mom," he says. From the bad reception, the static, and the time-lapse syllables I know he's on the cell phone; the one his grandmother got him, the one his grandmother pays the monthly fees for, the cell phone I strongly objected to for spoil-the-child reasons. For social-boundaries reasons. Not that the MIL listened to me.

"Where are you?" I ask.

"At work," he says, stating the obvious.

"And are you having a good time?" I add, stating the stupid.

"Yeah, right. Loading boxes onto trucks. Lugging stuff

out of the freezers. Stacking shelves. Pushing those dollies. What a thrill, Mom."

"I know. A dumb question. Still, a lot of kids would give—"

"Enough, Mom." He stops. He lowers his voice, though I can still hear scorn curl his syllables. "*And* the best part, the most fun about my *job* is all the razzing the warehouse guys give me about being the boss's *son*."

"That was your choice. Your father suggested you work in the office: On billing, wasn't it? Your grandmother, as I recall, wanted you to be the receptionist."

"Yeah. Right. And how would that look? A high school kid—the boss's *son*—with all those suits? And secretaries in hairnets."

"They don't wear hairnets in the office. In the testing kitchens maybe—"

"Lay off, Mom. I picked the warehouse. It's fine. It's cool. Except for the teasing, I'm one of the guys. Why, Ramon offered to share his beer with me today at lunch."

"Tommy . . ."

"And Sean said he'd sell me some drugs real cheap."

"Tommy," I repeat.

"Just kidding." He pauses. I hear shouts in the background. "Easy!" somebody yells. "This way!" another person calls out. Then the rumble and screech of heavy machinery. "Well, I talked to Dad about my so-called six-week visitation in Wellesley."

"Yes?"

"And he said he wouldn't mind if I cut it short here. If I came back to Somerville a little early."

"Great!" I look around at my lonely four walls. At the bed empty of the rendezvous compensation I had hoped for while I had the house to myself. "Terrific. Though I'm a little surprised. I mean, he never before agreed to that. Even that summer when you kept telling him you were bored out of your mind."

"I know. But there were a couple of factors."

"Such as?"

"Mom, I don't want you to get all hot and bothered, all crazy about this . . ."

Which immediately makes me crazy. "Just tell me," I command.

"Dad has a girlfriend."

"He does?" I shake my head. "Your father? A real girlfriend?"

"It's true. I couldn't believe it either. Dad!"

"And has this girlfriend moved in? Is this why you want to come home?"

"Dad would never do that." He laughs. "Never in front of the children. Never in the same house as the children. Maybe never. I mean, can you imagine Dad having sex?"

"Actually . . . ," I begin. Actually, I'm tempted to say, Dad once had sex, very good sex. But I keep my mouth shut.

"Well, I know he had it once."

"Very funny." *How old? How pretty? Race, religion, creed? Job, hair color, education, personality?* I want to ask. Not fair, I decide—if Rex has found a girlfriend, then I deserve a boyfriend. "That's nice," is what I say. Then add, "I'm glad for him." I wait. "Does Grina like her?"

"I don't think she knows yet."

"If I were your father, I'd make sure she never finds out." I stand up. I straighten the legs of my jeans. "So when are you coming home?"

"At the end of the week."

"I'll fill the fridge. I'll dust your old superhero collection."

"Yeah. Right."

I lower my voice. There's something in his. A mother always knows. "Has anything else been going wrong? Is Dad's girlfriend . . . ?"

"She's okay," he says.

"Young?" I ask. I can't help myself.

"I guess. Not my age anyway."

"Pretty?" So much for good intentions.

"Sort of." Then he adds, "Though not as pretty as you."

I allow myself a grin, which gets wiped off my face by his next words. "It's Grina."

I groan. "I'm not surprised. Tell me."

"She's acting weird."

And when hasn't she? I want to point out. "Really? In what way?" I ask.

"In many ways. Number one, she doesn't approve of my friends."

"You mean the other men at the warehouse?"

"Not them. They work for Pollock's; she can hardly object. No, it's—"

"Girls," I supply. That's what it boils down to. It always boils down to girlfriends and boyfriends in the end. And Grina has developed disapproval into a model so advanced and elaborate she deserves the Nobel Prize for the science of being mean to girlfriends.

"Well . . ."

"One girl in particular?" I ask.

A burst of static does not muffle the no-comment, you-got-it sigh.

I persist. "September?" I wait. "She came to visit?" I deduce.

"She caught the subway to the train, the train to the bus. She missed her connection. Then she had to walk the mile and a half to Pollock's. It took over two hours." His voice holds amazement.

Though I'm hardly amazed. Who wouldn't hike through a field of thorns, across a bed of burning coals to get to the side of my first and only born? September. I try not to let my own disappointment show. "She must have been eager to see you."

"Kind of."

"And Grina?"

"You know Grina."

"Did she find out?"

"She stopped by to take me out to lunch. She wanted to surprise me. You remember that horrible Chinese place that Dad likes."

China Sails. Which, in the first year of our marriage, Rex anointed as "our restaurant." "I do indeed. And she met September?"

"Yeah. September was hanging out in the warehouse with me and Ramon. She wasn't interfering with my work."

"I'm sure she wasn't." I pause. "Did Grina invite her to come along to China Sails?" I ask even though I know the answer.

"You must be dreaming. No way."

"I assume she didn't approve."

"You can say that again. Like it wasn't exactly love at first sight." He clears his throat. His voice fades and comes back. "Also . . ." He stops.

"There's more?"

"Hey, kid, how about some help!" I hear in the background. "Hate to interrupt your *cell* phone conversation for plain ol' work," adds somebody else.

"I can't really talk now," Tommy whispers.

"We'll discuss this when you get home," I promise. But he's already hung up.

I look at my watch. I'm late. I dial Darlene on her cell. It's not just spoiled kids who own cell phones, not just heirs to the chicken potpie millions whose grandmothers pay their tuition to fancy private schools and their monthly Cingular fees. "I'm running a few minutes behind," I explain.

"I'm standing in front of his house," she announces, her voice hushed with reverence. "I think I saw someone staring out the window, so I'm hiding behind a tree. He hasn't picked up his papers yet. They're still on the welcome mat."

"Factotum, Inc., is not the CIA. This is no mission impossible. March right up there and ring his bell. Hand him his papers—your first chore. Introduce yourself."

"Without you? I'm way too nervous. I couldn't. My heart is pounding like you wouldn't believe."

"Do it anyway." I pause. "That's an order," I add in the hammy manner of a cartoon boss.

I sit down. I try a few deep-from-the-diaphragm breaths as demonstrated on *Exercises to Manage Your Anxiety in Our Troubled World,* a cable program that plays every Thursday at three A.M. I've had an intermittent love/hate relationship with it. The breathing exercises are good in that I can actually follow them. The rest of the programming belongs to the Veg-O-Matic/Pollock's-Poultry-Persuaders twilight world of budget broadcasts. But still, on tossing-and-turning nights, there's a benefit to managing your anxiety in a troubled world. As opposed to simply zoning out on reruns of *The Brady Bunch*.

I take two more breaths. I'm so relaxed I could fall asleep in this chair. I get up. I grab my pocketbook and keys. Déjà vu all over again. My hand is on the doorknob when my phone rings once more.

An embarrassment of riches. Some nights when Tommy's at Rex's, my apartment is so quiet I welcome the chimes of telemarketers. *Maisie,* they say, and the very word mitigates my loneliness.

I rush back to the phone. I need to register for caller ID. Still, I'm sure it's Tommy, who's been able to seize a private moment to offer up, for my delight, a few more egregious examples of his grandmother's trespasses.

"Maisie!" the voice barks. I hold the receiver a foot from my ear.

"Mrs. Pollock." I start to cough. Her name on my tongue acts like a life-threatening allergy. All at once, my eyes sting; I feel my throat swell up. How far behind lurks the anaphylactic coma? Followed by death?

You'd think that after ten years of marriage, six of divorce, all umbilicalled by my son and her grandson, she'd give me the *call me Ina* version of *call me Ishmael*. You'd think that after bullying her way into the delivery room (more later about *that* nightmare) to witness the crowning of Tommy's head, intimate knowledge of my pudenda might qualify me for communication on a first-name basis.

I suppose I could have addressed her as Ina without the invitation. Who could have objected to my crashing that particular party? But I couldn't bring myself to do it. She was Mrs. Pollock. She was my enemy.

She *is* my enemy.

I cough some more.

"Stop that coughing," she orders. "Are you planning to pass on those germs to my grandson?"

"It's allergies," I excuse.

"Caused, no doubt, by all the dust in that apartment of yours," she growls, a cannibal with a carcass in view. "Maisie," she repeats.

"What do you want, Mrs. Pollock? I'm in a rush. I'm on my way to work."

"You call that job work?"

"I have to go." I jangle my keys for emphasis.

"Hold your horses, young lady."

It does not comfort me that she thinks I'm still young. "I'm already late."

Her voice lowers two octaves. "It's about Tommy."

I sit down. The way to grab an enemy's attention, the way to get to a mother, any mother, is through her kid. Who knows this better than I? *And* the woman on the other end of the line.

She doesn't wait for an answer. She's got me. "I'm worried about him," she says.

"Oh?"

"I found something," she begins.

I am not alarmed. How bad could it be? Bikini underpants? Condoms? Well, I hope condoms. Not that I condone carnal knowledge among sixteen-year-olds. But it's a new world from the innocence of my own teenage years. I'm a realist. And Rex and I have already had our separate but equal safe-sex conversations with our son.

Mrs. Pollock is now trying so hard to control her breath—she pants, then slows to deep, hard gulps—that I suspect she's a fellow insomniac watcher of *Exercises to Manage*

Your Anxiety in Our Troubled World. I toss her a bone. "The girlfriend?" I prompt.

"Oh, her," she dismisses. "Totally inappropriate. So cheap. Obviously from the wrong side of the tracks, the way she dresses, the way she talks."

Though I'm tempted, I do not mention her own wrong-side-of-the-tracks personal history. I wait.

"How can Tommy take up with a girl like that? Why, in Wellesley we have so many lovely, well-behaved young ladies from good families. What is wrong with my grandson that he has such bad taste?" She pauses. "Like his father."

I start to object. Then I let it go. After all, she could mean the current girlfriend, too. Whoops. *Whom she hasn't yet met.*

She continues. "Why didn't you do something? Why didn't you say something to him? Point out how unsuitable this girl is. Why didn't you forbid him to see the little tramp?"

"She's not a little tramp," I defend. "Besides, I learned long ago not to interfere in matters of the heart. I had enough good examples to show me how not to behave."

Any insinuation is lost on her. "You are ignoring your parental responsibility," she complains.

"He does have a father," I point out. "A parent in the full meaning of the word."

"I would *never* bother Rex. He works so hard. He has so much on his plate. A man's job is all-consuming. My Arnie did the office stuff, and I handled everything else. Even in the beginning, I was the cook; he was the brains. I never once troubled him at work. I knew my place."

Yeah, right. The iron-gloved lady of the hearth. The

monster behind the throne. *Don't tell the wife,* Arnie had whispered to me when he handed over our wedding check.

Mrs. Pollock sighs a how-I-miss-my-Arnie sigh, then adds, "That's the way it should be." Implying my marriage fell apart not only because I was unsuitable (code word for not rich) but also because I didn't take on the Ina Pollock role.

I could argue this—I *have* argued this, have trod the same unjust territory—till doomsday, but I no longer have the energy. "What's bothering you?" I ask. "What did you find?"

She gulps a few more times. She hems. She haws. At last, she spits it out. "White powder. In a Baggie. In his backpack."

To my own discredit, I don't ask, what were you doing snooping through his backpack? I don't bring up privacy issues or personal boundaries. I don't even dismiss her comments as troublemaking. Though I don't trust her as far as you could throw a chicken wing, I'm certain that she would never lie about anything less than exemplary about her grandson (except, of course, a potential girlfriend). I take my own deep breaths. "That doesn't mean . . . ," I protest.

But it's a weak response and she knows it. "I wasn't born yesterday. I watch the talk shows. I know all about those movie stars who go to Betty Ford. White powder in a backpack . . ."

"Doesn't necessarily . . ." I repeat. Yet what else could it mean? Right on my desk sits a letter sent home to all parents from the headmaster. ZERO TOLERANCE POLICY ON DRUGS, enlarged, boldfaced, and colored warning-sign red. The two stars of the school, the two most likely to succeed, had just been suspended for dealing drugs behind the library. I picture the Pit in Harvard Square where the pot smokers and worse are rumored to hang out. Didn't Tommy meet September Silva there among the skateboarders and truants and panhandlers?

"It's all that girl's fault," Mrs. Pollock concludes.

"You don't know that," I warn, though I am thinking the same thing. And because I am thinking the same thing, I hate myself.

"Who else could it be?"

"There could be a thousand explanations," I answer. "Some perfectly sensible reasons for that Baggie's presence in Tommy's backpack."

"Name some," she orders.

"Give me a minute," I say.

"Betty Ford," she says.

I ignore this. "So what did you do?" I persevere. "Did you confront him? Did you ask him?"

"Of course not!" She's so indignant I can hear her sense of insult crackle over the phone. "Not outright. But I did ask him if there was something he wanted to tell me. If there was something that was bothering him. He said no."

"See!"

"So I searched the pockets of his clothes. Checked the call list on his cell."

"That's an invasion of privacy."

"Hardly. Not when you think your grandson has fallen into bad company. Not when he may be heading for serious trouble. Not to mention the embarrassment of any kind of public discovery. We, the Pollocks, do have a position to uphold."

"I think you're getting a little ahead of yourself."

"How would you ever understand? *You're* not a Pollock."

And proud of it, I want to snap. "What did you do with the powder?" I ask instead.

"I thought about flushing it down the toilet. But then I just put it back."

"You put it back?"

"Well, I didn't want him to think his beloved Grina would snoop."

"Of course not."

"I know how he feels about me. We have such a warm and close relationship." She sniffles. She blows her nose. A real honk. "Besides, it's *your* responsibility. You're his mother. The only one he has. You need to find out what it is and deal with it."

"And his father? And Rex?"

She clicks her tongue in reproof.

"I shouldn't even have bothered to bring that up."

"Too much on his plate," she says.

"Too much on his plate," I mock.

We wait a beat. And then, together, we sigh. "Oh, God," we chorus, a duet of worried women. For once, for the first time ever, Ina Pollock and I, Maisie Grey, are on the same side.

SIX

I pull up in front of Seamus O'Toole's house. A ramshackle gingerbread sorely in need of paint, it sits on the unfashionable end of Fayerweather Street above Huron Avenue. A spreading chestnut tree right out of Longfellow hugs the curb, just beside the brick walk. As far as I can tell, there's no Darlene Lattanzio lurking behind it. There are no newspapers in their blue (the *Times*) and clear (the *Globe*) plastic wraps piled up on the welcome mat either. I open the back of my station wagon. I pull out the carton of Staples supplies—file folders, printer refills, fax paper. Later, I'll unload the six-pack of Guinness from the University Liquor Store. "Georgette is visiting her mother in South Carolina, and I feel quite abandoned," Professor O'Toole had complained to me. "In fact, my dear, I am in utter despair. I'm counting on you to take up the household slack."

I've been trying not to think of Tommy, of what the MIL had just told me. I drove all the way here taking such deep breaths I almost passed out at the Raymond Park traffic light. There's got to be an explanation, I reassured myself. Tommy, my son, would never take drugs. *That,*

I'm sure of. Then I pictured those two suspended kids, their high SATs, their intact both-parent families, co-chairmen of last year's triumphant fund-raising campaign. Can you ever know anybody? Even your own child?

By the time I got to Huron Avenue, I had made my decision. I was not going to do anything until Tommy came home. Until I could examine the Baggie myself. Until I could look Tommy in the eye and detect a guilty secret behind those clear hazel orbs. I would not tell Rex until I was sure. I would postpone all worries until the end of the week. Instead, I would throw myself into my work in general and the education of Darlene Lattanzio in particular.

Now I ring the bell. I have the key—I have all my clients' keys. But I always ring first. Ever since I walked in on a former client and found him watching the *Today* show dressed in the slingbacks and satin bustier pulled from the wrong side of the his-and-her bedroom closet. "I'm so sorry," I pleaded.

"You should have knocked first," he'd snarled between bared-teeth lipsticked lips.

A few days later I received a termination-of-services notice and two weeks' severance pay. *I trust I can count on your discretion* had been scrawled underneath his cross-dressing signature.

I punch the bell one more time, then fish for the key. Without my discretion, my business would fall apart. Is it a class thing, I wonder, this self-effacing service industry where even the sole proprietors of enterprises such as mine are rendered invisible? We're the faceless minions not worth hiding the stash of porn for or even wiping off the ring around the tub. Who cares if we notice the splayed-open pamphlets for fertility treatments, the vials of Viagra, the notarized subpoenas, the online-dating-service bills, the pathology reports. Perhaps people like Darlene have always been invisible. And I, entering that world temporarily, am temporarily invisible, too.

I walk into the hall. Where is she, anyway? I don't hear the whir of the vacuum that would muffle the bell or the scrape of books and files being moved about. All I do hear is—what?—laughter coming from the direction of Seamus O'Toole's study. No doubt enraptured students—*women* students—listening to stories about Professor O'Toole's drinking contests with Dylan Thomas, his la dolce vita dives into the Trevi Fountain during his fellowship at the American Academy in Rome, and his high jinks in the White Horse Tavern back when Greenwich Village was the center of all things Bohemian. "Hello!" I call out.

"In here," chime Professor O'Toole's robust syllables. He sounds pretty cheerful for someone whose wife's visit to her mother has cast him into utter despair.

I head toward Professor O'Toole's study. I halt at the open door. Surprise, surprise. Instead of the usual bevy of dewy undergraduates, I see only one woman in there. Darlene Lattanzio, sharing a love seat with Professor O'Toole. Well, it *is* early in the morning, I remind myself. The student acolytes may still be in bed. "Sorry I'm late," I apologize.

"Hadn't even noticed," he says. He waves a dismissive hand. Only a millimeter separates his other hand from Darlene Lattanzio's denim thigh.

"Hello, Mrs. Miss . . ." Darlene pauses. "Maisie," she just about manages to get out. She nods at my client. "Seamus has already given me the tour of the house."

Seamus? "Great," I say. "Maybe you can help me unload more stuff from my trunk."

She doesn't move.

I peek closer at the mise-en-scène. On the stack of books that acts as a coffee table lies a tray bearing a chipped teapot, two mismatched mugs, a half-pint of milk in its carton, a sugar bowl with a broken handle. Clutched between Professor O'Toole's knees is a bottle of Bushmill's Irish whiskey. I don't say anything. If I were to pass judgment on any of my clients' peccadilloes, antisocial behavior, or even near-criminal activity, I'd be out of a job.

Professor O'Toole pours a hefty four fingers of whiskey into his mug, then holds it out to Darlene. I clear my throat with a few warning, sun-not-over-the-yardarm rumbles. She ignores me. She is looking at my client; her eyes never leave his face. Her shoulders thrust backward, which causes her formerly shapeless turtleneck to cling to her suddenly remarkable breasts; she is actually smiling; unexpectedly animated, she's like a children's toy that has had its rusted-out batteries replaced. Professor O'Toole swings the bottle in front of her. She shakes her head. Keeping me from having to step in to state Factotum, Inc.'s no-drinking-on-the-job policy.

"I understand," he says.

My eyes move down to her lap. Cradled in her arms lies a Ziploc bag. Could it possibly be?

It is.

"Maybe you'd like to store that in the freezer," Seamus suggests. He nods at me. "My new little friend has been telling me her life story. What a catalog of sorrows." He shakes his leonine head. Toast crumbs scatter from his beard. "There's something darkly Irish about such suffering, almost Joycean." He takes a noisy sip from his spiked mug. "Even though she *is* Italian. Not that sunny Italia doesn't have its own stigmata." He points at her lap. Tucked into the backpack at her feet I can make out a corner of a plastic breast pump. He turns to Darlene. "My dear, give your little package to Maisie. She knows the way around my kitchen."

Darlene gawks at me. She hands me the bag.

I take it. The milk sloshes. It's warm.

"If that's okay . . . ?" She blinks a sequence of rabbity flutters. "I mean, if you don't mind."

I mind. I'm the boss. I don't fetch and carry. At least not without a creative component mixed in with a clear financial incentive. It's not my job to run errands for my brand-new mentoree, I want to protest. But the Factotum, Inc., Board of Grievances consists of only me. I take the bag into the kitchen.

Darlene may have been given the house tour, but she certainly didn't stop to do any organizing. Papers and books teeter on the table along with bowls of congealed foodstuff. A briefcase, a tote bag, a pair of hiking boots, a pile of drugstore paperbacks with seminaked women in full-frontal provocative poses take up the seats of all four chairs. Old newspapers are stacked next to an empty blue recycling bin.

Let's face it—things are usually neater when Georgette is on the premises. Lately she seems to be spending far too much time at her mother's. She must be neglecting her academic duties. Not to mention her husband. A situation, dare I point out, causing more than a little inconvenience to me. If this keeps up, I may have to have a talk with Professor O'Toole about increasing my fees.

I open the refrigerator door. Bottles of vodka and gin stock the shelves, flanked by two nearly empty jars of peanut butter and mayonnaise. Half a head of lettuce seems to have liquefied into algae. An onion is sprouting a stem. A hunk of cheese is cratered with mold. There's a sour smell. I breathe through my mouth. I slam the door shut.

Lord knows how long this milk will stay here. If my own specimen is an example, it could be four thousand years. I pull out the bottom freezer compartment. I can barely slide it open, it's stuffed so full. I tug. The whole compartment stops and starts along its tracks like a broken-down train. What could possibly be making it stick like this?

When I finally wrest it open, I know. But though I know, I can't believe it. There in front of me, there come back to haunt me like a boomerang of my recent past, a symbol of all I want to forget, lie box upon box of Pollock's frozen Chicken Potpies: the All-White Deluxe, the Turkey Trot, the Chicken and Pasta Plus, the Chicken with Petit Pois, the Tamarind Curry Select, the Wings à la King, the Sweet 'n' Sour, the Irish Cabbage Stew, the Drumstick Bangers and Mash, the Ulster Fry. Outside of the family firm, the supermarket chain, the MIL's supplementary basement Sub-Zero, I've never viewed so many in one place. One *unexpected* place. I study the bag of milk in my fist. There's not a single square inch of freezer to stuff it in. Where did such a surfeit come from? What does this bounty mean? A bounty, by the way, that incites thoughts of mutiny.

I smell a rat.

"It's awfully quiet in there," I hear Professor O'Toole comment from the hall. He lumbers into the kitchen, his hand rubbing his bad back. "Maisie," he says, "we were getting alarmed. We were worried," he tee-hees. "We were afraid you fell in."

"So many Pollock's Potpies," I gasp.

"Aren't there indeed?" he exults. He pats his substantial stomach. "Georgette's afraid I'll waste away. She feels the need to stock up for when she's out of town."

"On *these*?"

"She's enormously fond of them. From time to time she consults for the company."

"You're kidding!"

"Not at all. My better half is in demand throughout the food industry. She's in charge of her own lab at Wellesley College. Plus, she has just one class a week to teach, and she draws a full salary. If only Harvard were so generous. She's quite the accomplished biologist."

I think of the limited biology portion of the science-for-poets survey course I flunked at Wellesley College. Class. Species. I forget the rest. But not the pathetic little frog we dissected, the star of my freshman nightmares. His tiny splayed legs. His intestines like a tangle of thread. The advanced students—that is, the smart ones—got to take apart a formaldehyded cat.

"Not that she does anything so prosaic as dissect frogs and cats," Professor O'Toole goes on. "Even with the subspecialty of animal husbandry." He offers a few in-joke hoots. He makes gorilla thumps on his chest. "And I'm not talking about her animal husband."

I supply a polite giggle. "Of course not."

"Her doctoral thesis focused on the subject of poultry. You know, the chicken and the egg." He hoots again. He slaps his knee. He's a barrel of laughs.

A barrel I—client-sensitive—feel obliged to dip into. I force a smile. "Did she solve what came first?"

"Brilliantly. Though I am loath to hazard an explanation of her conclusion. I must confess I never read the thesis. I offered, but she kindly granted me absolution. All that *science*." He wrinkles his nose. "Not quite the medium for one such as I, for one so inadequate as to be solely and utterly and purely steeped in great literature. But feel free to ask her. She'll be thrilled."

"I will. The next time I see her. When she's back from her mother's." I point at the freezer. "And her payment for the consultation consists of"—I hesitate—"a lifetime supply of Pollock's Chicken Potpies?"

"That's just the lagniappe, my dear. That exceptional lass of mine brought home a gorgeous and substantial check. Which will support next summer's sojourn in the Emerald Isle." He pulls up a kitchen chair. He sweeps some heaving-bosom paperbacks to the floor and falls into the chair's splintered seat. He props his feet up on another chair bearing a DVD with the title—I look twice—*The Fuck of the Irish*.

He's wearing his usual argyle socks with sandals. Does he ever change them? His big toe sticks up through an unraveling diamond-shaped hole. I notice his chinos are stained and his shirt needs ironing. It's not only the household that is suffering from Georgette's away-visiting-her-mother neglect.

"I'm quite fond of the Ulster Fry pie. I just pop it in the microwave and in minutes I've got a madeleine of the old sod. Without the traditional black pudding, alas." He grins. "Georgette, southern belle that she is, prefers the all-white-meat deluxe, the one that uses just the breast."

"Speaking of which . . ." I lift up Darlene's milk.

"Your new employee is just a delight. An absolute delight. Untutored, unsophisticated, but I see real potential there." He stops. "If I might toot my own horn, I am renowned for spotting potential in the unlikeliest sources."

I bet. "Let's hope she takes to the *job,*" I say. "But there seems to be no room to store this bag."

"No problem at all, my dear. We will just remove a few pies from the freezer and put them on the counter to defrost for my supper. That, and the Guinness you so kindly arranged to purchase on my behalf . . . well, it'll be a feast beyond imagining." He stops. He jabs a thumb at his forehead. "In fact, maybe you and the delightful Miss Lattanzio—ah, how the tongue wraps around that name—will do me the favor of whisking a few home for your own delectation."

"No!" I exclaim. With more force than I intended, as Professor O'Toole startles. I soften my voice. "I mean, thank you, but I can't use them. Though perhaps Darlene . . ." I stop. "By the time we finish our work, they'll be spoiled," I conclude.

"Well, another occasion, then. I'll make you up a doggie—no, a chicken, chickie—bag." He waits for a laugh.

"Clever," I allow. I start to remove and rearrange the chicken potpies to find space for Darlene's milk. "Besides the Ulster Fry, is there another one in particular you feel like eating tonight?" I ask.

"Surprise me," he challenges.

When I can finally wrench Darlene away from Seamus O'Toole's love seat, his smiling Irish eyes, his musically blarneyed syllables, his passionate interest in the story of her life, not to mention the bulk of her milky breasts, she turns out to be a hard and efficient worker. So good, in fact, that I decide to pay her. Why should she give up her cleaning jobs to fulfill Jack's idea of an internship? How can I ask her to work for me without a fair wage? Having settled this, I feel the enormous relief of an employer who refuses to exploit those in her charge.

We clean up the study, organize files, sort bills, dust, and shelve reference books. I fax a syllabus to the department chair. I write down a list of voice-mail messages, none from Georgette, then clear the tape. Darlene sharpens pencils. She manages to change the toner in Professor O'Toole's printer by following the none-too-simple diagram on the box. I update his calendar. I type his lecture schedule into the computer and print it out. I lay it neatly beside Darlene's sharpened pencils. In our new four-hands-make-less-work mode and despite Tommy's delay-causing telephone call, we are finished with plenty of time to get to the Misses Elderberry.

"Thank you, my dears! Thank you," my satisfied client exclaims. He dances a bowing-and-kowtowing little jig. Seamus O'Toole seems more grateful than he has ever been in the past. Even that Christmas when I'd surprised him with the four cans of Spotted Dick I'd ordered off the Internet. Or that morning when I had to deal with the plugged-up toilet because using a plunger, let alone shoveling raw sewage, was not good for his back. "You're a saint, a real saint, Maisie," he'd said at the time.

"What an angel," he says now. "*Angels,*" he corrects. "Veritable Florence Nightingales!" He walks us to the door. "See you next week," he croons.

"I bet your pies are already thawed," I say.

"I'm salivating in anticipation." He smacks his lips. "Spill the beans. Which one did you choose for me?"

"Drumstick Bangers and Mash."

"Ah. You know me too well." He stops. He grins. "By

Gorry, I've just had the most brilliant idea. Would either of you ladies like to join me for a repast?" He looks at his watch. "Early lunch? Brunch? Elevenses?"

Darlene tilts her head at me, her eyebrows raised into question marks. She's got the eagerness of a puppy sniffing a dog biscuit hidden up her master's sleeve.

But I am the disciplinarian, the one-woman obedience school, the dog whisperer. "Sorry," I say. "Another time. We're expected somewhere else."

"Of course. Hopeless me, you've already mentioned that." The corners of Professor O'Toole's mouth turn down, then, slowly, clownlike, curl up again. "Well, how about later? When you've finished your estimable and very important work? Ulster Fry pie, Drumstick Bangers and Mash are simply splendid accompanied by a nice ruby red Guinness. And somewhere, in the recesses of the larder, I can dig out the loveliest Stilton. I'd be so honored if you'd accept."

Darlene's eyes open wider. *Oh please oh please?* her expression beseeches me.

I shake my head. "Not possible," I say, already planning, once we're in the car, my number two, don't-socialize-with-the-clients lecture reiterating the Factotum, Inc., code of business conduct.

Her face falls.

Her potential host, who has already spotted her potential, notices. He pats her shoulder. "Chin up," he orders. "A rain check," he consoles, "for a real Irish breakfast. Fried eggs, rashers, black pudding, sausages, tomato, mushrooms, soda bread. None of this frozen stuff." He shakes his head. "Not that it isn't delicious." He holds the door open for us. He hands Darlene a green trash bag stashed in the corner of the front hall. He waves good-bye as we walk to the car.

We climb inside. As soon as I turn on the ignition, I start the no-socializing-with-clients sermon.

"He's nice," she states. "And really smart."

"He's not your friend. You work for him. You don't chat, dine, drink, or flirt with him."

"He called me his new friend."

"Well, you're not. Darlene, you have to be careful. You can't always believe people. Particularly—as you well know—you can't trust men."

"But he says he'll teach me stuff," she defends.

I slam on the brake.

She braces her hand on the dashboard.

I stare at her. "What stuff?" I ask.

"Not *that*." She laughs. "Books and things."

"You are not his student. Anything other than Factotum, Inc.'s mandated duties will not be tolerated."

"Whatever." She shrugs. "You're the boss," she adds in the tone of one who understands that no matter how unreasonable, how unfair and biased—sad to say—in this unfair, biased, unreasonable, classist society, she must answer to me.

"As long as you understand," I stipulate. I segue into the no-drinking-on-the-job speech.

She sits up. Her hands fold into fists. "I'd never," she protests. "I'd never ever," she insists.

Maybe I've overdone it. I've certainly learned, with teenagers, anyway, you can't nail the complete list of your complaints to the door the way Martin Luther did. You have to spread them around. And intersperse them with niceties, leaven them with your own we're-all-human flaws. "Don't worry," I soothe. "I wasn't thinking. It's just the sight of the Irish whiskey that triggered the one-size-fits-all speech."

"I'm *always* careful not to drink too much," she scolds, "because of my milk." She folds her arms over her chest.

"Now that you bring it up . . ." I clear my throat. "Do you feel it's entirely appropriate to store your breast milk in the freezers of strangers?"

She turns to me. "Is that considered socializing on the job?"

"Not precisely. But still . . ." I veer onto Huron Avenue. A woman with two toddlers is carrying a stack of pizza boxes out of Armando's. I stop the car and wave them across the street. Oh for the days when we parents worried about nitrites in pepperoni and teeth-rotting sodas. An innocent time compared to white powder in a Baggie unearthed from a grandson's backpack by an interfering, secret-agent mother-in-law.

Darlene Lattanzio's own breast-pump-toting backpack lies at her feet. One sneaker-clad toe pokes at it.

"I know this is none of my business," I begin. I stop. "Actually it *is* my business. Are you planning to pump your breasts—however discreetly—in the houses of all our clients? Those on today's schedule, for instance?"

"If I don't pump regularly, my milk will dry up. It's my one connection with Anthony Vincent. I mean, since I can't see him. If I keep pumping my milk, then I feel like I'm still kind of taking care of him. Though Mr. Gordon says he's going to get me visiting rights." She tugs at her hair. "Once he—we—get all this mess cleared up."

"*That* will be good."

"It'll be *great*. My landlord promised to deliver a batch to, well, where Anthony Vincent's living now. But then the roof got these holes and he was kind of stuck trying to fix it. Then my boyfriend—who's not my boyfriend anymore—I want him to leave, but I need his half of the rent." She pulls a Kleenex out of her pocket and blows her nose. "He promised he'd bring the milk if I did—well, you know . . ." She casts me a meaningful look. Her hand rises to her mouth.

I don't know, but I can guess. "Yes . . . ?" I prompt.

She speaks from behind splayed fingers. "In the bathroom in this bar. Another bar. Not the one . . . the one that caused all the trouble."

"And . . . ?"

"I never left him alone. I would never ever do that. I did go to a bar with my girlfriends that other time. But my husband was right on the couch watching TV."

"You still have a husband?"

"Mr. Gordon's going to help me get the actual divorce once I get my baby back. But I already think of him as my ex even though it's not official yet."

"I see." I pause. "About the bar . . . ?" I press.

"Well, in the other bar, the second bar. Just so's I could get the milk to my Anthony." She stops. "He likes new places. And I did it. Against my will."

"You shouldn't ever do what you don't want. You have a right to refuse."

"I know. Mr. Gordon told me that. But you never met . . ." Her voice trails off.

I remember the man who answered the phone. *Why's there nothing in the fucking fridge*, he'd yelled, then slammed down the receiver. "And?" I coach. "Go on."

Darlene takes a deep breath. "But still, even though I did it—that bathroom was filthy, and there were people pounding on the door the whole time." She shakes her head. "Still, even though I did what he wanted, he didn't deliver the milk." She starts to cry. "Men," she sobs.

"My point exactly."

She sobs harder.

I pull to the side of the road. I slide into a handicapped spot. Right now I feel no guilt. I look at Darlene Lattanzio. Was there ever a person who so clearly screams disability?

"I thought of FedExing it," she weeps. "But do you know how much that costs?"

"An arm and a leg."

"And the witch probably wouldn't sign for it anyways." She leans her head against the side window. The now shredded tissue is useless. In the glove compartment I find a wad of napkins filched from Starbucks. I hand her some. She blows her nose. "And even if the milk got delivered, it doesn't mean it would end up in Anthony Vincent's mouth. *She* is probably feeding him Coke."

I lower my voice to the soothing tone a good therapist might use, not that I can claim firsthand experience, as the marriage counselor Rex and I visited—just once—possessed a nails-on-blackboard voice and an M.S.W. obtained during her third divorce. "How old is Anthony Vincent now?"

"Fifteen, almost sixteen months."

"A fine time to wean him," I advise. I don't add that maybe he already is weaned. And hooked on Coke, though I trust it's the Coca-Cola sort. I don't voice my personal relief at a future in which Anthony Vincent will no longer require his mother's breast. Not to mention letting Jack off that hook, and making room for what must be a tsunami of frozen pies overflowing Professor O'Toole's barely-up-to-the-task refrigerator.

"Don't you think he's still a little too young to switch to a bottle?" she asks.

"Not at all," I say. "In fact, I weaned my son Tommy right before his first birthday. I have a photo of him holding a Mickey Mouse cup and blowing out the candle on his cake."

"And he turned out okay?"

I cross my fingers. "More than okay."

"I'll think about it," she promises. "Though it'll be hard to give up nursing. That closeness."

A closeness that is currently at quite a remove, I refrain from pointing out.

"I'll do anything for my kid," she says.

I nod in sisterhood, we mothers together who would go to any lengths when it comes to our kid. I choose my words. "So if it's all right with you, maybe I can dispose of the milk. And tell Professor O'Toole to do the same? That is, if you're starting to consider weaning him, which, as we've already discussed makes perfect—physical and psychological—sense."

She sits up. "Oh, no!" she exclaims. "Even if I decide to wean him, I'll need the evidence."

"Evidence?"

"That I'm a good mother. That I wanted to breast-feed my child even when he was stolen from me. I'm sure Mr. Gordon would advise me to keep storing the milk. Oh, please please please don't throw my milk away."

"Not if you—"

"Promise. *Promise!*" she begs.

"All right," I pledge. "For the time being," I qualify. "But why don't we—you—wait to hear what Jack—what your lawyer says."

"I guess," she allows. "Okay," she agrees. For a moment,

we both gaze out our separate side windows. I watch a squirrel chase its mate around a telephone pole. Darlene picks up the Starbucks napkins. "Where should I throw these away?" she asks.

"I think there's an old Macy's shopping bag somewhere." I look in the backseat and spot the green trash bag Professor O'Toole handed her. I point. "We can stick the napkins in there. We should have left that in Professor O'Toole's garbage bin."

She shakes her head. "It's Seamus's laundry. I told him I'd darn his socks and iron his shirts."

"You can't be serious!" I exclaim. I picture Darlene scrubbing toilets, pumping milk, losing her child, living with someone she loathes because she needs half the rent, forced to do God knows what in the filthy bathroom of a bar. For whatever reason—class, education, just enough money, resourcefulness, the semiability to stand up to a mother-in-law, to leave a husband, to break up with a boyfriend (sort of), to hold on to a child, or just plain luck—I feel I've escaped that kind of victimhood. "Don't darn his socks. Don't iron his shirts," I order.

"I want to. It's no trouble."

"Is he paying you?"

"I didn't ask for money. It's an honor to do the laundry for a man like that."

"He should pay you, Darlene."

"I couldn't—"

"Well, *I'm* going to pay you."

Incredulous, she stares at me. "You are?"

I nod.

"But Mr. Gordon—"

"Forget Jack. You're doing a great job."

"Really?"

"Yes, really."

"Thank you." She hesitates. "*Maisie,*" she adds.

A car pulls up beside me. A card bearing a wheelchair logo dangles from the rearview mirror. A pink-cheeked, white-haired couple sit in front. The husband's hands grip the steering wheel at a perfect two o'clock. The wife beams at his side. Their seat belts slant across their shoulders, like banners. They're Mr. and Mrs. Santa Claus.

Just leaving, I mouth. I turn on the ignition. I pull away from the curb. Sweet Mrs. Santa Claus rolls down the window, pokes out her sausage arm, and thrusts up her middle finger. *Asshole* forms on her rosy Mrs. Santa Claus lips.

SEVEN

This morning I'm at the kitchen table reading the *New York Times*. It's nearly nine-thirty. I slept late. I pushed the snooze button twice, then ignored it. Last night I wandered the aisles at Whole Foods until eleven P.M. in search of organic, seven-grain, free-range edibles for my returning son. He comes home tomorrow, to a spick-and-span house, a bursting refrigerator, fresh sheets, and an organized closet, his sneakers untangled and paired if not deodorized. Back in the apartment, I scrubbed out the fridge before I filled it. At one A.M., I actually baked two dozen cinnamon buns. The whole apartment shines, smells of cinnamon and cloves, a model home of a model mother. Unlike Darlene, I'm one of the privileged ones, parents left alone to screw up child raising without the intervention of the government.

I swallow the rest of the coffee. I scarf down one of the delicious-if-I-say-so-myself cinnamon buns. If the DSS visited me now, they'd probably sign me up for a foster family. Boy, am I tired. I yawn, glad for a day off. Darlene's at Professor Alistair Livingston's, my client with the fused spine whose shoes she has to tie. "There's hardly enough work here for the two of us," she informed me when I called her cell from bed, prostrate with apologies. "Stay home. I'll handle it."

I feel a little guilty considering her past experience. "He's always trying to pat my butt, but, thank God, he can't bend down far enough," she confessed.

"In some circles, that could be cause for a sexual-harassment complaint. Not that we'd want to lose a client as loyal and as grateful for our services as Professor Livingston. Are you sure you don't mind?"

"Oh, I kind of like it. I'm used to handling guys who cop a feel."

I thought of Seamus O'Toole on his love seat, his fingers inching toward Darlene's thigh. What is it about academics? Is randiness a prerequisite?

"Besides," she continued, "Alistair likes to talk about this guy Kant. Spelled with a *K*," she added. "And when he, Alistair, explains stuff, the way Seamus does, too, educational stuff, it makes me feel real smart. Like you."

"Tell that to my old teachers," I said. *Smart*, I marveled.

Right now I don't feel at all smart. No wonder. Take a look. Am I reading the front page of the *Times*? Am I scouring the Op-Ed? Chastised, I flip fast from What's On the Runway to Science.

A headline and the accompanying illustration catch my eye: A Bacterium That Improves Your Work Habits. The illustration shows a construction worker in a hard hat drinking from a baby bottle, its exaggerated rubber nipple tilted at his mouth. Apparently, when workers take daily doses of a bacterium found in breast milk—*Lactobacillus reuteri*—they are less likely to call in sick and are thus more committed to their work.

Aha! Maybe the natural production of *Lactobacillus*

reuteri explains why Darlene, right now crouched over Professor's Livingston's wingtipped shoes to avoid his wandering fingertips, is the Energizer Bunny. Maybe I was wrong to suggest she wean Anthony Vincent and surrender such a biological boost. She puts me to shame. I see her ironing Professor O'Toole's shirts, starching the collars and cuffs, matching up the sleeves. "Miz Lattanzio never stops," my clients praise. "Your new assistant goes the extra yard," wrote Jeremy Marshall on a note clipped to his last check. Where was this magical substance sixteen years ago when I, exhausted, was nursing Tommy, unable to tap any Darlene Lattanzio source of energy?

Tommy. He'll be here tomorrow. I'm thrilled. I'm scared. I want to feed him, to grouse about his too-loud music, to scold him for wet towels on the bathroom floor, to feel him pat me on the head from his six feet of growing-boy altitude/attitude. I want to listen to his long-suffering but deeply affectionate "Aw, Mom."

What I don't want is to contend with the white substance filling the Baggie in his backpack. Okay, so he's a child of divorce, a teenager with a girlfriend he first met in Harvard Square's notorious Pit, a boy with a rich (and mean) grandmother and a poor (and, I hope, nice) mother. He attends a fancy private school and lives in an apartment in decidedly nonfancy Somerville. Big deal. A life divided. But you're not necessarily doomed by your childhood. Even the wrong choice in a mate—look at me—doesn't mean you say yes to drugs. Oh, Tommy, I sigh. I don't want to deal with this.

And because I don't want to deal with this, the phone rings.

"So," says the MIL with no preliminaries, "you need to deal with this."

"I plan to. As soon as Tommy comes home."

"Before," she orders.

"And just how am I supposed to do that?"

"I took the"—she lowers her voice—"*you-know-what* from his backpack this morning. You must come get it and arrange to have it tested before he moves back to Somerville. Then we'll know what we have to do."

We? I'm five steps behind. "You took it from his backpack?" I sputter. It's bad enough to spy on him, but to steal? I am not surprised.

"He'll never miss it. Have you ever seen what he keeps in there? If you ask me, it's a breeding ground for bacteria. Something I know not a small amount about due to Pollock's ongoing battle against salmonella." She waits. "I was going to suggest China Sails, but for some reason I feel like corned beef today. Meet me at Ben's Deli at Newton Center. On the dot of one." And she rings off before I can even RSVP.

It's only a couple of dots after one when I get there. Okay, okay, if you want to split hairs, exactly seven minutes and thirty-two seconds past. I had to circle the block twice to find a space, then hop into the drugstore to get change for the meter.

Mrs. Pollock is already sitting in the corner booth, barricaded by a giant pocketbook on one side and an equally humungous shopping tote on the other. She is looking at her watch. "You're late," she says.

"Your watch must be fast," I answer. I slide into the booth—the *dock*—opposite her. Guilty until proven guiltier.

"You're too thin," she pronounces.

"*Can't be too thin or too . . . ,*" I begin. For obvious reasons, I stop before I add the word *rich,* thus giving her one more nail for the she-married-him-for-his-money coffin. I touch my unbuttoned waistband. I'm ten pounds over my fighting wedding weight, probably even more due to a breakfast of cinnamon buns. No matter. Facts fall in the face of eye-of-the-beholder prejudices.

"As you get older"—she flashes me an appraising, nonflattering look—"a thin face shows its age much faster than one with a little flesh under the bone."

You should know, I want to reply, mistress of turkey wattles, incubator of jowls, those absolute measures of lost youth. But I keep my mouth shut, which has always been my problem when faced with the behemoth that is—was—my mother-in-law.

She orders corned beef on a bulkie roll, fries, coleslaw, and a knish.

What I really want is the whitefish salad. And, given that, alas, there's no wine and beer list attached to the atlas-sized menu, I'd settle for an iced tea. Since, however, I'm determined not to offer Mrs. Pollock any ammunition for my putative thinness to stir rumors of eating disorders and thus unfit motherhood, I order the chopped liver on whole wheat and a cream soda.

"Their chopped liver isn't bad, as we give them our leftover schmaltz," she informs. "Chicken fat," she translates for the Episcopalian side of me, "though it's much better on the onion roll."

"I like whole wheat."

"Too bad." She glances from side to side as if the elderly, deli-bellied waitpeople with their stained aprons and orthopedic shoes are undercover NARCs. She leans forward as if there are listening devices planted in the napkin dispenser and bowl of garlicky half sours. She reaches into her giant tote. She pulls out a Bloomingdale's plastic shopping bag. "Here," she whispers.

I take it. I peek inside. A smaller Costco's bag encloses an even smaller Saks sack, which holds the *you-know-what,* which, in turn, seems to be wound in layers of bubble wrap. Russian dolls within Russian dolls.

"Not here!" she commands. "Put it in your purse."

Fortunately I brought along my one pocketbook almost as large as hers, useful for stashing books, the odd file folder, a cosmetic counter's worth of emollients as well as your average contraband. I stick the bag inside the bag inside the bag inside the bubble wrap inside my pocketbook.

"I read about all those drugs," she says. "Whatever they're called. Cocaine. Crystal something. Ecstasy? And worse. Movie stars in *People* magazine are always going to rehab to get off of them."

"Betty Ford," I remind her.

"She had her own problems, but she did a lot of good. Unlike some other first ladies I could name." She lifts her roll and squiggles mustard on the corned beef. "Tommy," she sighs.

"I can't imagine Tommy—"

"All I ever use is aspirin. And the pills I take for my pressure and cholesterol. What could be in that bag? I don't know anything about drugs."

"And you assume *I* do?"

"It's that girl's influence. That January. That February."

"September," I supply. "September Silva."

"What kind of name is that? Silva?"

"Portuguese."

"I suppose she's Catholic."

"Probably."

She shakes her head. "I introduced Tommy to these fine young ladies in Wellesley. Granddaughters of my dear friends. All from very nice families." She stabs a fork into a French fry. "And he falls for this good-for-nothing with shifty eyes and a ring in her nose. It's all your fault, the way you raised him."

"What's my fault? That he's a wonderful kid?"

"Well, he *is* a very wonderful boy," she concedes. "You got lucky."

"Luck has nothing to do with it. It's how I brought him up."

"He takes after his father. That same sweetness." She looks at me. "Rex now has a lovely girlfriend. I assume you know."

"I neither know nor care," I lie. "But how do *you* know?" I ask, trusting both Tommy's assurances that Grina had no idea about the new girlfriend and Rex's well-hewn instincts to keep any female hidden from his mother's certain disapproval.

"I bumped into them at the dry cleaner. I'd just switched to a new one after the old cleaner lost three buttons from my best coat."

"That's too bad. About the coat, I mean."

"At first, yes, but then if those buttons hadn't been lost, I wouldn't have met her so soon. I liked her right away."

"Really?"

"In fact, I insisted they follow me home for coffee and cake. I'd just made my butter cream with raisins that very morning."

"Lucky them," I say.

"She's quite the catch. Perfect manners. Smart. Very refined. Well dressed. Lots of energy. Beautiful."

"Jewish?"

"You know, that question never crossed my mind." She vacuums up the knish in one bite. "If my grandson has, well, a little problem, I'm sure it's temporary. Due to bad companions. An unstable life."

"He has a stable life. He is unconditionally loved."

"No grandmother has ever loved a grandson more," she nods. "But I always think it's good to face the music. Dear Arnie used to say that God never gives us more in life than we can handle." For a second, her eyes hold a far-off, misty, missing-Arnie sorrow. I think of his tiny waist, his stock of clichés, his under-the-counter checks, and I miss him, too. "Thank God he's not around to have to witness this," she rallies. She points a fork, its tine speared with a potato, at my pocketbook. "We'll know tomorrow when you get this—the evidence—tested."

"Now that you've passed me the buck," I say, "or hot potato"—I pat my pocketbook—"it's not your concern anymore. I'll take it from here."

Her voice rises. "Don't you dare exclude me. I have a vested interest in this child."

I assume she means financial. The cell phone. The pager. The private-school tuition. The college fund. The unfashionable clothes appropriate for excessively pious bar mitzvah boys or Japanese businessmen.

"Financial, naturally," she goes on. "But he's also my closest grandchild. Tommy and I have a very special relationship." She leans forward. "A very unique relationship."

I want to tell her *unique* is a word that stands alone grammatically. You can't qualify it. It stands alone. Like me. Who, with white powder in her purse, an unwanted chopped-liver sandwich on her plate, and a reproachful mother-in-law sitting across from her couldn't be less unqualifiedly uniquely ungrammatically alone.

"In case you forgot, my grandson and I formed an instant bond at birth."

"Forgot?" I exclaim. "My own child's birth?"

She shrugs.

Wait a minute, I want to yell, *I'm* the mother here. If any bonding with newborns happened, it happened with me. The *mother.* The one and only. I push my sandwich away. The last thing I want is to revisit the scene of Tommy's birth. The first, and worst, not to mention the most prophetic, in the series of times Rex let me down.

Mrs. Pollock smiles. "I remember the moment he was born like it was yesterday." She's got strings of corned beef between her teeth. But I'm not the kind of girlfriend who would point this out. Not to her.

"His first cry. Those itty-bitty toes," she continues, as if I were as incidental to the miracle of birth as the hospital room's print of Cape Cod or its beige acoustical tiles. "I could have sworn those little eyes were blinking right at me."

Looking back, sixteen years ago, to the obstetrical section of Mount Auburn Hospital, you'd have hardly known I was there. She had pushed herself into the labor room. "Excuse me?" one nurse said and was elbowed aside. Could a mere medical team, an almost paterfamilias, and an ice-cube-sucking, deep-breathing primapara stop this armored tank, this Hurricane Ina that was my mother-in-law?

"Get her out of here," I screamed at Rex the minute his mother left to change into the uniform designated for watching a baby exit the birth canal.

Did nobody hear me? Did the ice cubes and the lollypop and the deep breaths followed by the fast pants and heavy groans I'd learned in my prenatal class muffle my clear-and-present-danger alarms?

Rex, in his father-to-be green surgical scrubs, his face as leached of color as a hospital pillowcase, stood paralyzed. Petrified. What was he afraid of? Blood? Death? A young father's responsibility? Me? The baby?

No, it was his mother. He was scared of facing up to her. All he needed to say was *leave*. With or without the appended *please*. He said nothing. Torn between his wife and his mother, he was forced to pick. Guess his choice. "It's her grandchild," he implored. "She missed my sisters' kids who were all born in Florida. It means so much to her to be in attendance," he begged. "She isn't that young anymore."

"No!" I screamed. She was not going to see parts of me that I hadn't necessarily seen myself. "No!" I screamed again.

"I understand how you feel," he placated, "but she's here now. We can't kick her out."

"Oh, yes we can. Four little words. *Get out of here.*"

"Maisie . . ."

"She wasn't in our bed when your sperm met my egg," I protested. "If she'd shown up at the door, would you have invited her in to watch us conceive?"

"Don't be ridiculous."

"So why does she need to be here when I'm delivering?" I raised myself up on one elbow. "I want her gone."

"Maisie, honey." He held a damp cloth to my brow.

I shoved it away.

"Sweetheart." He pulled the wrapper off a fresh lollipop.

I threw it against the far wall.

"You're being unreasonable."

You don't know what unreasonable is, I started to yell.

Just then Mrs. Pollock plowed through the swinging

doors swathed in matching mother-son surgical attire. She stood behind the doctor at my stirruped feet, claiming a center-aisle view of my (formerly) private parts.

"No!" I shouted. But right that second, the baby's head crowned; I needed to push; I didn't have time to edit the *Come-Watch-Maisie-Give-Birth* invitation list.

Everything happened fast. With a hearty cry, Tommy arrived. The doctor helped Rex cut the umbilical cord. The nurse cleaned him up, suctioned his eyes, swaddled him, then handed Tommy to his brand-new dad. I lay back, exhausted, spent, ecstatic, elated. My breasts ready for a trial run. My arms crossed in a cradle. What about the brand-new mom? "Give my baby to me," I demanded.

My mother-in-law moved to Rex's side; "Little Arnold," she crooned.

"His name's Thomas. Tommy," I said.

She grabbed the baby out of Rex's hands. She turned her back to me. "Twinkle, twinkle, little star," she sang, then segued into Brahms.

Rex's hands dangled at his sides. Helpless. Hopeless. Hapless. Stricken, he looked at me. He wanted pity. Sympathy. I hardened my heart. With the collusion of my husband—unwilling or not—his mother held my son, the fruit of my loins, the product of my womb, the final reward for my pain, the diploma for six weeks of birthing class. She held my own baby. She crooned to him his first lullaby. She staked her claim even before I got close enough to count his tiny starfish fingers and toes.

"Remember how Tommy used to love it when I sang to him," she says now.

"Not really," I reply.

She hums an off-key "Itsy-Bitsy Spider."

A few years ago, an article appeared about delivery

rooms crowded with extended families. The author highlighted the tension between the mother-to-be and the mother-in-law. One woman, kicked out of the labor room, started a grassroots campaign called "Attend Your Grandchild's Birth Day." The last paragraph described a popular parenting Web site that promoted an online discussion titled "Don't Want MIL in the Delivery Room." I would have typed in my own appalling story, but the article came out fourteen years too late.

I sent that article to Rex. I underlined the meaningful mother-in-law parts. I attached a Post-it with a red-penciled *FYI*.

I didn't hear back. Not that I expected to.

I realize that by now, you must think I rely solely on what I read. Vicarious experience, you might say, too much reading, not enough doing, get a life. I rather pride myself on being well informed, but I must admit that some of all the news that's fit to print seems to speak directly to me. The stuff I read doesn't so much reflect my life as give me hope: forty-year-old fashion plates, female entrepreneurs, mothers whose teenagers worship them.

One of my favorites is Sunday's Vows column, where soul mates find each other, their families celebrate, and the MIL, thrilled by the groom's choice of bride, heaps praise on a brand-new dearly beloved daughter-in-law. "*Fill-in-the-blank* has brought my darling son true happiness," this enlightened mother-in-law testifies.

Now Mrs. Pollock jabs a finger at my plate. "You've barely touched your sandwich," she complains. "What a waste."

Since I don't believe that leftover chopped liver will solve the starving-children-in-India problem, I feel no guilt. Nevertheless, I'm compelled to add, "These portions are so gargantuan a third-world family could dine off them for a week."

"Well, you've certainly made a mess of it."

"It's impossible to fit this sandwich in your mouth. Besides, being so overstuffed, it's falling apart."

"Only because you don't know how to eat properly. You should have picked the onion roll." She slaps the menu. "Dessert?"

I shake my head.

She chooses the cheesecake. "Just a taste," she orders. "The teeniest bite."

The waiter brings her a slab that could do double duty as a skyscraper's cornerstone. She digs in. "I worry that you're such a picky eater. Tommy might take after you."

"Tommy has a healthy appetite," I defend.

"Not if he takes drugs."

"We don't know that yet."

She shovels a brick of cheesecake into her mouth. "There are support groups for eating disorders," she says. "You can find them in the yellow pages."

"Where you can also find Weight Watchers," I counter. "As well as anger management."

She ignores this remark. Her eyes stay fixed on her plate.

I grab a pickle.

She tsks. "All that garlic. Bad for your breath."

I eat another one. And another. I empty the bowl. I blast my bad breath in a direct path toward Mrs. Pollock's disapproving sour pickle of a mouth.

All that now remains of the cheesecake is a scattering of crumbs. I can identify. I feel gobbled up, too. The way I always feel when I'm near her, eaten alive, until what's left of me is just a spit-out residue. Mrs. Pollock should enter the *Guinness World Records* for fastest eater and most predatory devourer of the young (and not so young) in addition to meanest mother-in-law, though I assume there's a lot of competition for that spot if you can believe the anecdotal evidence. "I don't have time for coffee," she says.

"I wouldn't mind a cup of decaf," I venture.

"Lunch is over," she states. She slams down her fork to signal the KO at the end of our boxing-over-Tommy bout. Some contest. Have two contenders ever been more unequally matched?

She holds up a finger for the check. She puts on her reading glasses. She studies the tally. "It's easiest to divide this down the middle," she says. She whips out a platinum American Express. "Your portion comes to $17.72. With tip."

EIGHT

Tommy calls to tell me he'll be home late in the afternoon. He's stopping by September Silva's first.

I'm about to answer, *Didn't you just see her?* I'm about to add, *I, on the other hand, haven't seen you in five weeks.* But I stop myself. Even if Tommy *is* the sun—the *son*—my maternal planet revolves around, I understand that it is lousy psychology for me to remain the center of *his* universe. I'm all for mental health. I want him to shift allegiances in due course and at the appropriate age level. Haven't I, more than others, suffered the slings and arrows of an outrageous mother/son relationship? I know all about Oedipus and Jocasta, and Hamlet and Gertrude, and the smothering Jewish mother Portnoy had every right to complain about. I, the anti–Ina Pollock, would never say a word against any young lady my son chose. Even if the young lady were, like September Silva, completely unsuitable.

"Say hi to September for me," I tell Tommy now. "Give her my best."

"Right," Tommy says. "Later," he grunts in the verbless, abbreviated code that passes for communication among teenagers.

I find the pocketbook I lugged yesterday to the awful lunch. I'm still bristling over the let's-split-this-down-the-middle bill, considering my meal cost a quarter of hers. Did I order the eight-dollar cheesecake? Or the seven-dollar knish? I'm not surprised she calculated my "share" down to the last cent. Did I ever receive so much as a lousy blender to mark my wedding to her son or a birthday card to note my existence on this planet or a potted geranium when I was in the hospital giving birth to the perfect object of a grandmother's idolatry? Though Rex always made a point of telling her that it was I who'd picked out the sweater, the scarf, the birthday sachets—causing her "you shouldn't have" to take on a whole new meaning—no matter what I did, it was never right.

Just as what I'm going to do now is doomed to be wrong. I check inside the pocketbook. The Baggie is still there, undisturbed. Did I think that it would disappear in a poof and that all my troubles would vanish along with it?

I transfer my wallet, my keys, my lipstick, my checkbook, my breath mints from my everyday purse to this one. I meant to have the white powder tested yesterday afternoon. I really did. But then Darlene and I got busy—Amelia Elderberry sprained her wrist and needed both of us to take turns transcribing her dictation of chapter 63 of her memoirs, which, by the way, takes her only to the age of twelve. In the middle of this, my obsessive-compulsive client, Robert Levin, called in a panic. His wife actually packed her suitcases this time; she gave him a forty-eight-hour ultimatum: She would agree to share his bed only if the floor underneath was clear of his twenty-year collection of old broken-down running shoes.

I suppose I could have stolen an hour to take the powder to the hospital lab. Darlene's such a good worker that I've now got more flexibility than I had in the past. Alas, I put it off because plain old human nature wants to delay the diagnosis as long as possible, particularly if it might turn out to be bad.

But since Tommy's due home this afternoon and it's getting harder to ignore the increasingly frantic on-the-half-hour messages about rehab and drug abuse and lax mothering that the MIL has been leaving on my answering machine, I'll need to act.

I act. I brush my teeth. I brush my hair. I put pearl studs in my ears. I throw on a blue blazer that gives off serious grown-up vibes. I get in my car. Crowding the backseat are a couple of Trader Joe's cartons that once stored the cheap wine aficionados call Two Buck Chuck. Darlene left the boxes there yesterday. They're filled with darned socks rolled into little balls and ironed shirts neatly folded and stacked. "Would you mind dropping them off at Seamus's?" she asked me. "I'd bring them myself but they're kind of big to take on the T."

"You're a sucker," I pointed out.

"Aren't all of us girls," she moaned, "when it comes to guys?"

Not this one, I thought. Not anymore, I argued.

Unless the guy is a son, I now amend.

Traffic is light. I hit green all the way and pull up in front of Professor O'Toole's house within five minutes. I park under the chestnut tree. I think of Darlene's first day at work, how she hid behind this very tree, afraid to ring

Seamus's bell. She was so self-effacing, so shy, so bent into herself. How far she's come in such a short time. Shoulders thrust back. Discussing Kant. Whizzing through apartments and condos and houses. Kicking out the good-for-nothing guy who shared the rent. I decide I can claim the credit for much of her personal and professional progress. She's building the kind of self-esteem that soon enough will show the DSS that she's the mother Anthony Vincent deserves. I glance at the pocketbook on the seat next to me. Am I the mother Tommy deserves? A sentence that can be parsed two ways depending on how you look at it.

I get out of the car. It takes me a couple of trips up Professor O'Toole's walk to leave the cartons on his front stoop. I ring the bell, then dash to my car. I have no time to be marshaled inside to defrost a few Pollock's Potpies for his lunch. I have no inclination to share that lunch. I'm already about to turn at the stop sign when I glimpse him opening his door. He crooks a finger to beckon me. I wave. I hit the gas.

Someone's pulling out of a space just as I drive up. I grab it. I feed the meter every quarter I've got. Though I'm an expert jaywalker, this time I wait for the light to cross Mount Auburn Street. I clutch my pocketbook against my chest. All I'd need is to be sideswiped and land on the pavement with suspicious white powder sprinkled all over my blazer from my run-over, torn-apart pocketbook.

In the hospital lobby I spot signs for LABORATORY, PATHOLOGY, INFECTIOUS DISEASES, ICU. The arrows all point in the same direction. I follow them.

I am convinced that my skulking body language cries

out *criminal*! The fact that I am transporting illegal substances must be written all over my face. I glance from side to side. But nobody—nurses, doctors, patients, techs—pays me the slightest attention. Though the corridors seem to loop around like a maze, I finally reach the laboratory, which I recognize by its rows of white coats hanging on hooks. It doesn't at all resemble the lab at Wellesley, the one where I dissected—or, rather, butchered—my sad little frog. That one was a lab right out of central casting with its shiny counters, black microscopes, deep sinks, and mysterious vials and sloshing pipettes.

This one is a series of rooms, some small, some large, all dominated by computers and big whirring machines dwarfing the occasional microscope. The rooms are messy—papers piled, trash barrels stuffed, lights blazing. Against one wall, hot pink rubber-topped tubes jerk unattended along a track, like an old Lionel electric train. Signs warning BIOHAZARDOUS MATERIALS are pasted against stainless-steel doors. Big red letters spell out DANGER. I feel as if I've entered one of those scary other dimensions you see in sci-fi flicks. A machine spits out a tube containing what must be blood.

This is a bad idea, I decide. I'm ready to flee. But the minute I turn on my heel, I face the DANGER sign. Are its red letters blinking just at me? *Be Careful* is scribbled on a Post-it that graces a bulletin board. I take a couple of steps forward. I recognize a group of refrigerator-sized incubators that look exactly like the ones used in the chicken industry. Maybe they are. I peek around a corner where, just at that moment, a little window in the wall opens and a ghostly gloved hand passes something—a body part?—to a technician standing over a machine rimed with frost. People walk past me with purposeful strides.

A clean-scrubbed young woman—September Silva's opposite, I can't help but observe—opens a door on which is written DO NOT STORE FOOD IN THIS REFRIGERATOR!!!!!! At a nearby counter a man in a lab coat cuts into something that resembles raw steak. I stand around, unsure what to do next. Not a soul seems to notice me even though I'm the only one not wearing white or surgical blue. I clear my throat.

A motherly woman with gray-streaked brown hair coming loose from a bun and rimless glasses looks up from her computer. SALLY HINKLE reads the ID card slung around her neck. "Can I help you?" she asks.

"I'd like to get something tested."

"Do you have the referral form from your doctor?"

"Do I need one?"

She nods. "Of course," she emphasizes. "People can't just walk in off the street."

I consider my just-walked-in-off-the-street status. "This is a community hospital," I defend. "I'm a member of the community." Or half member, I correct, which means, I comfort myself, I can always try the Somerville hospital next.

"There are procedures," she warns.

I must look completely crestfallen and pathetic because she softens her voice. "Well," she says, "what is it you want tested?"

I hug my pocketbook. "I found . . ."

"Yes," she encourages.

"I have a sixteen-year-old," I explain.

"Ah," she says. "I have three teenagers myself."

"Then you'll understand. Not that your children—"

"They are a challenge, aren't they?" She points at my pocketbook. "What did you find?"

"I . . ." I lower my voice. "In his backpack."

"Go on."

I say it fast. "A Baggie with white powder."

She clicks her tongue. "That would be for toxicology. Even with all the right paperwork, the proper referrals, we'd send it out. To the state lab."

"Where's the state lab?" I ask.

"Jamaica Plain. Near the Arboretum. But I wouldn't advise your taking the . . ." She stops. She chooses her words. "The *specimen* there. Ever since the anthrax scare, since all this bioterrorism . . ." Her hands, which fall to her sides, finish the sentence in pantomime.

"Oh, my God! I never thought of that!"

"Times have changed," she says. "Fifteen years ago you probably could have just walked this in." She frowns. "I'm afraid that now, the police would have to be involved. And social services."

I fall into the nearest chair. I don't bother to remove a *Health Today* and a *Good Housekeeping.* I start to hyperventilate.

"Are you okay?"

"I don't know," I gasp.

She puts a hand on my shoulder. "Can I get you a glass of water?"

I shake my head.

"Maybe there's someone you could talk to," she suggests.

Does she have a sideline in therapy? "I don't need a shrink. I need a lab technician."

Just at that moment a man walks toward us carrying a cardboard tray with two Styrofoam cups, thimbles of cream, packets of sugar. Steam rises from the hole in the spongy white lids. "Speaking of which," she says.

"Lab technician?" I ask.

"Not that," she answers.

"Here's your coffee, Sally," the man says.

She grabs a cup and one packet of sugar. "And here's someone with a problem just up your alley, Gabe," she counters. She points at me. "Sorry. Got to run. It's my break, and I have to call my boys." She stares at my pocketbook, which must be sending out *do-you-know-where-your-kids-are* messages. She puts her hand on the knob of a door marked STAFF ONLY. She stops. She smiles. "Be strong," she consoles. "No matter what it is, we're never given more than we can handle." She opens the door. "I'm sure everything will work out okay."

"Gabriel Doyle," the man says. "Gabe."

I look at him. Tall, slim, freckles, brown hair, a lopsided smile, perfectly pleasant, but no one who would grab your attention from across a crowded room. Or in the corridor of a hospital when your attentions are otherwise engaged on the possible juvenile delinquency of your only son. "Maisie," I manage. "Maisie Grey."

He nods. "Maisie Grey," he repeats. "I'm a social worker here."

"Sorry, but I don't need a social worker."

"I'm sure you don't." He puts down his tray. He sinks into the seat next to me. "Can I get you water? Coffee?"

"No, thanks."

He removes a cup from the water dispenser, pours half of his coffee into it, and hands it to me anyway. He passes me the sugar.

I tear open the packet and dump it in.

"Sally says you have a problem," he invites.

"You can say that again. But I'm not an official, signed-in

patient. I can't produce a referral. I just walked in off the street."

"Ah, the most intriguing of circumstances." He grins.

"Don't you have an official, hospital-approved, health-insurance-funded, forms-filled-out caseload of—what do you call them—patients? Clients?"

"I'm on my break. Is there anything I can do? Unofficially?"

Maybe it's the *unofficially* that gets me. Maybe it's the grin. Or the smell of the coffee or the intense professional interest. Or maybe I'm just too tired to move from this chair. I pull the magazines out from under my bottom and put them on the table between us. I look at the cover of one: Pregnant Celebrities. Maternal Bliss. Underneath are photographs of movie stars with million-dollar smiles and million-dollar wraps over their stomach bumps. "I'm afraid I crushed these," I confess.

"Good for you. Let's hope they'll get replaced with more current issues. I predict the articles inside some of those magazines date from the last century." He stirs his coffee with a little plastic stick. He tilts his chin, dimpled, I notice, now that I'm at closer range. "So . . . ?" he encourages.

"It's about my son," I say. "Tommy. He's sixteen."

"And that's the problem right there?"

"I suppose it *is* a difficult age."

"Tell me about him."

Though I'm tempted to pull Tommy's photograph out of my wallet and stick it in front of his face in a picture-is-worth-a-thousand-words gesture, I resist. The wallet, after all, is buried somewhere in what could turn out to be a drug-trafficking vessel illegally transported across the

Cambridge/Somerville line. Nevertheless, he's said the magic words. "Oh, he's adorable, charming, funny, smart, a mother's dream," I supply.

"And his father?" Do his eyes move to my bare fourth finger left hand?

"We're divorced."

"I see."

"But he's no child of divorce. I mean he *is* a child of divorce but seems to have survived intact."

"I'm sure he has." He leans closer. His voice is soft. I can smell the sugary coffee and a whiff of lemon shampoo. "Then what's the problem?"

I look at the magazines. *Maternal Bliss.* I take a windup breath. "I found some white stuff in a Baggie in his backpack," I exhale. A sentence that is starting to become my mantra, I've repeated it so much. I pat my pocketbook. "It's in here. Do you want to see it?"

He shakes his head. "I'm no chemist. I'm afraid I couldn't tell a suspicious substance from this sugar"—he brandishes the torn packet—"or from, well, detergent. He brightens. "For all you know, it could be a washing machine cycle's worth of Tide."

I picture piles of Tommy's laundry on the bathroom floor. "I have serious doubts."

"Then, why not a bag of powdered milk?"

I sigh. I'm the expert on milk in bags, though this is information I don't plan to share. "You might as well say stardust," I offer.

He laughs. "I guess we're getting carried away. We can't be sure. Unless we taste it, which probably isn't a good idea."

"The precise reason I brought it here to get tested. But the woman—Sally Hinkle—said they'd need authorization and then it would have to be sent out to a state toxicology lab that would no doubt feel compelled to notify the police and social services." I stop. *Social services!* Why didn't that phrase hit me earlier? I think of Darlene. I think of DSS. *Department of Social Services.* I imagine Tommy taken away, assigned to semibachelor quarters with Rex, shipped off to reform school. Or—I shiver—even worse than reform school, ordered, like Anthony Vincent, to live with his grandmother. I put down my coffee; I drop my head into my hands. "What should I do? I don't know what to do!" I wail.

"There, there," he soothes. His voice is low, kind. I assume he's good at his job. I assume he's got a huge waiting list of clients requesting to spill their troubles only to him. "There, there," he says again. He pats my shoulder. "Let me ask you this." He waits a beat. "Have you ever had any trouble with Tommy and drugs before?"

"Never." I cross my heart.

"Well then."

"What should I do?" I repeat.

"Ever since nine/eleven, the state labs, the hospitals are forced to take precautions. Going that route, therefore, makes little sense. Still, you should probably get those contents tested. If only for your own peace of mind." He looks up. "Do you know any chemists? You're a part of this community. Do you know anybody who might work in some of the labs over by MIT?"

"Not a single person," I say.

"Are you sure?" he asks. "Think hard."

I think hard. I try to concentrate. Chemists. Chemists. I scroll through my neighbors, friends, family, former classmates, mere acquaintances. Maybe there are chemists in the kitchens of Pollock's Poultry whose help I could enlist. I dismiss that possibility. Would my mother-in-law spit in her own soup? In her own potpie? Will an animal foul its own nest?

"Visualize," the social worker orders. "Close your eyes. Take a deep breath."

I close my eyes. I take a deep breath.

"Slowly. In and out. In and out," he coaches.

I breathe.

"Good. Now imagine beakers. Lab coats. Chemistry texts. Visualize."

I visualize. I see an apartment. I see plants. I see CD racks stuffed with all the greats of rock and roll. I see bookshelves buckling under the weight of chemistry texts. I inhale. I exhale. This visualization technique really works. I can even picture some of the titles that I've walked by on the way to water the Christmas cactus, the ficus tree, the split-leafed philodendron: *Carey Organic Chemistry Sequence, Skoog Principles of Instrumental Analysis, Advanced Organic Chemistry, Spiro Chemistry of the Environment, Pharmacology.*

Pharmacology!

"Got it!" I shout. I shoot my fist into the air.

"Great!" he says. To his credit he doesn't ask me what chemist I've come up with, even though, unlike him, I am not bound by laws of confidentiality.

"Excuse me for one minute," I say. I find the ladies' room. Though it's empty, I squeeze into a stall. I dial Jeremy Marshall on his cell phone. I leave a message. I ask for a personal favor. I ask if he can test some white powder for toxicology purposes.

Since I'm already on-site, I decide to use the facilities. I once read somewhere that Queen Elizabeth offered her lady-in-waiting this piece of advice—If there's a bathroom nearby, use it. Maybe the quote is apocryphal, but the advice is still sound. By the time I've finished washing my hands—ALL HOSPITAL WORKERS MUST WASH THEIR HANDS THOROUGHLY orders the sign over the sink—my cell phone rings. "Jeremy Marshall here," the voice says. "Your message got forwarded to me in L.A. But I'm taking the red-eye back tonight. Just leave the—the matter to be tested—on my kitchen counter, next to the coffee machine."

"Are you sure?" I ask. "Don't you want to know the whole story? Where it came from. How I got—"

"Am running into a meeting. No problem. Considering all you, and your Darlene, have done for me, it'll be a pleasure to return the favor. I'll call you with the results sometime tomorrow afternoon."

For an instant, I'm so happy and so relieved, I roll lipstick on my grinning lips. I comb my hair. I check my reflection in the mirror. But as soon as I start to consider the prospect of the next afternoon, my freshly crimsoned smile vanishes. The phone call tomorrow. The phone call that can change my life. And Tommy's. And Ina Pollock's. And . . . "Quit it, Maisie!" I tell myself. I'll worry about the results only after Jeremy Marshall gives them to me.

The social worker is reading *Good Housekeeping* when I come back.

He raises his eyebrows in two arched question marks.

"I found someone," I announce.

"Yay!" he applauds.

"He'll let me know tomorrow."

"Great." He puts down *Good Housekeeping*. He stands up. "Forgive me for being bold, but by any chance are you free for dinner tomorrow night?"

"You're asking me out?" I exclaim. My first flush of

pleasure turns to incredulity, then embarrassment. The guy's a social worker, I remind myself. I study his face. "Are you worried I'll do something dire? Do you think I shouldn't be alone after I hear the results?"

He laughs. "Not at all. It's I who don't want to be alone at dinnertime."

NINE

I drive to Jeremy Marshall's condo and leave the Baggie on the counter, next to the coffee machine. I attach a Post-it scribbled with my profound thanks. The leaves of his ficus tree look limp and dried out. I can identify. I douse it with water. Is it my imagination, or does it right away start to seem perkier? Free of my burden, I feel a little perkier myself. I sit on Jeremy Marshall's sofa and offer up a quick prayer to the god of suspicious substances. I lock the door behind me. I whisper amen.

By the time I get home, my answering machine is blinking furiously. Though I know this is technologically impossible, I swear that the light flashes a brighter, more frantic red than usual. I'm right because all eight messages are from Ina Pollock whose progressively louder shrieks could shatter the glass of the John Hancock building located three miles across the river in Copley Square.

Message 1: "Where are you?"

Message 2: "Pick up the phone!"

Message 3: "Did you get you-know-what taken care of?"

Message 4: "Why have you not called me back?"

Message 5: "How incredibly rude of you to ignore my concerns. Though I'm hardly surprised."

Message 6: "Where are you? Answer immediately!"

Message 7: "You must be home by now. Unless you can't find your own way."

Message 8: "How could you be so stupid not to have told me your cell number? I'm on pins and needles. Call me!"

I press Erase. If only I could make *her* disappear as easily.

I'm proud of myself that I never gave in to her torturous demands for my cell phone number. "But I'm Tommy's grandmother. You must be available to me!" she'd cried. "You're withholding crucial information. It's criminal!" Then she *really* turned the thumbscrews. "What if something—God forbid—happens to him and I need to get in touch with you?"

I swore Tommy to secrecy. My cell phone number was our own little undercover operation. "She's going to try to squeeze it out of you," I warned.

"All classified information is safe with me." He placed his hand on his algebra book. "I'll never squeal."

"She'll attempt a bribe. Offer video games and gift certificates. Or she'll stick a guilt trip on you. Your grandmother wears the crown of Miss Guilt Inducer USA. 'How can my own grandson keep from me a simple telephone number when that's the only thing I want in life? Don't you realize that not having that number is causing my arthritis to act up?' "

"Oh, Mom, don't worry so much."

Worrying is a mother's lot, I think now as I pull out pans and bowls from the kitchen cabinet. I'm making all of Tommy's favorites tonight—meat loaf, mashed potatoes, green salad with freshly picked tomatoes from the farmers' market, corn on the cob, blueberry pie. Not a menu-padding, hackneyed chicken in sight. Comfort food.

And there's comfort in cooking, stirring, dicing, peeling, in movements so familiar you never have to pay the least attention to them. I chop onions. My eyes stream. I remember a cartoon of a woman chopping onions whose eyes turn tearier and tearier with every stroke of her knife until she finally plunges that knife straight into her heart. I assume there must have been extenuating circumstances—like needing to escape a mother-in-law.

The minute I have this insight, right on cue the phone rings. I put down the knife. I wipe my hands. I pick up the receiver.

"What is wrong with you? You should have called. I've been waiting by this phone all day," the MIL accuses.

"I just got home."

"What about your cell? You're not fooling me. I am aware that you own one. And that for some crazy, selfish, misguided reason refuse to give the number out."

I let that pass. I change the subject back to Topic A. "I have nothing to report. The results will be available tomorrow."

"That long?" Implying that if she were in charge, those results would be instantaneous.

"These things take time. The chemicals have to—well—interact chemically."

"I expect you to contact me the second you hear. The absolute second. I insist on it."

"I'll let you know, Mrs. Pollock," I reply, "but . . ." And

then I say words for which the right context has never before presented itself. ". . . don't call me. I'll call you."

Soon after, wonderful smells fill my kitchen. The pie's cooling on the counter. The meat loaf's being kept warm on low. I've set two places at the table. The silver candlesticks, a wedding present from my parents, gleam. The supermarket daisies stick out of the pitcher shaped like a cow. Cousin Lucinda's heirloom monogrammed napkins rise into sharp starched pyramids. The wineglasses sparkle, one designated for legal-age-appropriate pomegranate juice. For the first time today, I feel relaxed. Tommy's on his way home. Whatever his problems, we can solve them. Whatever aberration the stress of living so close to his grandmother has provoked, now that he's back with me, things will return to normal. By dinnertime, he'll be here, right where he belongs. Come what may, we will handle any temporary trouble, the two of us.

I turn on the radio. I spin the dial to a program about animals. A baby penguin has been stolen from a zoo on the Isle of Wight. "He can't survive without the attention and care of his parents," the zookeeper informs. "He is completely dependent on them for food." The parents are distraught, the talk-show host explains. They have no appetite. They pace back and forth. Their feathers are falling out from all the stress.

I lean against the counter. I wipe my hands on my WORLD'S GREATEST MOM apron. I touch my hair. Maybe it, too, is thinning from all the stress.

After a public-service announcement promoting the Save the Children Fund, the program switches to a seabird mother who, leaving her newborn in the care of its father, has flown 2,500 miles to seek food for her baby until finally, a month later, she returns to her nesting site where she regurgitates a meal for her chick.

I stick a fork in the pie and sneak a tiny, inconspicuous bite. In its purest form, untainted by psychological baggage and warring parents and affection-milking manipulators, food is love. I think of Darlene and of all the trouble she's suffered through to nourish Anthony Vincent. I can only admire her efforts. The need to feed your child is primeval, an instinct universal to the animal kingdom and the human condition, to all of us mothers everywhere.

The radio program moves on to fund-raising solicitations. *If we reach our goal by the end of tomorrow afternoon . . .* an overanimated voice pleads. I turn it off. I make myself a cup of chamomile. I flop onto the sofa.

Just as I finish the tea, I hear a pounding of footsteps on the stairs. I put the mug on the table and listen carefully. Isn't that more than the noise made by just two feet? Even adolescent feet wearing shoes the size of Old Town canoes?

Alas, my ears don't deceive me because when the key turns in the lock, when the door swings open, on the threshold stand four flip-flops, two belonging to Tommy and two exposing the chipped black-tipped nails of September Silva.

My heart sinks. Then plunges lower when I notice two bulging, battered suitcases.

"Hey," Tommy says.

"Hey," I echo. I wait. I want to get up and fling my arms around him. I want to tousle his hair, squeeze his bony shoulder, kiss his patchy cheek. I want him to tap the top of my head from his gawky height, award me his disdainful *Aw, Mom,* while his aw-shucks smile gives away his private pleasure. I want all of this. I stay still, however. I decide, with admirable restraint, that maybe now isn't the time for public displays of maternal affection.

"September's here," he says.

"So I see."

September waves five fingers, each of which appears to be ringed with a silver skull. "Hi'ya, Maisie."

I flinch. At my own adult, property-owner door, she talks to me as if I were sitting next to her in study hall.

I think of sixteen plus years of addressing Mrs. Pollock as—well—Mrs. Pollock. I remember how I begged Darlene Lattanzio to call me Maisie. "I can't," she had said. "It's not right."

"How's it going, Maisie?" September Silva asks now.

I offer a noncommittal shrug. I point at the two unfamiliar suitcases wedging my front door. "Are these yours?" I ask Tommy.

"September's," he says. "She's moving in."

I grab the top of a chair to steady myself. My mouth opens and closes with the mute imploring of a goldfish in a goldfish bowl.

While I'm thus paralyzed with shock, September moves in. At least as far as the living room. She sinks into the sofa. She's wearing assorted frayed black garments that look like rejects from a Salvation Army bin. "Thanks for having me, Maisie." She picks up the newspaper. She sticks her pierced-nosed face in it.

I look at Tommy. I raise my eyebrows. *What?* I mime.

"Trouble at home," he says. "I told her she could share my room."

"Wait a minute, young man." I cross my arms.

He nods in the direction of September, who has flipped off her flip-flops and propped her bare feet up on the coffee table, their soles almost as black as her clothes. "I'll explain later," he whispers. He wrinkles his nose. He takes a diversionary tactic. "Something smells good," he enunciates.

I want to tell him about the seabird who flew 2,500 miles to find food for her chick. *Not for the chick's girlfriend.* I want to tell him about the kidnapped baby penguin who won't survive without his parents to feed him. *Only him.*

"I'm starved," Tommy exclaims.

What would Mrs. Pollock do?

Easy. Throw those bags through the door and kick September Silva out after them.

What do I do?

I set another place at the table.

"Dinner's ready," I chirp in my brightest, all-inclusive June Cleaver voice. I bring out my beautifully arranged platters. My tastefully heaped bowls. My presentation, dare I admit, is remarkable. Sprigs of rosemary march down the middle of the meat loaf like an allée in the south of France. Parsley dots the salad like the brushwork of Seurat. Butter glistens on the corn like gold on a medieval manuscript. Every lettuce leaf is crisp and pristine. The mashed potatoes swirl into Art Deco curves.

"Wow!" Tommy whistles. "What a feast, Mom."

"It's to welcome you home." I emphasize the *you*, its second-person singular.

Tommy deflects all subtle social signals. "Thanks," he says.

I slice the meat loaf. Good manners trump mother-of-son misgivings. Brought up properly, I have no choice but to serve the lady first.

Some lady. September spreads her skull-ringed hands

across her plate. Her hair sweeps the rim. "Sorry, Maisie," she informs, now hunched over her place setting as if I'm the enemy storming a barricade, "but I'm a vegan. Also lacto-intolerant. Besides, I'm trying to cut down on fats and carbs."

I pass the meat loaf to Tommy.

"I think Tommy should cut down also," she continues. "His diet isn't, like, the healthiest."

Tommy chooses the thickest slab. "I probably should start paying more attention to additives and stuff," he concedes.

I serve him two giant scoops of mashed potatoes. I add two buttered ears of corn. His plate runneth over.

"Thanks, Mom." He winks at me.

"Tommy's diet is fine," I instruct my uninvited guest. "He's still growing. He needs a variety of different foods."

"If that's, like, how you see it." She shrugs. One sleeve falls off her shoulder to reveal a shredded black bra strap attached by a safety pin.

I pour water into her wineglass.

"Spring?" she asks. "Mineral?"

"Tap," I say. Then add, with a certain amount of glee, "Otherwise known as *l'eau municipal*."

"I never took French. It is French, isn't it?" She looks up. Mascara is smudged around her raccoon eyes. Her face is feral. What particular chunk of Tommy's childhood became so dislodged as to cause him to pick a girl like this? I study my clean-cut model-of-a-young-man son. Is that his hand resting on September Silva's rag-swathed knee?

September executes a boardinghouse reach and grabs the salad bowl. "Mind if I ask something, Maisie?"

Do I have a choice? "Ask away."

"Like what's in the salad dressing?"

"I doubt it's on your forbidden list. Balsamic vinegar. And olive oil." I pause. "Virgin."

"Pardon?"

"*Virgin,*" I emphasize.

I catch Tommy's eye.

He looks away.

"Extra-virgin olive oil," I explain. "From the best groves in Italy."

I pour myself a glass of wine. I gulp it down and pour another. My need outweighs any hope of setting a good example. "So what's the trouble at home?" I ask.

"Mom!" Tommy yelps.

"My mother," September says. "She kicked me out."

"For what reason?"

"Mom," Tommy repeats.

September puts a restraining hand on his shoulder. "It's okay, babe. I don't mind." She ruffles his hair. She nods at me. "Like she doesn't give me any space. Like I'm supposed to be her clone or something. She expects me to make the same mistakes as her. She always says, 'Well, it was good enough for me.' Like I'm not an individual in my own right. Like I'm not old enough to make my own decisions. But when I make a decision, she shows no interest in it. 'Whatever,' she'll say. She's not much of a role model. She just doesn't care." She starts to cry. Fat tears sketch black tracks down her cheeks. She picks up one of Cousin Lucinda's starched, ironed, hemstitched Grey family monogrammed napkins. She daubs at her face. Blotted with mascara, the napkin metamorphoses into a Rorschach test. I turn away.

Tommy leans toward her and pats her back. His brows are knit with concern. "Mom, can't you see this whole experience has been traumatic for September? Maybe we don't need to talk about this now."

September blows her nose into Cousin Lucinda's napkin. "It's okay," she allows. "Venting is good for my grief."

"What decisions doesn't your mother care about?" I persevere.

"Like that I'm sick of school. Like that I want to drop out."

I clutch my fork. "You want to drop out of school?" I ask, my voice rising in alarm.

Enough alarm that Tommy rushes to her defense. "It's September's decision," he argues.

Is this a contagious decision you catch by sharing close quarters? I wonder. Is Tommy in danger of being contaminated with a dropping-out-of-school virus? I make myself stop. Maybe a lifetime of Pollock private-school tuition has granted him immunity.

"I want to start my career," September insists. She thrusts out her chin.

"Which is . . . ?"

"Music."

"Oh, do you play an instrument?"

"No, I'm a composer."

"September writes these great songs," Tommy cuts in. "Lyrics. And some poems, too. She's a real poet. You should hear 'Back at Black Billy's Blues.' "

I think of the Pollock Pie-Perfect Persuaders. "Very alliterative," I say.

He turns to her. "How about reciting a few bars? For Mom?"

September shakes her head. "I don't think I'm in the mood right now."

"I understand," I allow. Spare me, I pray.

"Mom, she is so talented. Wait till you hear her."

"Tommy's my greatest fan. My number one fan. If only my mother gave me a quarter of, like, what he gives me . . ."

"Someday you'll get the recognition you deserve," affirms her greatest fan. He takes her hand.

It must be uncomfortable, all those rings cutting into his soft sweet palms. I bet they leave little skull impressions when she pulls her hand away. "I hope you will get the recognition you deserve," I offer. "We all should end up getting what we deserve."

"I don't read music," she confides, "which, like, never stopped any of the greats. Reading music probably turned them in the wrong direction. Cut the purity. Gave them false starts."

I want to ask who those greats are. The musically illiterate? The undereducated? I'm sure I won't recognize any of the names in that particular pantheon. "And I suppose finishing high school, too, has a negative impact on poetry and—well—composing?" I ask instead.

"That's right. I don't need to waste my time sitting in a classroom. Bor-ring." She turns to Tommy. "See, Maisie totally gets it. She's really cool."

"Well," Tommy fudges. He flashes me a steely eye, one that says you haven't pulled any wool over it.

September is oblivious. "I just sing my songs into a tape deck. And that preserves them." September spears a tomato wedge. She starts to bring it up to her mouth, then stops halfway, so she looks as if she's holding a microphone. "I promise I'll let you listen to them, Maisie. Sometime when I'm, like, not so upset. When I'm in the right mood."

"You'll love them, Mom," Tommy chimes in.

"I'm sure I will," I reply. "I can hardly wait." I spear my

own tomato. I chew on it. I have to chew extrahard to keep it from sticking in my craw. Could I imagine a worse girl for my son? As soon as I have this thought, I can sense Mrs. Pollock perching on my shoulder in Oedipal unity. *I know all about unsuitable girls,* I can hear her crow as her talons claw into my flesh.

You can't compare me to her, I want to protest. Me from a good home, me with a high school diploma, me freshly showered, employed, Henry James novels on my shelf, silver candlesticks on my table, a loving mother, a formerly devoted wife, a woman who can cook a meat loaf unequaled in culinary history. Add to this, French speaking, grammatically and politically correct, half Jewish even. Unlike Mrs. Pollock with her son, I, with mine, *really* have something to complain about.

But, unlike Mrs. Pollock, I am smart enough to keep my big mouth shut.

I bring out the dessert.

September's vegan, no-carbs, no-fats regimen doesn't seem to apply to my blueberry pie or my cinnamon rolls. She takes two rolls. She accepts a fat wedge of pie. She requests a larger second slice. When all that's left is a powdering of sugar and a blueberry smudge, she checks her watch, the size of a salad plate, with a black rubber strap and silver studs. She jumps up. She scrapes back her chair. "That was great, Maisie. Sorry we can't help you do the dishes. Tommy and I have, like, this opening band we promised we'd go listen to."

Does Tommy look a little sheepish? Does his head hang in apology? Or am I just projecting his chagrin and imagining—hoping for—a flash of regret?

"But you just got here, Tommy. I haven't seen you for weeks," whines the Jewish-mother part of my heritage.

Tommy stands up. "I'm home now," he announces.

I study him. "Will there be drinking? You know you're underage—"

"No problem, Maisie. We haven't even once used our phony IDs."

"Well, that's a consolation," I sputter.

September threads her arm through Tommy's in a way I can't help note is in-your-face proprietary. "Don't wait up."

"That was great, Mom," Tommy echoes. "Great," he repeats. He pats me on the head—the old familiar gesture that this time doesn't give me the old familiar pleasure. "Don't worry. We'll be fine. Don't wait up."

"Have fun," I begrudge. "I'll make up the living room couch for September," I add, my voice larded with housewifely martyrdom.

"Don't bother," September grants, *her* voice dripping with noblesse oblige. "I'll sleep in Tommy's bed. We're already having sex."

To his credit, Tommy's eyes stay glued on his feet. He pulls her to the door.

I go on as if her last sentence has been delivered in Hungarian. "On second thought," I say, "September must want her privacy. I'll make up the couch for *you,* Tommy."

"Mom," Tommy sighs.

"You may consider me old-fashioned, but under *my* roof you follow *my* rules."

September looks back at me. "Don't worry. I'm on the pill. Tommy's got condoms. 'Bye, Maisie." She holds up two fingers. She salutes. Her skull rings glitter. "Safe sex."

TEN

The phone rings. I jolt awake. The images in my dream—my nightmare, rather—now interrupted, were so clear I could have been watching them unfold on the Davis Square Cinema screen: A rain of white powder. The Beatles chanting *Lucy in the Sky with Diamonds*. Mrs. and Mr. Pollock in Laurel and Hardy costume smashing potpies against each other's chins, Sweeney Todd's glinting blade. A lab-coated chorus line of chickens, their synchronized yellow webbed toes kicking out a cancan to the strains of Offenbach. September Silva starring in a revival of *The Bride Wore Black*. I sit up. I look at the clock. It's six A.M.

"Well?" Ina Pollock shouts into my ear.

"It's six in the morning! I was fast asleep!"

"Sorry," she lies, then appends, disparagement powers unmitigated, "since I'm such an early riser, I forgot that ladies of leisure like you don't share the same work ethic."

"You probably woke up Tommy, too," I grumble. "Not to mention . . ." I'm about to add *September Silva*, but I catch myself.

"Ha! When he's not working or in school, that child is

dead to the world until at least noon. A stampeding herd of buffaloes wouldn't disturb his slumber."

"Unlike some of us," I point out.

"Nonsense. The older you get, the less sleep you need. Of course I didn't sleep a wink with all the worrying. Frankly, I'm surprised you were able to."

You don't know the half of it, I want to cry. Instead, I make my voice firm, the tone I use to warn Jehovah's Witnesses to leave me alone. "I told you, Mrs. Pollock, I'll call you as soon as I have any information." I say good-bye. I yank the sheets up to my chin. I stuff my head under the pillow. I want to hide here for the next decade, until Tommy's out of college (if he stays in school!), until Mrs. Pollock is in a coma in a nursing home (if she'd ever go to one!).

I got less than four hours' sleep last night. After I did the dishes, after I made up the sofa with sheets, a down comforter, and Tommy's childhood teddy bear on the pillow (a reminder that he *still* was a child), after I soaked Cousin Lucinda's napkin in bleach, after I stood in Tommy's room staring at September Silva's disreputable suitcases, after I convinced myself that drug-making equipment lurked between the layers of a wardrobe suitable for the Addams family, after I decided to point the finger at the one responsible for Tommy's fall from grace, after I acknowledged that even if there was no evidence of narcotics on those particular premises, the physical rather than verbal reassurance of birth control pills would go a long way to ease other anxieties—after all of this, I did nothing. I am not Ina Pollock. I would never search the belongings of a stranger. I would never go through my own flesh and blood's backpack either. *Never. Ever.*

Still, there it was, sitting right on the floor next to all

of September's worldly goods. *Open me! Open me!* it seemed to cry. I had to take a peek. Just in case another Baggie was stashed inside. Just in case Tommy had left behind something that any psychologist would interpret as a cry for help and thus approve of checking under the circumstances.

Fortunately, I found nothing incriminating—at least in *his* bag. Books, a sweater, a few CDs, an odd sock, a moldering chicken salad sandwich that his grandmother had made and, with anal, squared-off corners, wrapped for him. I threw it out.

Then I got in bed. I picked up the latest P. D. James on loan from the sisters Elderberry. I read the same paragraph over and over. Dalgliesh's ruminations on murder replayed like a scratched track on an old LP. I put down the book. I turned off the light and stared at the dark ceiling. I was having murderous ruminations myself. Funny how when he's at his father's, his grandmother's, overnight at a friend's, I don't have these worries. Strange how an out-of-sight, off-site sleepover for him can often mean a good night's sleep for me.

I waited for the footsteps on the stairs. I listened for the key in the lock.

It was after two when I heard them. Footsteps. Keys. Giggles. Bathroom noises—the flush of a toilet, the splatter of a faucet. "Shh," their voices whispered.

"Shit," September hissed.

"Don't wake Mom," Tommy hushed.

"She'll never hear us," September assured.

I could detect no slurring of words, no staggering of feet, no bumping into furniture. Because my walls are thick and because Tommy's room is across the hall, I didn't have to try to separate the sounds of bedsprings from the creak of the sofa. Ineffectual leader that I am, I didn't jump up to make sure my no-shared-bed rule was enforced. It was enough that I set it, I tell myself. I accept full responsibility for my ignorance-is-bliss/don't-ask-don't-tell policy. Still, safe sex or not, such too-young sex worries me. For health concerns. For what-is-this-world-coming-to laments. And maybe, if I'm honest, because of the tiniest stab of envy somewhere below the belt. *How about us middle-aged?* I want to implore. *How about us for whom the joy of sex denotes merely the title of a book?* I stop. Why am I using the editorial *we* here when I seem to be the only one of my in-their-prime acquaintances who is the sole, serial, and single occupant of a mattress built for two?

I think of Rex and his new mysterious woman, of Tommy pressed up against a near-dropout's teenage pulchritude. Of Darlene pursued by a never-ending supply of masculine brutes. I picture all my married friends whose husbands snore at their sides; the unmarried ones whose medicine cabinets hold their lovers' shaving cream. It all boils down to a Noah's ark of two by two whatever the variations. Perhaps I'm even worse off than the MIL, who keeps Arnie's pajamas archively folded under the pillowcase still matrimonially abutting hers. At least she has her memories. Good memories.

Unlike mine. For three more minutes I continue to feel sorry for myself. I allow a few seconds' worth of supplementary whining. *Everybody's got someone except me. I'm nobody until somebody loves me.* "Enough!" I order. I decide to count my blessings. I have a son, a home, a job. Besides, today is Tuesday. My daily planner lists a dinner date with social worker Doyle.

Now I roll over onto my stomach. I spread my legs

across a length of Sealy Posturepedic designated for the his-side of his-and-hers. I check the clock again: 6:15. I don't think I'm going to be getting any beauty sleep.

The ring of the phone ensures it. "Maisie!"

"I haven't heard any reports in the ten minutes since I talked to you. I promised I'd call when and if."

"It's not that," Mrs. Pollock protests.

"Then what?" I ask in the perfected pitch of long and needless suffering that I've copied from the master, my former mother-in-law.

"Do you have the news on?"

"I'm still in bed. I never watch daytime TV," I boast. *Subtext:* my spare time is devoted to reading all of Proust.

"I'm not surprised that you, of all people, would choose to miss out on exceedingly useful information."

"The news?" I press.

"It threw me. I actually overpoached my egg when I heard."

"Heard what?"

"A college freshman, just a little bit older than Tommy, was arrested at the airport on drug-trafficking charges . . ." She stops.

What is her point? Arrest? Drug trafficking? The bad influences of college? All of which could make me crazy with worry if I weren't so determined to resist. "And? Go on."

"He was carrying condoms filled with powder. Which he swore was flour. Said they were for squeezing to relieve stress."

"Which makes sense," I grant, all too familiar with the dozens of rubber balls stamped with corporate logos adorning the desks of my clients. "Businesses give rubber stress-reducers to their employees."

"These turned out to be filled with cocaine."

"So? This isn't our problem. Just because one college kid was stupid enough . . . I hardly see the relevance."

"I never even knew what a condom was at his age. I never even saw one, even after I was married. Arnie took care of all that."

I pause to process this new information. General generation gap? Specific Pollock gap? Maybe she never used birth control. Maybe she never saw Arnie's manhood in its full flower but felt only some southward fumbling under the counterpane. Maybe if she hadn't produced a son after the three sisters now in Florida, she'd have kept going until there'd been a dozen daughters just like her, populating a palm-treed, gated, golf-coursed community. But perhaps, mission accomplished, Arnie's penis, latex sheathed or not, retracted inside those iconic pajamas now stashed under his pillowcase. It wouldn't surprise me that all post-male-heir concerns with reproduction and fertility were focused more on breeding chickens than on suburban-lawn-moving intercourse. Maybe there was no sex after Rex.

Now I concentrate on the condoms no doubt stockpiled at this very moment next to Tommy's narrow childhood bed. "Why are you telling me this?" I ask. "Why this condom talk?"

"I assumed you shared my concerns. You are his mother."

"Well, I'm glad you're willing to concede that."

"I assumed you'd want to know that young people are carrying drugs all over the place."

"One doesn't need to watch daytime TV to be aware of our country's problems with drugs. But there is no reason to expect the worst. Or to use the Pollock family analogy: Don't count your chickens before they're hatched."

For the second time this morning between six and six-fifteen, I hang up. I get out of bed. Though I tiptoe into the living room, I'm not surprised to see the sofa sheets dramatically ruffled but empty of the body of one sleeping son. Do I collude in the charade? Do I yank two exhausted children out of bed and take a stand? *Not under my roof,* I want to scream. It's all too much. Besides, if I triage my worries, drug addiction trumps sex.

I choose the cowardly route. I make coffee. I eat the last remaining slice of blueberry pie. I turn on the TV news. Let me confess, in the interest of full disclosure, that I don't own one single volume of Proust. I stir sugar into my mug. And because it's true that a stampeding herd of buffalo wouldn't wake Tommy up, especially when he's behind the ostensibly forbidden door of his own room, and because whether September Silva is or is not a light sleeper is hardly my concern, I grab the remote. I press the Volume button hard and then harder on its little red Plus.

I surf the news stations. I don't find a single report on a college kid arrested for filling condoms with drugs. Maybe the MIL made it up. Could she possibly induce more guilt than the burden I'm buckling under right now? Could there possibly be any more room for self-flagellation in the remorse-bearing crevices of my anatomy? If there is, she'll home right in on it.

I watch a segment on celebrity marriages. The camera pans several couples whose two bodies merge into as much one as television propriety laws and nudity rules will allow. The "entertainment reporter" elides their names. I try my own version. *Rexmai*. Jack turns into *Jamais*, which I can't help but note is the French word for *never*.

I look closer. One blond bride with the kind of perky breasts that cry bottle-feeding totes a baby strapped against her impossibly flat stomach. I touch my own stomach, which hasn't recovered from a pregnancy sixteen years ago. A honeymooning Mr. and Mrs. kiss. I want to throw up. They're not awake at six A.M. breakfasting on blueberry pie. They're not stranded alone on the desert island of their bed. Their pink and perfect newborn doesn't know what a condom is. Yet.

Just you wait, I warn their model familyness.

I take a shower. I wash and dry my hair. I dress carefully in grown-up clothes, pressed linen pants, a crisp cotton blouse. I stick pearl studs in my ears, slip on my best Cuban-heeled black flats. Am I setting an example for September? Who won't see me until I return from work inevitably wilted, linen pants rumpled, shirt cuffs blotted with polish from tying Alistair Livingston's shoes, hair dusty from organizing and boxing the cookbooks Genevieve Rochester intends to give to the Schlesinger Library. That is, if September's there when I get home. Oh, let her not be there, I beg. It's only Tommy I want. Back in his single room. Back in the apartment where the mailbox bears just the two names of a mother and her son. I pile the breakfast dishes in the sink and leave them there.

Because it's still early, before eight, I decide to go to Genevieve Rochester's first. She's out of town giving a lecture on Victorian ices at the Culinary Institute of America. I've put Darlene on plant patrol for our other clients, those lucky ducks summering on the Vineyard, the Cape, in the hill towns of Tuscany, the olive groves of Provence. Not only is sorting, cataloging, and packing up the donated books according to Genevieve's precise and near-illegible instructions a one-person job, but also Genevieve's cluttered rooms aren't big enough for both of us. We'd be bumping elbows and hips and arguing over whose turn next to climb the rolling ladder to the top shelves.

When I pull into her driveway in Watertown, the first thing I see are the newspapers bagged and unbagged crisscrossing the steps to her front door. Preoccupied with ices and sherbets and sorbets, she forgot to cancel them. *Welcome, burglars,* these papers invite.

Of course those thieves are due for a disappointment once they jimmy the lock and enter the warren of cookbooks and recipe boxes and Bundt pans and wooden spoons and ceramic chocolate pots that provide their burgling opportunity. Not a stereo or laptop or plasma TV in sight. No cash stuffed into an old sock. Only ancient *Gourmet*s and the odd whisk. It would take an antiquarian book dealer/chef to recognize the treasure and an *Antiques Roadshow* expert to assess the considerable value of those tin ice-cream molds. Though I doubt there's a gang of larcenous librarians or felonious foodies casing the neighborhood, I make a note to stop deliveries. "Why do you subscribe to so many?" I asked once, tying together great stacks of yellowing broadsheets for the recycling bin.

"I read the food columns. As far as the news and the world, well, I couldn't care less."

At first I was horrified. Who would ever admit such bad citizenship? In the grand scheme of things, hers was a bird's-eye view scaled down to the size of a Birds Eye pea. But the longer I thought about it, the bigger its appeal.

Tunnel vision. Selective awareness. Could I block out the MIL the way censors blacken paragraphs of text? Ignore the dire warnings of the war on drugs the way writers claim never to read their reviews? Could I flash-forward the second the disastrous fallout of divorced motherhood dances across my screen? Delete those graphs that chart the dwindling chance of a middle-aged woman's finding a man?

Right now, as I scoop up the papers and turn the key in her door, I ponder Genevieve Rochester's personal philosophy. I'm sure I could learn a lot from such a woman, a woman who lives alone, who has never married, who has never wanted to be married. "I prefer self-sufficiency. I'm not a people person," she explained the day she hired me. Once, when I was quoting some cute phrase Tommy had uttered earlier, she shook her head. "I don't care for children much," she volunteered. "Never wanted them. Never liked their company."

Her life is focused on food. Despite this, she's limpet thin. She's in her early fifties, I believe, though her publicity photos show her looking middle-aged at her graduation from Bryn Mawr. She wears her almost-all-white hair pulled into a spinsterish knot. Good bones frame the kind of features-with-potential that bring other women to exclaim, "Such a pretty face—if only she'd try a little lipstick, a dash of blush!"

One time I found a vibrator behind the stack of *Bon Appétit* magazines she'd asked me to file.

"Oh that," she dismissed. "Stick it back in the drawer."

I must have hesitated. I must not have hidden my astonishment because she added, "Oh, don't look so surprised, Maisie. We all have our needs. I'm just glad I can satisfy them without the help of anyone else."

Now I see myself in full old-maid regalia, Tommy grown and working in Los Angeles or Singapore, all the men in my life married to younger women or living in retirement communities. I'm still running Factotum, Inc., which, by this time, has branched out all over the eastern seaboard. My job consumes me. In my measly non-CEO moments, I eat. I sleep. I play with the sex toys filling my night-table drawer.

Somehow this is not a future that promises me a Genevieve Rochester–type satisfaction. Even with the career-enhancing possibility of Factotum franchises. I'm afraid I'm a people person. I'm afraid I can't satisfy my needs without the help of anyone else.

I get to work. I decode Genevieve's illegible list. I pull off the Post-its that direct me to a particular shelf, cabinet, closet, drawer like so many clues in a scavenger hunt. I catalog the cookbooks. I sort them into the cartons crowding the front hall. I climb up and down the rolling ladder until I'm certain why Genevieve stays so thin.

I take a break. I make myself a cup of coffee in her old French *cafetière*. This is a production: grinding the beans, figuring out the proper proportion of coffee to water and the steeping time, pressing and turning the top with just the perfect amount of torque so as not to ruin the wobbling ancient knob.

I push aside a tower of index cards to make room at her table. I decide to call Darlene's cell. I want to check on her progress. I want to offer the collegiality that's so welcome when you're a people person who has to work alone.

"Jeremy Marshall's aspidistra is dying," she announces.

"I hate that plant," I confess.

"Me, too. On its best day, it looks like crap. But he's nuts about it."

"There's no disputing tastes," I marvel.

We discuss varying degrees of life support. We decide to cut it down and try some new fertilizer before writing its obit.

"You'd think that a *chemist* would be able to work out what to do for an ordinary houseplant," Darlene says. "Him with all those doctor certificates up on his wall. Wouldn't you figure it'd be a no-brainer? Wouldn't you figure a chemist would be able to save its life?"

I wish this particular chemist would save mine. And Tommy's. And get Mrs. Pollock out of my hair. Well, not even an Einstein could perform that Houdini miracle. I finish the rest of the coffee.

Don't worry about things you can't do anything about, Rex used to instruct me, a phrase that never failed to infuriate me however much I was used to it. *Don't count your chickens before they're hatched,* I'd told Tommy's grandmother. I can't take advice. I can't even take the advice I dole out myself. Soon enough, the what-ifs start clashing their cymbals and beating their drums inside my head. How long does it take to test that white powder anyway?

I swallow two aspirin and get back to work. I am dusting a volume about Sherlock Holmes's love of Yorkshire pudding and Cornish pasty when my cell phone rings. I slam the book shut. The signs are not good. Sherlock Holmes's most brilliant deductions occurred under the influence of cocaine. For a second, I feel myself on the verge of turning a minus into a plus, of justifying Sherlock Holmes's drug dependence for the brilliance it induced. I take a deep breath. I prepare for the worst. I snap open the phone.

"Gumdrops," Jeremy Marshall says.

"What?" I scream.

"Gumdrops. It's the sugar from gumdrops. You have nothing to worry about."

The world stops. My heart stops. Silence follows. Stunned silence. Are these the symptoms of post-traumatic stress?

"Maisie?" he asks. "Is there a problem with the telephone?"

I try to get a grip. Though he's in Cambridge and I'm in Watertown, I fall at his somewhere-over-by-MIT feet. "Thank you. Thank you," I croon, bowing toward the mecca of his lab. "I am so grateful. So grateful," I wail. I touch my metaphorical nose against Genevieve Rochester's pine-planked floor.

"It's nothing," he assures.

I pledge my eternal gratitude in increasingly hysterical increments until he replies with the measured syllables you'd use to detach from a demented relative. "No problem at all. Sorry, but," pause, "I," pause, "have," pause, "to," pause, "go," pause, "*now*."

I sit down. I bathe in the sauna of my relief. All anxiety exudes through my pores. I am worry free. At least free of that particular worry. There's always September Silva. Since the worrying nature abhors a vacuum, Tommy's-unsuitable-girlfriend concerns rush right in. I push my concerns aside. I know I should call the MIL and put her at ease. I know I should offer her the same burden lifting I am enjoying right now. But I wait. I wait as long as I can stand the guilt. I wait savoring my sole knowledge of innocence until I feel too mean not to share. Even with her.

I pick up the phone.

She answers on the first ring.

"Gumdrops," I say. "It's the sugar from gumdrops."

"I knew it!" she exults. "So much fuss about nothing. I know my grandson. I know he would never do such a thing. Unlike you, Maisie, I never had a single doubt."

I spend the rest of the afternoon whistling while I work. I sing along with Stevie Wonder's "You Are the Sunshine of My Life." I finish my chores hours ahead of time.

On my way home, I stop at the plant store. I wander the aisles until I find just what I want. I buy for Jeremy Marshall three glowing, growing, gorgeous, glorious, luscious, healthy aspidistras. I pay extra for express delivery.

ELEVEN

At five o'clock, the sky darkens. Rain pounds with the thunder-clapping ferocity of a sudden summer downpour. I run around my apartment closing windows against what may be, I'm afraid, a stormy-weather-ahead warning for my first date with Gabriel Doyle.

I'm getting ready for our dinner. He called me earlier to find out about Tommy. When I told him gumdrops, he yelled *Great!* so loud I almost jumped. "It's nice that you're pleased," I said.

"I'm *thrilled*. I know how worried you've been."

"I really appreciate your support." Was his empathy professional or personal? I asked myself.

"We'll celebrate tonight," he promised. In the background I could hear the rattle of gurneys and a loudspeaker calling for Dr. Sondra Levenson.

You have to give him credit even if his interest was strictly professional, I decided. Did Tommy's grandmother show such delight? Such relief? No. She used gumdrops as a stepping-stone to even more criticism of me. She accused me of a lack of faith in my own child.

"Can't wait to see you again," he added.

"I'm looking forward to it, too." I pictured Gabriel Doyle's freckled face and brown hair. His essential plainness, the opposite of Rex's dazzling looks. There's comfort in the ordinary, I realized. And as soon as I thought this, his nondescript features began to shift into a kaleidoscope of charm and attractiveness and intelligence. Maybe, I started to hope, there are possibilities here.

Possibilities immediately deflated, as evidenced by this next sentence, the first warning sign that our planets might not be aligned, our stars not compatible: "How about five-thirty?" Gabe asked.

"Excuse me?"

"Dinner at five-thirty."

"Five-thirty?" I repeated.

I must have sounded incredulous because he, early-bird sensitive, jumped right in with a compromise. "Let's switch to six."

"Do you have to be somewhere afterward?" I imagined a therapy session with another distraught mother in the waiting area of Mount Auburn Hospital. I could see the coffee, the sugar packets, the crumpled magazines displaying ecstatic pregnant celebrities, the sympathetic ear tilted just so.

"My whole night is yours," he pledged.

"I didn't mean—"

"Speaking figuratively, of course. But six o'clock is really fine for me. I hope it's okay for you, too."

I couldn't bring myself to match his sis-boom-bah *Great!* "If that's what you want," I managed.

He gave an apologetic laugh. "I'm afraid I'm an early eater. At home my mother would have food on the table at five o'clock sharp."

But we're not in Kansas anymore, I wanted to point out. I stopped. I understood how old habits died hard. "Eating early is probably better for the digestion," I said. Not that I would know, never having eaten at six since college, when you had to show up at the dining hall before the chicken breasts ran out and you were left with charred drumsticks on which the stubble of feathers was still visible.

Then he asked me about restaurant choices.

"It's up to you."

"I'd love your input."

I mentioned Legal Seafood. The Indian place in my neighborhood. Chinatown. The good Thai restaurant near him in Arlington, the Italian in the North End famous for its wild boar. "I could recommend a decent Vietnamese," I suggested. "And there's always sushi in Porter Square."

"Hmmm," he mused.

Silence followed.

I waited. I may not be a social worker with a perfected *hmmm,* but a mother knows all about the pregnant pause and the art of listening.

He cleared his throat. "At the risk of not making the best impression . . ."

"Go on."

"I've got a few food issues."

I tried not to groan. "So have you seen a therapist or a social worker to deal with that?" I asked.

He chuckled in good-sport camaraderie. "My food problems don't rank up there in the *Diagnostic and Statistical Manual of Mental Disorders*. I'm just a meat-and-potatoes guy."

"We all have our personal tastes," I offered.

A statement which seemed to provoke additional

from-bad-to-worse culinary confessions. "I'm not fond of fish," he went on. "I hate ethnic food. And Chinese I really loathe."

"I get the picture," I said, though I wasn't sure. Who didn't like Chinese? Even in the tiniest New Hampshire village, you can find wonton soup along with burgers and fries.

He must have been reading my mind because he started to explain. "A bunch of colleagues took me to a dim sum place. But when I saw those chicken feet . . ." His voice trailed off.

"An acquired taste. In fact, those chicken feet are considered a delicacy. Believe me, they cost more than the rest of the bird, even pampered free-range baby-chicken breasts."

"You know a lot about chickens," he said.

"Runs in the family."

"Well, that's an intriguing topic we'll have to explore. Once we pick that restaurant."

"Do you drink?" I asked.

"I'm Irish," he answered.

Now I tug on my jeans and a shirt. Just for novelty's sake, I would have preferred a place more conducive to romance, a place where I could get dressed up. High heels. The sparkly earrings Jack gave me when we were each in the-other-person-is-perfect phase. It's been a long time since I've rolled on panty hose to have dinner with a man.

And it will be longer still. Fred's Steak House, where Gabe has made a reservation for six "sharp," is a restaurant popular with dressed-down families, sports fans, and local pols. It's big on gigantic-portioned fifties fare—shrimp cocktail, steak, baked potato with sour cream, salad with blue cheese dressing, Boston cream or lemon meringue pie.

I pull up to the tiny parking lot behind Fred's at five-fifty-seven. Gabe is standing at the entrance like an attendant. Over his head, he holds a WGBH public television umbrella. He's wearing an odd-shaped, skimpy-looking raincoat that barely reaches the top of his thighs and, though belted, doesn't seem to close in front. Underneath, I can discern a just-come-from-work-Fred's-inappropriate suit and tie. He's making crossing-guard motions.

I lower my window. He moves his umbrella to protect my poked-out nose. "The lot seems full," I say.

"I snagged the last space," he offers. "I'm saving it for you. Just wait here. I'll back out and you can pull in."

"That's so thoughtful."

"I'm a thoughtful guy. Remember that when you're dreaming of chop suey and Dover sole."

"I will." I look around. "But where will you park?" I ask.

"I'll circle the block. There's bound to be something."

"But you'll miss your six o'clock deadline."

He grins. "I'm not *that* rigid. Though the booths might be all taken. They don't hold them, even with a reservation." He turns to walk to his car.

"Wait," I yell. "You go claim our booth. I'll find a space." This is no eat-at-a-fashionable-hour crowd. Already I see a phalanx of the early-bird set splashing through puddles in a rush toward the front door and skirting the two sentinel cement pots planted with marigolds.

Gabe must have noticed the hungry hordes, too, because he's crouched in a starting-gate stance. "Are you sure?" he asks.

"Positive."

"Then you take the umbrella."

I point to the backseat where my own WGBH umbrella lies seesawed across some cleaning supplies. "I've come equipped," I explain. I set the car in reverse and back out of the parking lot.

It takes me a couple of loops until I spy a spot just clear of a hydrant. By the time I get inside, Gabe's already snared a booth and is hanging his raincoat on the hook beside it.

"Great call," he says. "We got the last booth available." He shakes some drops off the raincoat's hem. He holds out one of its buckled sleeves and waves it at me. "I caught you staring at this," he accuses. He smiles.

"It looked a little odd," I confess. "Maybe my sight was distorted by the weather."

"Ah, you're one of those always-give-the-other-guy-the benefit-of-the-doubt people. That's a good quality." He slides into his side of red vinyl upholstery. "No, that raincoat's my mother's London Fog. I grabbed the wrong one."

For a second, it occurs to me that I should wonder why his mother's London Fog is sharing a closet with *his* London Fog. Stay in the moment, Maisie, I warn myself. Enjoy the joke.

"Great first impression," he laughs. "Great cross-dressing first impression."

"I can think of worse," I allow. "Besides, it suits you."

He taps the raincoat behind him. "Then I'll have to wear it more often," he says.

We order martinis, salad, steaks, and baked potatoes

with sour cream from a grandmotherly waitress whose bosom could serve as its own tray. "How you doin', Gabe?" she asks.

"Can't complain, Mary." He points at me. "This is Maisie."

"Oh," she grunts. She lifts a pitcher and fills my glass so full the water starts to cascade down the sides. She hands me extra napkins, then pivots and marches off in squeak-soled shoes.

I mop up the table. I stick the sodden napkins behind the A.1. sauce. The Red Sox are at bat on the TVs hanging over the bar. Every few minutes, cheers rise from the men downing beers and looking as if the bar stools growing out of their bottoms like mushrooms are permanent parts of their anatomy.

"So?" Gabe says.

"So," I echo.

He raises his martini glass. "To gumdrops," he toasts.

I clink mine against his. The olive wobbles. He's got three to my one. "To gumdrops," I repeat.

We do the usual first-date dance. Place of birth, schools, music, films, the gentrification of Arlington Center, of Davis Square, the brilliant renovations of the Capitol Theater and Davis Square cinemas and their superior popcorn as compared to the chains, the desecration of Harvard Square, the loss of the Tasty lunch counter where Gabe had his daily egg-salad sandwich when he was getting his master's in psychology, the demise of Wordsworth bookstore. Kids, my one, his none. Marital history. Mine.

I supply a quick tour of Rex. The lowlights, mostly, including a glancing blow at my mother-in-law.

His eyes ooze compassion. His eye-contact capabilities soar into the 100th percentile.

"And you?" I ask. He's forty-three. There must be an ex-wife or two to account for those bonds of empathy.

He ignores the question. He tilts his head heavenward.

I follow his gaze and see only chipped acoustical tiles and a brass chandelier in need of polish.

"Ah, mothers," he sighs.

The hairs on my arm stand up.

"Mothers," he says again, his eyes still directed on the ceiling and presumably the wild blue yonder above the restaurant's peaked roof.

I lean forward. "Tell me about yours," I ask, a question that seems the requisite choice in the good-manners category.

"She passed three years ago." He touches his heart.

Uh-oh. "I'm sorry," I offer.

He rubs his eyes. "Thank you." He finishes his martini. He signals for another. "She was a saint. My father died young. She raised five daughters and a son. Me. I was an afterthought."

I think of Rex, of the three-daughter hurdles that had to be cleared on the way to the Y chromosome. "You mean they didn't keep trying until they produced a boy?"

"That's not the Catholic style. Or at least not my mother's, who never missed a mass, even in her last weeks. You accepted what you got. God's will and all that." He blinks. "I was a rhythm-method casualty. My father died before my first birthday, so I was the end of the line."

"I bet you were adored."

"I was appreciated." He fishes out an olive. He pops it in his mouth. "You know what James Joyce said."

"Not really. I mean, I should. I work for a James Joyce scholar, Professor Seamus O'Toole," I boast, as if proximity confers knowledge. Why didn't I pay more attention to the contents of Seamus's bookshelves rather than the chicken potpies in his refrigerator? "Sadly," I confess, "the only Joyce I've studied is *The Dead*." Which is a blatant lie since my Joyce erudition springs solely from the movie I saw on a late-night-cable Angelica Huston festival. "But I've got *Dublin* on my night table," I fib some more.

"*Dubliners*," he corrects. "'Whatever else is unsure in this stinking dunghill of a world, a mother's love is not,'" he recites in a hammy brogue.

"There's no disputing that," I chorus.

"But ours was an undemonstrative family." He points to his plate. "Exhibit A: plain food. No frills emotionally, either. Minimal touching. Praise was considered bad for you. Not a lot of talk, which is probably why I became a professional listener."

I ponder this. I am grateful to my own mother, her hugs, her kisses, her always-available lap. Her endless *good jobs* and *well dones*. Is that because she is Jewish? I can't believe religious affiliation has any effect on degrees of coldness. My Episcopalian father is as lavish with praise as he is with bracing pats on the back. In contrast, just look at the MIL, whose devotion runs as hot and cold as the divided taps of my childhood and whose love for her son is so smothering that no good could or did come of it.

Gabe must be reading my mind because he now adds, "Not that a lack of physical warmth can be blamed on one's ethnic background. In fact, I had an Episcopalian friend in college who converted to Catholicism because the people who raised him, who showed him real love and tenderness, were the Irish nannies and maids who worked in his parents' house." He holds up his hand. He crooks his little finger in a parody of an English lady raising a translucent china teacup to her lips. "When my mother was being affectionate, she'd link her little finger with mine. And hold it there for a couple of seconds."

I imagine the woman from *American Gothic,* a pitchfork pointed to keep any affection-seeking children away from her bony chest and icy heart. "You're kidding! That's all?"

"It was enough." He looks heavenward again. "It was a privilege to take care of her in the last years of her life."

I stare at him. Something in his favor: He's a mensch who loved his mother. Something also not in his favor: Did he love his mother too much? "You lived with your mother? After you grew up?"

"It made sense. Most of my sisters married and moved away. The youngest, Sheila, is in grad school on the West Coast. It's a big house."

"And you still live there?"

"She left it to me."

"So you still live in your childhood house?" I press.

"Yes. I imagine it sounds odd. Somewhat regressive. A classic case of arrested development." He squares his paper place mat. "I'm single. I suppose if I had a family of my own . . ."

"You never married?" I stop. "Sorry. You must feel stuck at a table with the Grand Inquisitor. I mean, it's none of my business."

"Of course it is. You told me all about Rex."

"Not *all,*" I correct.

"Enough. I was engaged once. The same old story. She ran off with my best friend."

"That's terrible."

He waves a dismissive hand. "It's okay. She wasn't right for me. My mother hated her. Not that she actually came out and said anything, but I knew."

I can hear the warning bells. I should probably get up and leave this minute. Then I remember that his mother died three years ago. A fact that doesn't seem as consoling as it should—even though daughter-in-law hatred, girlfriend disapproval, dinner-companion dislike could be scientifically postulated to end at the grave. I offer an encouraging nod and a good-listener ear.

"I had a mother-in-law, too," he confesses. "For about a month."

I wait. Maybe *I* should get a master's in psychology.

He goes on. "I was married. It was annulled two weeks after the honeymoon."

I try to keep my face neutral to mask my astonishment. Doesn't annulment involve the pope? Doesn't annulment mean the marriage wasn't consummated?

I study Gabe. He looks normal. What is normal? Am I having dinner with a forty-three-year-old mother's boy who is a virgin?

I put down my glass. I must not look as expressionless as I hoped because Gabe says, right away—well, he's a psychologist who *is* trained to interpret people's thoughts—"Don't worry. I've had sex."

"I wasn't—"

"Let me reassure you, all the pertinent body parts are in full working order. As a result of plenty of practice through the years." He lifts his fork. His face reddens. "Though not currently."

I can feel my own cheeks heat up. "I never—"

He moves his potatoes to the side, away from his steak. "My marriage in a nutshell: She cried all through the wedding. She cried all through the reception. She cried all the way on the plane to St. Thomas. She cried on the beach. She cried on the motorboat. She cried onto every parasol stuck into every piña colada. She cried through sex, which kind of put a literal damper on things. Not that either of us was a virgin, mind you. Not that we hadn't had"—he pauses—"entirely satisfactory intimate relations before the wedding."

"You don't have to—"

"She went home the next day. She missed her parents. She couldn't stand to be without them."

"Was your mother glad?"

"Typically, she never said anything. She put fresh sheets on my bed. Renewed my subscription to the *New York Times*. And aside from one phrase—'that silly girl'—she never once spoke another word about it."

Unlike the MIL. God knows the bad-mouthing Rex has been subject to: Maisie's shortcomings, chapters one through fifty. Before, during, and after the marriage. How much brainwashing can a person take until Stockholm syndrome sets in, until you start to identify with your captor? "You're lucky," I remark. "Silence has its virtues. What happened to her?"

"My mother?"

"No, your . . ." I can't quite bring myself to say *wife*. "The runaway bride."

He grins. "She was no Julia Roberts, alas. She went to Library Science school and runs the Emmanuel College Library. At forty, she married a fellow librarian. They have twins. One named Dewey, if you can believe it."

"The other called Decimal?"

He laughs. "I wouldn't be surprised. They all live with her parents. Probably very happily."

"At least she didn't become a nun."

"I wouldn't have wanted *that* on my conscience." He pauses. "Maybe if I had worn the right raincoat . . ."

"Did you love her?"

"I thought I did. I was twenty-four. What does one know at such an age?"

I can only agree. What *do* you know when you're young? At sixteen you think you're immortal. You're sure your first love will last till eternity. You assume the joy of sex, just like a thing of beauty, will be a joy forever. You never imagine that money and jobs and mothers and mothers-in-law and kids and current events and the tricky hot-water heater and too many frozen chicken potpies and a bad cold and a thoughtless word could even penetrate the thick protective shell of your perfect love. What did I know when I married Rex? I was a child.

I study Gabriel Doyle. Have I learned anything between then and now?

The waitress clears our plates. Gabriel's is scraped clean. Because he likes the food? Or because of a mother who reminded him of the potato famine every time he sat down to his skimpy lamb chop and canned peas? Perhaps both. "You eat a lot for a skinny guy," I say.

"And don't think I haven't taken advantage of my lucky metabolism. In parochial school, the parents would send in cakes and cookies for their children as a special treat. The nuns used to take the packages away from the more conspicuously better-fed and distribute them to us skinny kids. I made out like a bandit. I never told my mother, who would have written a note to the nuns to declare that Gabriel was not starving and that she was more than able to put food on the table and please do not stuff him with any more sweets, thank you very much."

"That's amazing. But what must those parents have felt when the goodies intended for their darlings were diverted to somebody else's?"

"Sacrifice. Martyrdom. Qualities held in high esteem."

The waitress comes back. A stub of a pencil is tucked behind her ear. A notepad sticks out of her pocket. She doesn't touch either. "What will you have for dessert, hon?" she asks Gabe. "The usual?"

"Boston cream, Mary. You know me, I'm a creature of habit."

"That you are. It's sure nice to be able to count on some things in life staying the same." She turns to me. She scowls at the wasteful mound on my plate. "A doggie bag for that?" she asks. No *hon* for me.

And not the slightest chance of a *hon*, ever, when I reply, "No, thank you." Right away I realize I've given the wrong answer—by her expression and by the line of now departing diners carrying Styrofoam boxes of leftovers and foil bags twisted into swans.

"On second thought, sure," I amend.

"Dessert?" she asks.

I pat my stomach. "I'm afraid I couldn't possibly."

"She'll have some of mine," Gabe offers.

"I've never seen you share before," the waitress observes.

Before? I get it: Creatures of habit take all first dates to the same restaurant even if Fred's Steak House might not be the most suitable spawning ground for romance. Though perhaps, I begin to realize, its inauspicious atmosphere is the very point.

"I've never known you not to gobble down every bite of that pie," she persists.

"There's always a first time."

A loud cheer rises from the bar. "Manny's the man," someone yells.

"Go, Sox!" another voice slurs into his Bud.

"Who's up?" the waitress asks, and sails her prowlike chest toward the greener, Green Monster pastures of Fenway Park.

Gabe tilts his chin in the direction of her departing back. "She's a bit of a character. It takes a while to appreciate her charms."

What charms? I yearn to ask. Maybe she lit candles for his mother on her day off. "I don't think she likes me," I venture.

"It's not personal. She's suspicious of all . . ." He stops.

"All women who might share your booth?" I supply.

"Let me put it this way: She's the mother of sons."

A busboy slaps the pie onto the table. Gabriel slices it into two triangles so geometrically exact he might have used a protractor to measure them. He extends his plate.

I shake my head.

"You're sure?" A rhetorical question since he doesn't wait for my response before he wolfs down both halves. A glob of whipped cream mustaches his upper lip. I want to reach over and wipe it off. Just motherly instinct, I excuse, and lower my hands to my lap.

"Isn't there anything else I can get for you, do for you?" he asks. "Coffee? Tea? Milk? An after-dinner liqueur?"

"Uh-uh. Although . . ." I fiddle with the napkin on my lap. I study his open, ordinary face. His nice smile. His dimpled chin. I think of his social worker degree, his master's in psychology. His help at Mount Auburn Hospital. His genuine pleasure at the gumdrops report. "Maybe I could take advantage of your professional expertise?" I suggest. "Maybe, yet again, I could ask your advice?"

He gives a modest shrug. "I wasn't much help."

"Oh, you were!" I exclaim. "You helped me calm down. You helped me breathe. Without your visualization exercises, I would never have come up with the person to test the powder. I would never have got the results so fast."

"You give me too much credit."

"I'd be really grateful." I twist the napkin around my fingers, then smooth it flat. "Although I would completely understand if you feel social occasions are no place—"

He holds up a traffic-cop hand. "Social occasions," he repeats. "Some social occasion. I'm afraid I forced you to a restaurant you'd never choose, a meal you could barely finish, a waitstaff that would never last a day at a dive in France, a blaring Red Sox game, not to mention a lack of tablecloths, candles, any kind of atmosphere. For you, this must be less a social occasion and more a job babysitting a Boston cream pie."

"Not at all. I'm having a very good time." Actually, I note, to my surprise, I *am* having a very good time.

"You're much too kind." He moves his empty plate to the side. "Shoot. Ask me anything you like."

"Well," I lean forward. "It's about September Silva. Tommy's girlfriend . . ."

"Go on," he encourages. He bends forward, too, and meets me halfway, until all that separates our elbows are the salt and pepper shakers and the card promoting the cocktail of the week, a Fredaiquiri.

"Sorry." I hesitate. "It's hard to start. I mean, I'm not sure how . . ."

"Just jump right in."

I jump right in. "I've got doubts—serious doubts—about the way I'm bringing up my son."

"I thought this was about his girlfriend. The creatively named September Silva." He leans even closer. I can smell the pie on his sugary breath, his lemon shampoo. From this perspective I see that his eyes aren't the dull brown I once dismissed but the soft warm color of chocolate milk.

I take a running-leap breath. I sketch a broad and general outline of the saga of September Silva, how she's Tommy's girlfriend, how she planted her suitcases in my front hall, and how she's sharing Tommy's bed, the narrow bed of a sixteen-year-old *child* despite my efforts to set up the living room couch as a bundling board. I leave out such editorial window dressing as her hair, her clothes, her pauperish unsuitability for the prince who is my son. I don't want Gabe to think I'm superficial or prejudiced. "He's only sixteen," I cry. "Isn't he too young for sex—let alone having the person he's having sex with move in with him?"

"Not to mention, move in with *you*," Gabe clarifies, giving the words such shrinklike emphasis they sound ominous.

"That, too," I grant. I get your Oedipal insinuations, I want to inform him. I can recognize displacement. I understand projection. I'm no psychology-for-dummies candidate. But I keep my mouth shut.

He strokes his chin. "My sister Eileen had a similar problem."

"*My Sister Eileen*?"

"I know." He laughs. "I don't think my parents had a clue. They weren't theater people."

"Sorry. I didn't mean to interrupt. Continue."

"My nephew Kevin fell madly in love at summer camp. They were both fourteen. The girl was from New York. Manhattan. Eileen lives in Springfield. Kevin spent a weekend at her family's apartment. When it was the girl's turn to visit him, Eileen made up the guest bed. *But, Mom,* Kevin said, *Mrs. Lewis lets me sleep in Rebecca's room!*"

"'How can I, the mother of the *boy*, insist on separate rooms when the mother of the *girl* is putting them in the same bed?' my sister asked."

"What did you say?"

"I told her I understood exactly how she felt. I advised her to act within her own comfort zone no matter how many accusations of being square. And that, ultimately, whatever she did would result in only the appearance of keeping them apart, not the fact."

I shake my head. "It's hard when people come from different backgrounds, have different standards to uphold."

"Is that your problem with September?"

"I'm not exactly sure how to put this," I falter. "In case I'm misunderstood."

"Try," he instructs.

"I'm afraid this makes me sound as disapproving as my own mother-in-law, *ex*-mother-in-law," I qualify.

"Let's hear it."

"Well, she doesn't seem Tommy's type."

He smiles. "Maybe that's the appeal."

"You mean teenage rebellion?"

"A phenomenon that has been known to occur at the age of sixteen." He do-si-dos the pepper shaker around the salt. "What specifically is bothering you about her?"

How do I begin? That she calls me Maisie? That she wears rags? That the soles of her feet are filthy? That her fingers sport rings with skulls on them? That she's a lacto-intolerant, vegan food nut? (Perhaps I'd better not make an issue of *this*.) That her mother kicked her out, no doubt for a good reason? That she sticks a proprietary hand on Tommy's arm? That she's deposited what looks like all her worldly goods in Tommy's room? That she seems so—well—confident? That she's clearly more sexually sophisticated than my son? That she's dropping out of school?

Of course. "That she's dropping out of school" is the politically correct complaint I seize upon.

"That's easy."

"*Easy?*"

His knuckles tap the table with the verdict-arrived-at finality of a gavel. "A piece of cake. Just put your foot down and declare that if she drops out of school, she can't stay with you."

My mouth falls open in astonishment. "You're a genius! I never thought of that."

"You would have. In due course."

"I doubt it." I lean back. "You're one hell of a psychologist," I marvel.

"It's more the wise-lady-from-Philadelphia solution. Common sense."

"The wise lady from Philadelphia?" I ask.

"A character in an old children's book I found at the Arlington Public Library when I was a kid. *The Peterkin Papers*. The Peterkins get a new piano. It's moved in backwards. As a result, the daughter has to play it through an open window while sitting on the front porch. In winter, her hands freeze. The family doesn't know what to do until the wise lady from Philadelphia advises them to turn the piano around."

I laugh. "It sounds like a great book. Would that everything were so simple."

"Sometimes everything is that simple." He pauses. "Can I give you another piece of wise-lady-from-Philadelphia advice?"

"Please."

"Why don't you call September Silva's mother? What mother would want her daughter to quit school? I bet you could put your heads together and figure out a solution that will work for the two of you."

"The two-heads-are-better-than-one solution?"

"Tried and true." He stops. His eyes hold mine. "The way two people eating together are better than one forlorn soul dining alone. Even in the least promising restaurant."

The waitress comes back. She hands me the twisted-swan-slash-doggie bag. She takes away the card promoting the cocktail of the week. "They're changing it tomorrow," she explains.

"To what?" Gabe asks.

"Beats me. Nobody ever orders those fancy cocktails with those silly names anyhow. Complete waste."

"You never know, Mary. Maybe *I'll* order the special cocktail next time," Gabriel says.

"As if. I've never heard you order anything but a martini in all the years you been coming here. Creature of habit you are." She digs into her pocket. She fishes out the check. She slaps it not quite in the middle of the table—six inches closer to me. She adds three foil-wrapped mints. It hardly takes a genius to deconstruct *that* symbolism.

Gabe picks up the check before I can make any equality-of-the-sexes motions. "Not on your life," he says. "I invited you."

When we leave the restaurant, the sun is shining in all its clunky symbolism. Except for puddles in the gutters and a few drops glistening on parked cars, you'd never have known that a torrential storm had passed through a couple of hours earlier. Gabe insists on walking me to my car even though it's only eight. Skateboarders and window-shoppers and leisurely strollers and kids with dripping ice-cream cones crowd the sidewalks. The remains of rush-hour traffic still clog Mass Avenue.

He snatches the key from me and opens the driver's-side door. "How about tomorrow night?" he asks.

I must look utterly surprised because he takes a step back. "Am I being too forward?" His face turns sheepish.

"No, it's not that . . . Believe me, I'm flattered. It's just—"

He smacks his forehead. "Of course, you have another date. A smart, charming woman like you must have her dance card all filled up."

What do I tell him? That tomorrow night is my dinner with Jack to rake over the dying—if not dead—embers of our relationship? That even though Jack is the boyfriend on the way out, there's still some unfinished business there? Do I admit to him that two dinners in a row with members of the opposite sex is a highly improbable statistic in my personal database?

I search his face, which lays bare disappointment and a certain endearing woebegoneness. You'd think a therapist would be better able to hide his feelings. But maybe outright emotion is part of his psychologist's bag of tricks, because now I feel so sad on his behalf I reach into my pocketbook for my blank-paged calendar. I riffle through it. "How about the day after tomorrow?" I ask, my Good Samaritanness fueled in no small measure by being called charming and smart. "I think I'm free," I add.

"Great!" he exults. "Come to my house. I'll make you dinner."

I laugh. "Pizza?"

"My favorite." He pauses. "Except for . . ."

"I know. Except for anchovies. Broccoli. Pineapple chunks. Pepperoni. Jalapeño peppers . . ."

"You got it." He reaches into his pocket. He takes out his card. On the back, he writes his home address. He gives me directions to his street from Mass Ave at Arlington Center.

"Six o'clock?" I ask.

"Seven," he says. "I'm going to start living on the wild side."

I turn on the ignition. "Seven it is."

He leans his head through the open window. "It's been a lovely evening, Maisie."

"Thanks for dinner," I say, "and all the wise-lady-from-Philadelphia advice."

He moves closer. For a minute I think he's going to kiss me. I sense his lips near my cheek. I feel the soft brush of his breath. But he seems to think better of it. Discreetly he pulls back. Just as well, I tell myself.

TWELVE

My horoscope this morning warns of gray skies ahead, even though sun streams through the kitchen windows. In addition, we Sagittarians are also advised to steer clear of the telephone and not to venture outdoors. I can't. Despite the risk of an MIL call, I could no more ignore the telephone than Pavlov's dog could stop salivating at Pavlov's bell. The minute I scan the other months to check out Tommy's sign, Aries—*love is in the air, celebrate*—the phone rings. I reach for the receiver. Too late. I should have listened to the astrologer. "Something's come up," Jack announces.

"Hello to you, too, Jack."

"Yeah. Hi," he concedes.

"So how are you?" I ask, mistress of bright preliminaries to delay the dark inevitable.

He lobs back a perfunctory, "Okay. How are *you*, Maisie?" then doesn't wait to find out before he adds, "I'm going to have to cancel tonight."

"Surprise. Surprise."

"I've got a memo due on a merger, a partners' meeting,

clients coming in all day, a bank reception for trust accounts, a desk piled so high I can't find a spare inch to sign a document—"

"I've kept this particular date clear for two weeks," I remind him. "At no small inconvenience."

He blows his nose. "And I may be coming down with a cold."

He gets no sympathy from me. "You're not the only one busy. I've set this time aside. Even though I've had some very tempting invitations."

"Which you should have accepted. God knows, I'd understand. You needed only to have said the word—"

"And you wouldn't have been disappointed?"

"I would have been glad for you. Totally." I hear some papers shuffle. He lowers his voice. "After all, we're not a couple anymore."

"Pardon?"

"You and me. Not a couple."

"I thought this was the topic up for discussion. At Redbones tonight. The state of our coupledom." I pause. "Or non-coupledom."

He offers up a few phony-sounding change-the-subject coughs. "And also, I have to prepare for a hearing tomorrow for one of my pro bono cases."

"Really?" I ask. "Darlene?"

He waits. I hear the tap of a keyboard. I hear the ping that signals a just-arrived e-mail. He is in the office early. And I can recognize the signs of multitasking. I can sense when a caller's attention is not focused on his callee.

"Is it Darlene?" I repeat.

"I'd rather not say," he obfuscates.

"What do you mean?"

"Attorney-client privilege."

"Bullshit. Attorney-client privilege was hardly an issue when a particular client's bodily fluid needed a storage facility outside her privileged attorney's refrigerator."

"Now now, Maisie," he says. "Let's be reasonable."

"Don't you dare use your placating-a-toddler, pacifying-a-demanding-client voice on me!"

He sighs. "I'm just up to my ears."

I know those ears. How they redden with anger or embarrassment. How, like Pinocchio's nose, they signal a lie. I know the taste of them, the texture. Right this second, I can only imagine the intensity of the scarlet now setting those ears aflame. "Forget it. It doesn't matter. Darlene will tell me herself," I say.

"Fine," he replies.

I look at the calendar hanging on the refrigerator. "Just for the record, I assume you don't want us to reschedule?"

I hear nothing. I hear the sound of silence.

"Fine," I echo. I fold the newspaper in front of me. I wonder what Jack's horoscope advises. Wait, I tell myself, we've been seeing each other for a year and I never even found out his birthday date. Talk about signs.

"I've been thinking," he goes on. He drums his fingers against the telephone.

"Yes . . . ?"

"Maybe we should call it quits. Permanently. Officially. Why rehash what isn't working?"

"Ah, the editorial *we* . . ."

"Maisie . . ."

"Never mind. Go ahead."

"What I meant was, why bother to meet when it's so clear we've both gone our separate ways."

I take a few deep breaths for generic breaking up's sake. I consider. "You're right," I agree.

"I knew you'd be reasonable."

"Not hard when very little is at stake."

He lets that pass. "Well, thank you."

"Though I, for one, was looking forward to those ribs."

He squeezes out a token chortle to acknowledge the comic relief. "They're so bad for you."

Who is speaking here? Lacto-ovo-vegetarian September Silva? Or the man who on more than one occasion brought a Big Mac to bed? "Which is why they taste so good," I explain.

"It's all in the barbecue sauce."

"Not to mention their slow-cooking techniques as well as their wood-burning pit," I add.

We seem to be stuck on a culinary theme, so I'm glad when he switches to, "No matter what, I'm sure we'll stay friends—"

"And we'll always have Somerville," I finish.

"One of your best qualities is your sense of humor, Maisie," he grants. "We shared some great times. We'll have good memories."

"We'll mull them over in our rocking chairs in our assisted-living facilities. I'll tell the toothless geezer next to me about the man who broke our date and cheated me out of some ribs."

"Sure. Right. Whatever." He blows his nose again. "I'm glad you agree it is time for each of us to move on. To find other companions."

"So you've already moved on. So you found—quaint phrase—another companion," I state. Am I surprised? I pretty much guessed he was a serial companion finder when I met him. Who better to fit that profile than a commitment-phobe who'd never park his toothbrush in a companion's medicine cabinet. How do I feel? I take my romantic pulse. Hurt in the sense that it's better to be the dropper than the one who is dropped. But not hurt in the sense that the love of my life is in the arms of another. I'll miss *the* boyfriend more than I'll miss *this* boyfriend. The ribs I can get on my own.

The phone clicks. "Hang on a minute," Jack says now. "I've got another call."

I wait. I pull out the Redbones menu from the kitchen drawer. In true save-our-planet Cambridge/Somerville tradition, Redbones offers bicycle delivery as well as free bicycle valet parking. At five o'clock, I'll call the take-out number and have the ribs bicycled over by dinnertime.

I sigh at the prospect of my dinner for one. No doubt Tommy and September will be chomping on celery in front of a thumping electric guitar. Still, a woman who eats ribs by herself is hardly as pathetic as a woman who drinks alone or who lives with cats. If I'd only known that the end of Jack's and my two-week moratorium was going to be neither celebrated nor extended tonight, I would have Magic-Markered Gabriel Doyle into my calendar right over the scribbled *dinner with Jack*.

"Sorry," Jack returns. "But I had to take it. An *important* client." He stresses the word *important*.

Believe me, I get the hint. "Sure," I say.

He coughs three times as prelude to the verdict. "Okay, then, we're both on the same page," he summarizes.

"So I gather."

"Gotta go." His voice drops all trace of a cold as fast as you can say Lourdes. He chimes with vigorous health. "You take care, Maisie," he orders.

"You, too."

"It's been great," he grants, magnanimous now that he's made his escape.

By the time I get to Seamus O'Toole's and put my key in his front-door lock, I don't feel so great. That I should have heeded my horoscope's warning to stay home and shirk those astrological gray skies is further underlined by what I see in Seamus O'Toole's living room: a sobbing Darlene Lattanzio, head nestled against the professorial chest, the two of them jammed together on the sofa, mop and pail at their feet, wadded Kleenexes under both their eyes. *Both* their eyes?

I stand transfixed. "What happened?" I exclaim.

Four tear-washed red eyes, two rubbed-raw red noses tilt up at me.

I stare at them. Death, rape, a stolen *Ulysses* first edition, salmonella in the chicken potpie, strontium 90 in the breast milk—all these race through my mind. "My God, what happened?"

Seamus extends a hand with a squalid tissue at the end of it. He points to the nearest chair. "Sit down, Maisie. Neither of us should have arisen from Morpheus's arms this morning. Such a perfect day. Glorious sun. Azure skies. Birdsong. All of which to an Irish soul can only portend disastrous storms both real and fantastical."

I assume Darlene's work was interrupted, or only progressed as far as liberating the bucket and mop from the broom closet, because I have to move a dozen items—papers, books, an empty pie plate with bits of burnt crust, a broken pair of reading glasses, one semi-invisibly darned argyll sock—before I can sink my stunned body into the faded, patched corduroy upholstery. I stick the key in my tote bag; I put the bag on the floor. I lean forward, my body language coiled into a question mark.

Seamus turns to Darlene. "Ladies first," he stage-whispers the way a Celtic tragedian might declaim Yeats.

"Darlene?" I prompt.

In between her sobs I can just about manage to string together these words: *Hearing. Lawyers. Tomorrow. Mother-in-law. Custody. Fight.*

"You've got a hearing tomorrow about Anthony Vincent's custody?" I translate.

"Not an official hearing. More of a meeting," Seamus explains.

"No wonder she's so upset."

"I'll say. This poor little thing has been served a citation. Her diabolical mother-in-law has petitioned for sole guardianship of the angelic child."

"What does that mean?"

Darlene's body heaves. "Court. A *trial*. The *kidnapping* of my baby. *The end of my life.*" Her words accelerate into a frantic pitch, then drop into a low, keening moan.

Seamus rubs his own eyes. "Her lawyer has arranged a meeting with the mother-in-law and opposing counsel tomorrow to see if they can negotiate something before the case heads to court."

"*The case!*" Darlene exclaims. "That's what it comes down to. Me and my baby, we're just a case." She pounds her fist against the sofa arm, raising, I'm professionally alarmed to note, a cloud of dust. "I've already been given a court date," she bawls. "On the very day we're taking the Elderberry sisters to their doctor's appointment and then to tea at that Athens library in Boston they've been telling me about."

"Athenaeum," Seamus corrects. "I've spent a bit of time there myself. They have in their possession seminal volumes on the Irish in Boston. And quite a decent bust of Joyce, if I do recall."

"Not that I'll ever see it. Not that I'll ever see anything." Darlene wipes her nose on her sleeve. "I'll be in *court*. Me, whose only crime, besides marrying that good-for-nothing, was shoplifting a Milky Way when I was six. I gave it back. Now I'll be in a real courtroom with a judge and the DSS notified and everything! For what? Leaving Anthony Vincent with his father? His own father even if he *is* worse than no father at all. And because his nightmare of a mother always had it in for me for marrying her no-good son." She bows her head. She lowers her voice to confessional mode. "Okay, I made some mistakes. I shouldn't have had those tequila shots, since I was nursing. Okay, I shouldn't have—well—flirted with the bartender."

"As if it were a crime to flirt," Seamus defends.

"Maisie, will you come with me?" Darlene pleads. "Oh, say you will! Seamus really wants to, but he has to teach his class."

"Of course," I promise. "Sure," I add with an alacrity fueled by the surprise I imagine on Jack's face when he spies the just-friends friend to whom he's given the boot, and despite the realization that I was asked only after Professor O'Toole said no.

"You're a saint," Darlene cries. And cries some more over the miracle of my saintliness. The Kleenex box is now empty. Wadded tissues dot the rug like the crumpled manuscript pages of blocked writers in the movies just before they hit it big. Seamus takes something from the back of the sofa—a dish towel? a pillowcase?—and hands it to her.

I shuffle in my seat. I nod encouragement while she emotes. When I decide she's off-loaded a sufficiently healthy and therapeutic amount of feeling—I wish I could consult Gabriel Doyle on this point—I stand up like my sixth-grade teacher signaling the end of class.

She quiets down to a snuffle. She nestles her head back against Seamus's chest.

"There there," he soothes.

"And do you want to know the worst of it?" she asks his now sodden blue oxford-cloth shirt. "I've been so upset ever since I got that notice, my milk's dried up."

That's hardly the worst of it, I think. In fact, there might even be a few advantages. For her, of course. Not to mention the benefit to my own storage space, especially now that I've got my extra, if uninvited, guest. I check out Darlene's breasts, which look untouched by tragedy however smashed against the shirt of Seamus O'Toole.

"But I've been so selfish," Darlene says. "All *me me me* when Seamus himself is suffering."

Because there are always the starving children in India to make your own gruel look good, I turn to Seamus. "And what's *your* disaster?" I inquire.

The Old Faithful gush of blarney seems to have deserted him as his mouth opens, then clamps shut. Darlene hands him the dish towel/pillowcase. He blows his nose.

"What happened?" I press.

Darlene answers. "Georgette's left him."

I sit back down.

Seamus hoists himself up out of the sofa. He starts to pace. "She's abandoned me. She's deserted me," he says. "All those visits to her soi-disant ailing mother. All those science conferences. All those research grants. All those phone calls. All that mendacious concern about my health. All those chicken potpies she left in the freezer. With careful instructions in her own infelicitous, *infidelitous* hand about how to heat them in the microwave. All that uxorial nattering about my nutritional needs." He halts.

Darlene turns to me. "Doesn't he speak great?"

I nod. You've got to give him credit for a wide-ranging vocabulary.

Seamus leans an elbow on the mantel. He raises a theatrical hand to his brow. "Nutritional needs! What about my emotional needs? My sexual needs? And all the while she was . . . she was . . . she was—"

"It's okay," Darlene intervenes.

"It is *not* okay, most emphatically not okay," Seamus yells. "She was cohabiting with someone else! She was bestowing sexual favors on another man. She was performing her intimate gymnastics for an entirely new audience. She was unfaithful! She broke our marriage vows!"

"How terrible," I chorus. I try to dismiss any who-is-calling-the-kettle-black thoughts. I've heard the rumors about this Celtic Lothario. About the student he trysted with on his office floor, the writer for *Playgirl* he married and divorced, the two nymphets—Melissa and Melinda, the infamous M&M's—he left one of his wives for, and now the miniskirted Georgette. The word on the academic street was that he alone provoked the emergency formation of Harvard's policy on sexual harassment and faculty-student relationships. And yet it's hard not to feel sorry for him, especially while your chair vibrates with his pain as he stalks the living room, a caged beast with an arrow through his heart.

"Georgette," he cries. "My darling Georgette!"

Darlene grabs his hand. Gently she pulls him back to

the sofa. He sinks his head on her shoulder, a head that slides a little too fast, I notice, to her chest. Oh, God, will Darlene be next? He's older now. He has a bad back. He must be a shadow of his Gaelic-Casanova self. Though I personally can't see his appeal, perhaps for Darlene his mellifluous big-words voice might be the sexual instrument that matters most.

I look at her. Tears stream down her cheeks as she holds him the way she must have held Anthony Vincent, in full pietà mode. Is she crying for herself? For him? For both of them?

"And can you believe it?" Seamus roars. "She left me for a businessman. *A businessman!* Which certainly proves Hannah Arendt's theory of the banality of evil. And on top of this indignity, she had the gall to choose a person with the most asinine, most pretentious, most logic-defying name." He stops. He burrows farther into Darlene's mammaries, but his words aren't sufficiently muffled that I miss what follows: "Can you believe it?" he gasps. "Georgette left me for some idiot by the name of Rex!"

THIRTEEN

By the time I get home, the skies have turned charcoal. A half hour after I place my order at Redbones, it starts to pour. The bicycle messenger drips all over my welcome mat as he passes me my ribs and slaw. He is wearing a Paddington Bear–style bright yellow slicker. Bicycle clips fasten the sodden legs of his jeans. I offer him a warming cup of tea, although I myself have already opened the wine. He cheerfully declines. Doesn't touch the stuff, he explains, and he's got three more deliveries to make in the neighborhood. "It's only a little rain," he adds.

Is rain just rain? Maybe a banana is just a banana, a chicken breast just a chicken breast and signify nothing else. A philosophical discussion on this topic could be the diversion I need to get through this dreary night.

Though this particular delivery boy is not about to be my deliverer. "I'm afraid I've got to go," he excuses. "Is there anything else? You don't want your ribs to get cold."

I give him a five-dollar tip.

"Awesome," he says. "I love it when it rains like this. People get way generous."

Oh, to be young. To have dreams. The young can withstand a lot. And I, as ancient as Methuselah, can neither withstand—nor stand—all that much anymore.

I got through the rest of my day thanks to my strong work ethic and my Scarlett O'Hara–like abilities to displace and delay. At four-thirty, even though it was still sunny, my own personal storms could no longer be denied. I left a windowsill of begonias unwatered in Jeremy Marshall's living room. I felt bad, especially since Jeremy Marshall's laboratory skills had granted me such blessed relief. But just when everything is looking fine, ominous weather, as well as thunderclouds of misery, can surprise you.

I dump my dinner on the table. I pull up a chair. The begonias will rally. I'm not sure I will. I realize some flowers do better without overscrupulous attention. As do some kids. Both might actually thrive on benevolent neglect. Why can't I apply some benevolent neglect to this latest lightning strike? Seamus O'Toole's current wife and my ex. A combination that sounds like one of the odder-named Pollock potpies: Southern Belle à la King? Hester Prynne Drumsticks? I want to cry *Foul!* Or, rather, *Fowl!* Why does it matter? Why do I care? I no more want Rex back than I want Jack in my bed or my ex-mother-in-law across from me calculating her half of a check. It's the surprise, the too-close-for-comfort shock.

Rex and Georgette. What do they have in common? Georgette's a biologist; she can dissect a chicken breast. Rex owns the chicken breast Georgette can dissect. Well, at least she's a fan of Pollock's products, confirmed by the pie-stuffed freezer to tide her husband over while she's out dallying with his employee's former spouse.

Then, there's the geographical connection. She teaches

at Wellesley, where Rex lives. Did they meet at that pizza place in Wellesley Center, where I served Rex the house special with extra cheese? Did they flirt in China Sails, "our restaurant," over moo shu pork and parasoled drinks? Though our parallel lives subsequently diverged, the key question remains: Did Rex kiss a woman—did Rex go to bed with a woman—who was already married to somebody else?

Okay, enough, you might say. Give it a rest. Eat your dinner before it gets cold. Why are you so relentless on this subject when you yourself have offered your own postdivorce Sealy Posturepedic to a member of the opposite sex?

Who wasn't married, let me protest. And whose romps in my bed took place when Tommy was at his father's.

Speaking of Rex—does he know Georgette's husband is a client of mine? Is that part of her I'll-show-Maisie charm? Wait until Georgette comes smack-dab up against Ina. That business about Rex's "very lovely new girlfriend" doesn't fool me.

What's more, does Tommy realize Georgette is already somebody else's wife? Maybe the adulterous coupling of Georgette and Rex counts as the traumatic experience that propelled Tommy to rebel against an education-prizing, well-brought-up, virginal young woman and forced him to choose the pierced and ragged likes of September Silva. Perhaps Rex's example is the reason Tommy's having sex before he can legally drive.

I open the Redbones box in front of me. I grab a rib and dip it into its plastic cup of sauce. The rib is too big, the cup too small; the sauce overflows into a brown puddle. Soon enough I am gnawing at these ribs the way I am gnawing on my problems—as if chewing them will get me to the heart of the matter. But what I get to is only the hard, tooth-breaking, thought-stopping bollard-like fact of the bone. I examine the bone in my hand, now picked so clean it could be the subject of one of Georgia O'Keeffe's desert still lifes. I study the table in front of me. I am appalled. If Tommy were the diner, I would lecture him: "Are you a barbarian? A caveman? Get a plate, a glass, some silverware."

Clearly this is a case of do what I say, not what I do, because if you were in this room, this is what you'd see: a woman with a flattened and stained brown bag for a place mat, her hands dripping with grease and sauce, eating from a take-out box, dipping a rib into assorted too-small plastic cups of hot, mild, sweet, tangy barbecue sauce; and, in between, scooping up coleslaw from another paper container with a tiny, two-tines-broken-off white plastic fork. What's more, you'd see a woman convinced that her lame excuse of I'm in a bad mood, or I've had some startling news, is enough to justify this slovenliness.

I finish everything in the box, in the bag, in the plastic cups. I get up. I open the refrigerator door. I swing my head back, checking for spies from Emily Post, then I swig grapefruit juice right out of the carton. The rain splashes against the windowsill; thunder starts to roar. I'm sure Tommy, unlike the bicycle messenger, is not wearing suitable bad-weather gear. And, God knows, every inch of September's clothes—inner and outer—seems to be bulleted with holes. The two of them are in Harvard Square, trying out a new organic restaurant that has Om and Zen in its name. "Sounds expensive," I said as they were about to leave.

"Dad upped my allowance," Tommy answered.

As a buy-your-silence bribe? I wanted to ask. "Remember the time Dad took you to the Boston Marathon?" I said instead.

"Aw, Mom, not that again," Tommy groaned.

He was five. When they came back, Tommy's pockets ballooned with candy; he wore a marathon T-shirt, a marathon hat; his hands clutched enough posters, banners, and marathon Frisbees to open his own marathon memorabilia store. My suspicions soared into high alert. "Did you have a good time?" I asked.

"Yes," he said.

"It was *great*, wasn't it?" Rex boomed. "Super. Tremendous. My boy and I, we had a blast."

Tommy lowered his eyes. He lowered his voice. "Except for one thing."

I leaned closer. "What one thing?"

"Daddy losted me."

Now I picture the restaurant that Rex's guilty generosity has made possible. I imagine white walls, blond furniture, tofu on white plates, a single white lily in a recycled ginkgo biloba jar, Tibetan music—is there Tibetan music? The only unwholesome, incongruous note: Tommy's un-Zen-like date.

I look at the mess on my table that seems to symbolize the mess of my present situation—Jack, Rex, the MIL, my unwanted guest, Darlene's distress, Seamus's abandonment, wilting plants—and decide to atone. I need to take some positive action. I am going to save September Silva's life—or, at least, her future. I am going to do an intervention and make sure she stays in school. I am going to follow Gabriel Doyle's advice. My brain may be muddled but I can still manage to re-create Gabriel's wise words during our dinner at Fred's: *Why don't you call September Silva's mother? What mother would want her daughter to quit school? I bet you could put your heads together and figure out a solution that will work for the two of you.*

I pick up the phone book. I check out the Silvas in Somerville. There are fifteen of them. I start with the first: *Silva, Alcestis.* "Is this the home of September Silva?" I ask. "I mean, is this where her mother lives?"

"What?" a man shouts.

"September Silva," I repeat.

"September?" the voice spits. "You must be joking."

How can somebody named Alcestis call this particular kettle black? "I'm looking for her mother," I explain.

"What is this? Some kind of 'Do you have Prince Albert in a can' joke? You kids," he grunts. "Let him out yourself," he orders and slams down the phone.

Under the circumstances, I am not so flattered to have been called a kid. Though I've certainly been as naive as a kid to assume I might reach September's mother on my first try. I put the phone book aside. I realize that calling fifteen—no, fourteen—Silvas in Somerville is not the best use of my time. So how *do* I figure out which particular Silva is responsible for adding September to our overpopulated universe? In a normal situation, a mother might reach her child on his grandmother-provided cell to ask a girlfriend's address, a parent's name. In an even more normal situation, a mother might already have in her address book the legal residence of the person living in her child's bedroom, sleeping under her child's lovingly laundered sheets. But, as you are well aware, these are not normal times in the lives of Maisie Grey, mother, and Tommy Pollock, son.

What's my next step? I weigh the morally reprehensible act of rifling through her private possessions against the morally high-minded deed of keeping September in school. Is there any choice? Who wouldn't condone the lesser evil? Besides, I've already sinned once, the search through Tommy's backpack, excused on parental-privilege grounds. Subversive activity in the pursuit of securing the future of a misguided teenager has to count as a forgivable offense.

I go into Tommy's room. Speaking of messes . . . I resist the maternal instinct to pick things up. I resist the fresh-air-fiend urge to open the window on the doubly ripe smell of unwashed socks. My exemplary behavior, along with my correct moral choice, is instantly rewarded because right away I spot an address on the luggage tag adorning September's rope-wrapped valise, which means I don't have to commit a criminal search-and-seizure to open it. As soon as I check the scribbled tag, I am further rewarded for righteousness—the address matches that of one of the Somerville Silvas: *Silva, Olidia J.*

I check the name against the phone book. I copy down the number. I dial.

"Mrs. Silva?" I ask. "Olidia Silva?"

"Depends on who wants to know," rasps a smoker's voice.

"Actually—" I begin.

She interrupts. "Depends if you're the IRS. Bill collector. My deadbeat ex. My no-good relatives. Or someone calling to tell me I won the lottery. Ha. Ha."

"I'm not any of those—"

"Then who the hell are you?"

Before she can accuse me of Prince-Albert-in-a-can pranks or extortion attempts, I rush to explain. "I'm Tommy Pollock's mother. My son is a"—I hesitate—"a *friend* of your daughter."

Immediately her voice turns as cautious as if I *were* the IRS. "Oh?" she manages.

"I assumed you might want to know about her. The people she hangs out with. Your daughter's friends."

"Sure, why not," she grants. "So how's she doing?"

"Okay," I allow. "Considering."

"Considering what? What's the big deal?"

"I thought you might be worried. I wanted to tell you that she's moved in with us."

"I never worry about her." She coughs. In the background a television blares. A dog barks. Dishes clang. "That girl always lands on her feet."

"I'm not so sure. If my son hadn't brought her home, she would have had no place to stay. As a matter of fact, I heard . . ." I stop.

"Yeah?"

". . . that you kicked her out of the house."

"You heard right. She's all grown up. Boy, is she all grown up. Something you must know real good by now. Besides, it's time she was on her own."

"At sixteen?"

"I was fourteen when I had her. In some places, Miss, kids grow up fast. That girl can take care of herself."

"But she's a child. Legally . . ." I start to stammer.

"Don't throw that legal crap at me."

"Now wait a minute." My back stiffens. All my sympathy for the underdog, the underdog *child*, rises to the surface.

"*You* wait a minute, lady. What are you doing calling me up? Butting into stuff that's not your business. You've got some nerve."

"I thought that as her *mother*"—I pause—"you might

be concerned about your daughter's whereabouts. About her welfare."

"You've already told me she's fine and living with you."

"And with my son," I feel compelled to add.

"Is that the problem right there? Hey, I'm no prude. That she's shacking up with a boyfriend doesn't bother me. More power to her, I say." She laughs. "Though I can tell from your voice that it friggin' bothers you."

"What bothers me is that she's dropped out of school. I hoped we might put our two heads together and figure out a way to keep her in."

"You thought that, did you?"

"Well, yes . . ."

"Well, *no,*" she mimics. "Let me make one thing clear. I don't give a flying you-know-what about whether or not she stays in school. I didn't finish school myself. It was good enough for me. Let her go out in the world and get a job. It's time."

"Don't you want something better for her? With an education, she might be able to make something of her life."

"Are you nuts? You think that girl is going to be a big cheese or something? If she doesn't want to go to school, that's fine with me. As long as she stays out of my hair."

"Wait a minute. I'm sure you have a legal obligation. As her mother . . ." I step back. All at once I understand that September Silva wasn't kicked out of the house because she decided to drop out of school. I had viewed her situation through the veil of my own middle-class values; I had role-played the scene substituting Tommy and myself and our own motivations. I take a wind-up breath. "But if you didn't kick her out of the house because she dropped out of school, then why—"

"I suppose you think it's your business given that you're her boyfriend's mother and all . . ."

"I'd like to understand."

She lowers her voice to a whisper. "Look. I'm getting my life together. I've got a new guy just moved in. He doesn't like kids. It wouldn't work if September was always hanging around."

"Only seconds ago you said September wasn't a kid."

"Whatever. Kid. Not kid. You know what she looks like. I just can't take a chance—"

"But you're her *mother,*" I persist.

"So what."

I hear a crumple of paper, what could be the strike of a match, the long rasping inhalation of a cigarette.

"Hey," she breathes out. "You sound like you're just dying to take that job. Go ahead. She's yours. I give up all rights to her." The dog barks. *Shut up, King,* she shouts at it. Obviously cowed—no wonder!—the dog falls silent. "Now that you understand," she finishes.

"I understand nothing."

"Then listen close. Don't you go sticking any lawyers, any DSS on me. I've got my own problems. My own life to think of. Leave me alone. I wish her well, but she's made her bed."

"Even though she's your flesh and blood? You just can't . . . ," I argue, stuck in a broken-record groove of incredulity.

"Oh, yes I can! I was worse off than her when I was her age. Leave me alone! And you just tell that girl to leave me alone, too!" She coughs. King barks. She's the second Silva within a half hour to bang down the phone.

I reel back from words that feel like pelted stones. I drop into the nearest chair. I survey the remains of my meal: the picked-apart bones; the spilled, puddled sauce; the stained paper bag; the tub of coleslaw, down to the last few shreds of cabbage swimming in its milky dregs. My stomach turns.

Olidia Silva's remarks might just as easily have come from Ina Pollock's mouth. The only difference between the two mothers is that Ina's rejection would be directed at me and not at her own child. I could never be that mean to someone close to my son, however much I might disapprove. Poor September. Poor motherless girl.

Okay, so I've done a one-eighty. Now, instead of regarding September's clothes as a rebellious red flag, I can evaluate them as the rags Oliver Twist might have been forced to wear. Instead of being annoyed by her "food issues," I can now understand how a person whose mother never cooked her a nutritious hot dinner might choose rigid rules of health to achieve actual and emotional nourishment. Instead of being appalled by her dropping out, I can appreciate how someone who lacked a mother to monitor her homework, read to her, show by example the merits of a good education might decide a diploma is not worth striving for. No wonder she quit school.

Even her sexual precociousness can be interpreted as a cry for love and physical contact. Here's someone under my own roof, someone who needs an *in loco maternis* to take the place of her own loco mother. I am going to change her life.

The minute I decide this, I hear the key turn in the lock. I walk toward the door. Over the threshold step Tommy and September, looking like drowned kittens in need of rescue.

And I am just the person to rescue them.

"Hi, there," I chirp, a perky Miss Congeniality.

"Something smells good," notes Tommy.

"If you like fat and sugar and the body parts of dead animals," September scorns.

My smile flags slightly. *Motherless child, abandoned baby,* I remind myself and pump up the level of cheer.

Tommy moves closer to the table. "What did you have?"

"Ribs, slaw, the usual."

There is such longing on his face, I wrap up the remains of my dinner and whisk it out of temptation and into the trash. "And how was *your* meal?" I ask.

"Tofu," Tommy says. "And more tofu." He rolls his finger along a pool of barbecue sauce splattering the table and puts it in his mouth.

"Yuck, Tommy!" September screeches. "That stuff was, like, probably just touching pig."

For a second I cling to the delicious certainty that if she keeps up this way, she will soon hoist herself on her own nagging, vegetarian petard and I won't even have to step in à la Ina Pollock to save my boy. Then guilt rises.

"You're right," Tommy confesses. "I forgot."

September flops onto the sofa. She sticks her feet, in their scratched black-platformed, sharp-buckled shoes, on top of the coffee table. I'm about to say something; I'm about to say what I'd say to Tommy if he didn't know better. Which of course he does, so well trained, so *mother* trained is he. And September, on the other hand . . . I cement my mouth shut. I remind myself of *Silva, Olidia J.* Of a child so neglected that life lessons about shod feet and coffee tables were never passed down from mother to daughter as automatically and irrevocably as genetic traits and a string of good pearls. "All tofu?" I ask now. "Your dinner was all tofu?"

"Pretty much," Tommy says. "One hundred ways to cook tofu to make it look like real food. Bonus points for presentation, though." He casts a longing glance toward the pedaled garbage can.

September laughs. "Oh, you," she says. She turns to me. "It wasn't just tofu, Maisie. There was seaweed and seitan casserole with soy cheese. They had these Tibetan Goji berries, just delicious. Brown-rice cakes, chickpeas with hemp seeds. They put the cutest little flowers on top for decoration. You could totally eat them. The café had an excellent stereo system with this awesome drumming music that was really, you know, calming. I got, like, some amazing ideas for my own work, in fact."

"Well, that's always a good sign. To get inspiration."

She nods. "And everything was white and bare and totally spiritual." She stops. She takes some swamilike centered breaths. She sighs a few mantralike *oms*. "Maisie, maybe you could come with us sometime."

This catches me unawares. "I'd enjoy that," I say, flattered in spite of myself.

"You'd hate it, Mom. It's not your scene," Tommy counters.

"You can always teach an old dog new tricks," trips platitudinously off my tongue.

"Maisie, you're not *that* old," September defends. She rakes her black-polished nails through her rat's nest of hair. Her shirt is ripped under the sleeve. Intentional? There are red marks on her neck. Insect bites? Tommy bites? It's not going to be easy, my new social-work project. Is it a Zen thing, embracing what you most dislike?

"If Tommy doesn't want to go, maybe you and I can go, Maisie. Just the two of us."

"How lovely," I say. "I've always wanted to sample one hundred ways to cook tofu."

"You're funny, Maisie. I can see who Tommy gets his sense of humor from." And she looks so happy, my heart melts. Under all that makeup, the clothes, the defiance, the intolerable behavior, there is a real child. One in need of guidance. One in need of me.

"And maybe we can, like, go shopping sometime, too," she suggests.

My eyes fix on her clothes. "Good idea," I agree. I smile at the two beaming teenagers in my living room who, I realize, I'd have eating out of my hand if my hand held anything they'd eat. I press my advantage. "Now I know you've settled in with us for the time being . . . ," I begin.

"And I really appreciate it, Maisie," she hastens to add. "Though I want you to know I totally plan to get my own place as soon as my music career takes off."

"She's really talented, Mom," Tommy supplies.

"I'm sure she is," I hedge. "As you've told me, Tommy, more than once." I look at September. I put on my sternest face. "I'm sure you *are* really talented, September," I emphasize. "But I have one condition for your staying here."

"The couch? It seems sort of unfair to make Tommy sleep there since we already . . ." She shrugs. ". . . and, like, with our hours and stuff, he'd really be in your way if he slept in the living room."

"That's not my condition, September. I've given up locking those barn doors after the horses have fled," I state. "Alas," I add.

"I know I'm a little messy, Maisie," she goes on, "but I'll

really try to get my crap together and help you with the cooking and cleaning and stuff."

Cleaning? I think. Cooking? I imagine a mound of tofu. I imagine scouring cloths indistinguishable from her clothes. "No, it's not that. Though I am glad for your help. And if you decide to accept my terms and settle in, we'll make a list of chores. My condition—which is nonnegotiable, let me say at once—is . . ." I stop. I raise my voice a notch. "My condition is that you stay in school."

"Mom!" exclaims Tommy, horrified. "You have no right. September is an artist. A lot of artists find school way too boring, way too"—he searches for the words—"middle class so they need to drop out to create their art."

"That may be true. And I admit I am uncoolly middle class. However, artists who are sleeping under my roof have to stay in school."

"Mom!"

"A high school diploma is important, no matter who you are, no matter what you plan to do. Musician or plumber or cleaner. Learning the basics, studying literature and math and science and history and languages—these can only enhance a person's art."

"You are not September's mother," Tommy protests in the familiar outraged-toddler voice that used to scream, midtantrum, *You are not the boss of me!*

September pulls herself off the sofa. She takes Tommy's arm. "He's so sweet. He always sticks up for me." She pats his hand. "It's so excellent having someone on your side."

"Mom, you are not September's mother," Tommy repeats.

"No, I'm not. I'm *your* mother. And this is *my* house."

September leans into Tommy. She nuzzles him. His

whole body seems to soften. His thrust-out, Ina Pollock-ish chin relents and retreats.

September turns to me. "Maisie, I know you're not my mother. I know you're Tommy's mother." She stops. She flashes me a triumphant *cogito ergo sum* smile. "But since I love Tommy, how's about you'll kind of, like, be my mother, too."

I grab the corner of the table. *Be careful what you wish for,* my own mother used to warn.

Tommy kisses her on the lips. A real lip-lock that I'm fairly sure involves tongue. I look away.

"That's not quite what I meant," I begin. Also, not what I want, I tell myself.

Though it's easy enough to see what *they* want; they are in such a clutch now that not a sliver of light shows between her body and his. In two minutes they'll be heading for his bedroom. And I will be pumping up the volume on *This Old House.*

September detaches her head—lips, cheek, and nose—from Tommy's lips, cheek, and nose with the smack of pulled-away Velcro. "And since you agreed to let me now think of you as my mother," September continues, addressing me with lipstick-smeared lips and sleepy eyes, "I need to tell you something."

"Go ahead," I say. I prepare to stand my ground. I'm determined to stick to my principles and accept her Little Match Girl fate. Hard-hearted, I'm all set to kick her out even into this thunderous rain. And to toss her tattered possessions after her. A clap of thunder just now erupts to applaud my resolve.

"I've decided I'll do what you ask, Maisie. I'll stay in school."

I cough. Maybe Olidia Silva's germs flew through the

telephone wires and poisoned me. Maybe I'm choking on the sweet taste of victory. Or the bitter aftermath of a war. Or perhaps I'm just disheartened that September's surrender wasn't the triumphant result of a much bigger fight. I cough some more.

Tommy fills a glass with water from the sink. He brings it to me. "Are you okay, Mom?"

I gulp it down. "Never better," I say. I turn toward September. "Well, what do you know."

"Are you glad?" she asks.

"Thrilled."

Tommy steps between us. "Sep, don't let her boss you around. You're your own person."

"It's okay, honey. Really. Like all I ever wanted, Tommy, besides you of course, was for a mother to give me good advice, a real mother to tell me what to do."

FOURTEEN

The meeting over the custody of Anthony Vincent is planned for ten o'clock this morning in one of the rotating conference rooms at Somerville Legal Services. It's an informal gathering, Darlene told me when she telephoned to remind me. Its purpose, she explained, to come to an agreement and avoid court. Not that she expected her mother-in-law to agree to anything. "My lawyer . . . ," she said.

"Jack," I snarled.

"Wants me there at nine-forty-five."

"Does he know I'm coming?" I asked.

She stopped. She clicked her tongue. "Not really. I told him I was bringing a friend. He didn't ask for any details. He seemed to get real down after he heard Seamus couldn't cancel his class. I mean, I think he was counting on the surprise of Seamus showing up. It would be a big deal: a professor who wrote all those books finding the time to come to this meeting to support a single mother who never finished high school." I heard a sharp intake of breath, a slow exhalation. "Not that . . . don't take this the wrong way." She paused. "Maisie, do you think it will make a difference if I bring you?"

I could sense her anxiety. I could almost sympathize with her anxiety. The externals, who you bring, what you wear, how early you get there, the color of your pen, the size of your notebook, are the only things you can control. I understand the no-choice choice between a Joyce scholar and the woman who dusts that scholar's books, even if the duster is the CEO and founder of her own company.

"I'm sure it won't make the slightest bit of difference," I soothed, "to your *case*," I stressed. "In fact, it might help you to have a fellow woman, a fellow mother there."

She sighed. "Oh, Maisie. I hope you're right."

I suggested we meet at nine-forty, at the door to Legal Services.

Her voice went silent.

"Darlene?" I prodded.

"What if I bump into . . . you know?" she asked. "On the street? In front? Before you get there? All by myself?"

"Say no more. I'll pick you up outside Walgreens."

"Do you mind?"

"Not a bit." I should have anticipated this reasonable fear. Who knew better than I what it's like to be blindsided by a mother-in-law, to be undefended, to be up against such powerful hormone-fueled, Oedipal-fueled dislike that even the toughest, street-smart woman might falter in her resolve.

"What's her name?" I asked. "In all our conversations, you've never actually spoken her name."

She gulped. "You're not going to believe it."

"Try me."

She giggled. "Carlene. Carlene Lattanzio."

"Come on."

"Afraid so."

I considered. Maybe some names, like certain planets, just couldn't be aligned. Wouldn't a Carlene be threatened by a too-close-for-comfort Darlene? Wouldn't an Ina get along with a Miriam better than a Maisie/nee Margaret? Which led me to wonder how to chart the zodiac compatibility of a Georgette, and the degree of dominance implied by someone called Rex.

Darlene cleared her throat.

"Sorry."

"And, Maisie?" she went on.

"Yes?"

"My lawyer says to—quote—'dress appropriately.' I kind of sense that should include you."

Though I'm sure my neatly pressed white shirt and navy pants, my low-heeled, shined black pumps, the delicate Tiffany silver hoops that were a first-anniversary present from Rex announce *well-bred professional,* I question the definition of "appropriately" when I pull into the Walgreens parking lot. Within seconds, I spot Darlene crouching behind a mailbox and looking, at this hour in the morning, like an actress ready for her cocktail party close-up in *Dynasty.*

She swivels her head in all directions. She jumps into the front passenger-side seat. She slams the door. She scoots below the level of the dashboard. "Thank God," she whispers.

"Are you being followed?" I ask.

She shakes her head. "I started to have a panic attack that Carlene might want to stop for Alka-Seltzer or something on the way to the meeting. For a couple of minutes, I almost couldn't breathe." She tries out a series of pants to test that her lungs are in working order. She bends toward me. She pats her sprayed hair, which has been permed into an Orphan Annie frizz. The shoulder pads on her gold Lurex jacket might be hand-me-downs from an all-American quarterback; her rhinestone earrings match the rhinestone buckles on her sling-back satin shoes. There's something touching about these efforts to dress up, like a child playing make-believe in the old clothes from an attic trunk. "How do I look?" she asks.

"Wow," I exclaim.

"Thanks." She beams. "I got my hair done."

"I can tell."

"And I've only worn this outfit once. For my girlfriend's wedding." She smooths a lapel. "Brenda. She's got kids now in junior high." The mention of kids turns her sober. She sniffles. "It's too bad I have to bring it out, after all this time, for something awful like this."

"Yes, I completely agree. A dress like this has special occasion written all over it."

She digs into a pocketbook studded with appliqués of tropical fruits. She finds a Kleenex. She blows her nose. "I didn't sleep a wink last night."

"Me, neither."

"That's so nice of you, Maisie, to be so worried about me. About my Anthony Vincent."

I pull out of the parking lot. I feel a stab of guilt. I'm afraid worries about her and Anthony Vincent were not at the top of my list during my tossing and turning and obsessive checking of both the illuminated green digits on my clock radio and the level of activity in the room across the hall from me. As much as I relate to her troubles, she and Anthony Vincent made up only a portion of the crowd scene in my roaming, disturbing, dark-of-the-night thoughts. These included Tommy, September, Jack.

But, if you want the shameful truth, mostly I was fixated on Rex and Georgette. Of course I could not care less, believe me, that Rex has a girlfriend. I'm not the kind of person to begrudge him a significant other just because I don't currently have one myself. Honestly, after all this time I wish him well. I'm more than happy that someone else exists to suffer the slings and *poison* arrows of Ina Pollock. I only focused on them because I feel sorry for Seamus, who is my client, and for Tommy, who has to adapt to yet another unsuitable person in his life.

Then my thoughts once more skirted Anthony Vincent and settled on the other unsuitable person in Tommy's life: Who is staying in school, thanks to me. Who is entrenched in my apartment, thanks to me. Who is going to be a greater and greater part of my life, thanks to my own social work.

But as soon as I projected this scenario, I imagined its opposite. What if they break up? A likely prospect given their age and divergent backgrounds. In the be-careful-what-you-wish-for category, I'd then end up dealing with a devastated Tommy and having to evict a child whose proximity has caused my heart to grow almost fond of her.

I shake away these concerns, which will be there when I'm ready to return to them. I shift attention back to Darlene. Right now she deserves a bigger share of my worrying. I try to focus every ounce of sympathy, every bit of concentration on her particular misery. I pat a glittery elbow.

"I'm scared, Maisie," Darlene admits.

If only I could switch on the lights, open the windows, vanquish all the bogeymen the way I used to when Tommy was five and had bad dreams. But a custody hearing is not a scraped knee a mother can produce a Band-Aid for. "I know you're scared," I say. "And why wouldn't you be? No mother could feel otherwise."

"There'll be social workers at this thing, and my mother-in-law, and her lawyer . . ." Her voice trails off; she puts her hand to her hair. "Are you sure I look all right?"

"Positive." I reach for her. I lace my fingers through hers. "You look beautiful."

"At least we don't have to go all the way into Boston," she says. "I figured the meeting would take place in Mr. Gordon's office. That's where the social worker told me they are usually held. *In your lawyer's place of work.* She was surprised it was set up for Somerville. But Mr. Gordon was really stubborn. So much more convenient, he explained." She shakes her head. "It would be hard to take the T downtown in this outfit, in these shoes. He's so thoughtful."

"Isn't he just?" I snap.

All sarcasm is lost on her. She smiles, touched and delighted by her lawyer's concern for the welfare of her wardrobe.

I remember the one time I went downtown to meet Jack in his office. Correction: not in his office but in the building's lobby. "Don't bother to come up," he said. "Just head to the security desk and they'll buzz me." We had tickets for a Celtics game. "I assume you won't be wearing your jeans," he added.

"I'm supposed to get dressed up for *basketball*?"

"You're coming by the office, my *building*, first. *I'll* be in my suit."

Considering this exchange, I'm hardly surprised he didn't want the likes of Darlene, in jeans or gussied up in Lurex and flower appliqués, defiling the corridors of Lah, Dee, and Dah, Attorneys-at-Law, to claim her status as a client of Jack's. Not to mention a style-deficient squad of noncorporate opposing counsel, Somerville DSS representative, and a mother-in-law who might conceivably have an even worse fashion sense. Let me ask you. Would Jack ever eat at Fred's? Would Jack take the trouble to flirt with one of Fred's robust waitresses?

Now Darlene folds her arms across her breasts and shuts her eyes. I fiddle with the radio dial, but all I can find are reports of war, of death, country songs about men who done us wrong, and a hip-hop warning of bad things going down in the hood. I switch it off. I drive along Somerville Avenue, past car washes, auto-body shops, and Portuguese and Haitian groceries. I follow a maze of intersecting one-way streets. I park facing a sign of bullet-riddled letters that spell out DEAD END.

I turn off the ignition. Darlene opens her eyes. She sits up. I lean against the steering wheel. Neither of us moves toward her respective side door.

"Well, here we are," I state.

"Here we are," she echoes.

Across from us stands a yellow-brick nondescript building with cracked concrete steps and a SOMERVILLE LEGAL SERVICES sign in its dusty ground-floor window. Half a bicycle is lashed to a guardrail. A few wilted dandelions poke through the fence. Fast-food wrappers litter the pavement. A uniformed policeman, holster bulging, pushes through the front door. He stops on the sidewalk. He lights a cigarette. He kicks a soda can into the gutter. He caresses his gun.

Darlene shudders. "Seamus promised he was going to fax a letter in support of me," she offers, "to explain how responsible I am, what a good worker, honest and reliable, what a concerned mother. He promised to write it on his office stationery, with those *veritases* all over it. Seamus told me that means 'truth' in Latin."

"Jack will be thrilled. I'm sure everyone will be impressed."

"Oh, I hope so. I imagine a letter from him is pretty good. Of course it would be better if he could be there in person."

"*I'm* here," I remind her. I am starting to feel annoyed. I am starting to feel jealous and a little marginalized by the power of the *veritas*. After all, *I* hired her. It's only because of *me* that she came to sit at the feet of the great man himself. It was *I* who coaxed her out from behind the chestnut tree and up the walkway to Seamus's front door. Stop it, Maisie! I tell myself. Keep your eye on the prize. The goal here is to get the baby back.

She crumples into her seat. Her eyes fill. "And don't think I'm not grateful, Maisie. I owe you everything." She sniffles a couple of times. She points out the window. "If it hadn't been for you, I wouldn't be here now trying to get custody of my own son."

"No, it's all you. You're a wonderful mother. You've gone through so much for Anthony Vincent's sake. We have to believe that everything will work out. That justice will prevail."

"You don't get that from the TV news. Usually, the way I figure it, the bad people come out on top."

"Not this time," I say. I follow her gaze to the shabby

home of Somerville Legal Services. A pigeon pecks at the roof. A young woman runs out the front door sobbing into her sleeve. I am trying to have positive thoughts despite the course-of-true-justice-never-runs-smooth vibes of our immediate environment. "You have so many people on your side," I add.

"That's true," she agrees. "The Elderberry sisters each sent a note," she goes on. "Handwritten on paper that smelled of fancy flowers. One rose, one lily. I mailed them from the post office on Mount Auburn Street. They didn't trust the box on the corner. Said they were sure kids put lit matches down it. And Mr. Marshall, too, e-mailed Mr. Gordon and said that if I cared for Anthony Vincent half as well as I cared for his plants, then I would be the best mother on earth."

"See! You have a real cheering section."

"I planned to ask you to write a letter for me, too, but Mr. Gordon said not to bother. He figured a Harvard professor, a famous scientist, and two ladies from a mansion in west Cambridge were enough."

"He did, did he?"

Her voice rises in alarm. "Oh, do you think I should have tried to get more letters?" She slaps her knee. "I never should have listened to him."

"It's okay."

"You're sure?"

"Really."

"You're not mad?"

"What you already have is fine. The court will get the general idea about your competence. Besides, it's important to avoid overkill." I unclip my seat belt.

"You don't mind that I asked you to come kind of at

the last minute? That I invited you only after I knew Seamus wasn't able to?"

"Spilt milk," I say and instantly regret such words, under the circumstances.

Darlene doesn't seem to notice.

"What matters is that I'm here," I emphasize. "And as your *boss*, I will certainly speak up in your favor. I'm sure that my actual presence will carry plenty of weight."

"That's what I was hoping. That's what I'm counting on." She grabs my hand. We each squeeze. Twice. The secret handshake of the worried-mothers club.

FIFTEEN

The conference room, which resembles the teachers' lounge of a soon-to-be-condemned junior high—Formica-topped metal table, metal chairs, buzzing and flickering fluorescent lights—is already filled when we arrive except for two empty seats marking the Siberia end of the table. Darlene and I both freeze at the threshold. I am sure that she is having the same junior-high-conspiracy theories I am. Briefcases gape open, papers fan out, pens lie uncapped, coffee cups, a few lipsticked, are already half emptied. Five faces spin in our direction. The room hushes. Darlene and I gawk at each other. Did they all get here early to talk about us?

The silence stretches. We both shift our weight from foot to foot. Already I feel guilty even though I have no idea what I've done wrong.

"Here they are," a woman states at last.

I check my watch: 9:43, two full minutes before the estimated time of arrival, before the *suggested* time of arrival. "Are we late?" I ask anyway.

"No. No. Not at all." Jack jumps up. His jacket hangs

over the back of his chair. His tie is loosened. "Take a seat." He turns toward me. He frowns. "Maisie, this is a surprise." The unstated *and not a pleasant one* dangles in the dust-moted air.

"Darlene wanted me along for moral support," I protest. "And to speak in her favor."

"Very nice of you. Not that it's necessary, given legal representation"—he points to a squared-off stack of papers—"and more than enough letters of endorsement." His eyes track my dressed-for-semisuccess outfit. Do I detect a flicker of approval? "But since you're already here . . ."

Darlene and I tiptoe toward the end of the table. We are both slinking sideways, like criminals who need to watch their backs. When we sit, our chairs seem lower than those of almost everyone else—or maybe I'm just paranoid. Darlene's gaze stays fixed on her knees. I raise my head and study my fellow conferees:

First of all, Carlene, Darlene's—and now my—archenemy: Eyebrows drawn on where no eyebrows would ever grow. Pearlized eye shadow of a blue unknown in the natural world. Fuchsia lips smeared beyond the boundaries of her actual mouth. Matching fuchsia cheeks. A platinum blond ponytail. Breasts popping out of a tank top with HOT MAMMA! outlined in sequins.

Let me ask you, does this person look like someone suitable for taking care of, let alone guiding the future of, Anthony Vincent? Does this person even resemble a grandmother? Though, in all fairness, I doubt that too many turkey-platter-toting, sweetly smiling Norman Rockwell grandmothers are stepping out from behind their ovens in this day and age. Carlene adjusts an earring the size of a shower-curtain hook. I notice she is wearing two bracelets of black leather studded with silver thorns. All the better to caress a child with. Why didn't her lawyer instruct her in appropriate granny garb?

Clearly *her* lawyer seems the opposite of a crackerjack Jack. He sports a droopy short-sleeved shirt yellowed under the arms; ink from a plastic ballpoint pen stains its pocket. A navy necktie flaunts red scales of justice and is secured by a pin of crossed hockey sticks; frayed suspenders, the elastic stretched out, couldn't possibly hold up pants. But who knows better than I that appearances deceive. Maybe this getup is deliberate, a rumpled Clarence Darrow ploy. I am well aware, from my reading in the *Somerville Journal*, of the local prejudice against big-shot downtown Boston lawyers crossing the river to bulldoze home-grown attorneys wiser in the ways of their particular community. I'm sure that such bias hobbles the course of justice in this airless room.

My eyes move to the social worker with her mass of coarse salt-and-pepper curls scrunchied off her face. Dangling earrings of African beads. Reading glasses on a chain of linked cats. A faded batik dress of a flour-sack shape. Birkenstocks. An expression of humor-banishing earnestness. No makeup except for a trace of bitten-off lipstick.

Across the table, a young woman—secretary? stenographer?—doodles on a yellow legal pad. I can make out flowers, smiley faces, and linked hearts. She's pretty in an understated coed sort of way. Casual Friday on this Tuesday morning, she's wearing jeans and an Indian tunic. She stops, swigs from a bottle of water, and yawns.

"Now that we're all here," Jack begins.

"Time to get this show on the road," the other lawyer adds.

"I'll say," groans Carlene Lattanzio. "My baby's at home

with a sitter. Fifteen bucks an hour she charges. And boy does my little guy cry when I'm not right there with him."

Darlene snaps to attention. "He's not your baby. He's not your little guy."

"Oh yeah? Let's see about that."

"Wait just a minute. *I* am the mother."

"You just a minute yourself." Carlene smacks the table. "In your case, *mother* is only a name."

"Who are you to . . . ?"

"What right do you have . . . ?"

"I have every right. *I* am the mother," Darlene repeats.

"You wish. You've got no idea how to take care of a baby."

"I can do a better job than an alcoholic."

"*Darlene*," Jack warns.

"*Carlene*," her lawyer cautions.

The two women glare at each other. They glare at their lawyers.

The secretary stifles a giggle.

"Ladies," Mrs. Lattanzio's lawyer says.

"Women," Jack corrects with a glance in my direction. "This is not a legal hearing," he adds. "This is a *friendly* meeting to see if we can work things out to avoid appointing a guardian *ad litem*. To avoid going to court."

"No way," says Carlene. She crosses her arms over her chest so that HOT MAMMA! reads as HA! "I can tell right now that we'll never work things out. This is a waste of time. My daughter-in-law's got no sense. Imagine leaving that baby home all alone to go to a *bar*!" She shakes her head. Her drawn-on eyebrows knit. "Nobody loves that child like me," she shouts.

Darlene's hands are clenched into fists. "Bull . . . ," she begins, then covers her mouth.

"See!" says Carlene. "What kind of language. What kind of example. Why, there's the fucking evidence."

"She's got nerve. What does *she* know about bringing up a child? Look at how she raised her own son!"

I put a hand on Darlene's arm.

Carlene's lawyer grabs his client's elbow. She wrenches it away. He pulls her back. "Lay off," she orders.

I can almost hear the announcer's voice: "Ladies and gentlemen, behold the battling Lattanzios, junior and senior. In this corner, Darlene. In this, Carlene." Though court looms, the future of a child hangs in the balance, though evil mothers-in-law might triumph, for a second I identify with the giggling secretary.

The social worker scribbles something into a notebook bordered by peace signs. Her left hand curls around to barricade her words from prying eyes, an all-too-familiar action that floods me with even more junior high school memories.

Jack raps his knuckles against the table. "Calm down, everybody," he commands. "This interchange is nonproductive to say the least." He rakes his hair. A gesture I know. Hair I know, or once knew, its bristly texture not that long ago buried into my flesh. I dismiss this thought. "Does anyone want coffee? Water?" He points to the young woman. "Karen over here will be glad to get you some."

We shake our heads. I'm sure I'm not the only one who longs to ask for a Scotch.

"Okay, then. Let me introduce all the participants before we proceed in the kind of civilized manner that will be most helpful. I'm Jack Gordon, Ms. Lattanzio's lawyer. That is, Darlene's. Perhaps for clarity, we can use first names since we have two Ms. Lattanzios here," he suggests.

"Sure," agrees Darlene.

"No problem," Carlene speaks up, "though personally I never went in for that Miz stuff. Missus Lattanzio has always been fine by me."

"Not that there's any Mister Lattanzio," Darlene puts in.

"Mind your own business."

Darlene addresses the table at large. "In case you don't know, my mother-in-law had her son out of wedlock."

"So what?"

"I, at least, was married to him."

"Which was the worst mistake my boy ever made."

"As if . . ." Darlene hunches her shoulder pads. "Truth is, it was me that got the short end of *that* stick." She zeroes in on Jack. "Wouldn't that be something in my favor?" she entreats. "The fact that I was married and she wasn't? Wouldn't that make me more," she pauses, "more stable?"

Carlene lunges forward. "Why, you—"

"I'm just bringing up a fact."

Jack raps against the table once again.

Carlene's lawyer clicks his ballpoint. "All this back-and-forth is wasting everybody's time," he states. "These accusations are not helpful."

"And really mean," adds the mother-in-law.

"Though could go to issues of character," Jack considers.

"Not in the heat of argument," the other lawyer rebuts.

Jack shrugs. "If I may continue." He points across the table. "And my colleague over here is William Belcher. Billy, as he prefers to be called. Who represents *Missus* Carlene Lattanzio."

William/Billy nods.

"On the other side of him is Fern Ross-Gratowski of social services."

"Good morning," says the social worker. "Just pretend I'm not here. My job is mostly to observe. You might say I represent Anthony Vincent. My interest is solely in the welfare of the child."

"And mine isn't?" challenges Carlene.

"That's the only thing I want, what's best for my baby," declares Darlene.

"Well, then, we're all on the same page." Jack's voice is mild, his expression noncommittal, as if the Solomon-like implications of this, its biblical ramifications, have never crossed his mind. He turns his head. "And last but not least, Karen Hannigan, our intern, chief cook and bottle washer. Jack-of-all-trades." He winks at her.

I give her a sharp look. What trades? Can the word *intern* ever be spoken without the connotations of that blue dress from the Gap?

"You're the jack-of-all-trades, Jack," she giggles.

"Karen's pre-law at Tufts. Majoring in sociology," he explains.

Which makes her what? Twenty? Nineteen? And he, I know for a fact, is forty-five.

"Her primary interest is in family law. With your permission, of course, she's here to learn something and take notes for me."

"You can bring the *National Enquirer* in here for all I care," says Carlene.

I study the young, pretty intern. So what? I think. *Life is unfair, never mind the law.* I notice that Darlene's hands, now clutched in her lap, are trembling. And nothing is more unfair than the potential loss of a child. I turn my attention to Billy Belcher.

"So now that the pleasantries are over . . . ," he begins, ". . . let me offer up the list of Anthony Vincent's grandmother's complaints." From under a pile of papers, he digs out a pair of crescent-moon reading glasses; he wipes their lenses on his tie; he slides them halfway down his nose. "If I could proceed without interruption . . . ?"

Jack nods.

"Okay. My client claims Darlene Lattanzio is an unsuitable mother because she has consistently neglected her son—"

"I never—" Darlene inserts.

Billy Belcher tsks. "So much for interruptions. Could you please restrain your client, Jack? Let me finish. There will be plenty of opportunity for debate."

"Let him finish," Jack instructs.

Under the table Darlene reaches for my hand.

Billy Belcher clears his throat. "If I may continue . . . My client feels that Anthony Vincent is suffering from insufficient nutrition because his mother insists on breastfeeding beyond the time that makes nutritional sense. Considering that the milk has been moved around so much, it's hard to trace or even identify; there is, in addition, always the possibility of contamination. Thus, my client worries about infection. Hepatitis. Or AIDS." His tongue lingers on the last word.

"No way," says Darlene.

He scowls. "My client is also concerned about pumping, storage, and retrieval, unnecessary complications that may be harmful to the milk because of its age and the way it's been frozen. I've done some research." He unfolds a sheet of white paper. He holds up a Xerox. He adjusts his glasses. "Here are the guidelines for storing breast milk. It can be kept in the freezer compartment of a refrigerator for three to four months. Longer than that, milk requires a deep freezer with a constant zero degrees Fahrenheit. It is my client's contention that such a freezer does not exist, nor has it ever existed, in her daughter-in-law's apartment and thus the breast milk might actually constitute a hazard to the child."

I sneak a glance at Darlene, who has gone as pale as the milk under contention. I think of my own icebox, of the water that sloshes in its insufficiently cooled ice-cube tray. I hate to admit it, but I'm sure that for all those months traveling from freezer to freezer in the greater Boston area, Darlene's breast milk has not been deep frozen at a constant zero degrees Fahrenheit. In fact, the only domestic deep freezer I know resides in the suburban pantry of Ina Pollock, its sole purpose not to prevent a hazard to a child but to warehouse the Pollock potpies.

Billy Belcher puts down the Xerox. "Let's face it," he laughs. "The child has a full set of teeth."

Leave it to a man to come up with such an inanity.

Obviously the social worker has the same united-in-sisterhood reaction. She stops writing long enough to shake a finger at him, a gesture that states, unequivocally, *Shame on you.*

He is not daunted. "Thus she has decided to buy grade-A, pasteurized, homogenized milk at the store. In addition," he goes on, "my client fears that the child has been left home alone on more than the one documented occasion of when the mother abandoned the child to go to a bar. Also, she is concerned about moral issues; there are witnesses at that bar who could testify not only to excessive drinking, but also to inappropriate sexual congress with someone who is not the father of the child."

Next to me, Darlene groans. *"Oh, shit,"* she curses under her breath.

"Moreover, my client states that she is financially and psychologically prepared to stay at home with the child. That she has earned her grandson's trust and love. She feels that with her Social Security checks, her early-retirement pension plan from Paradise Groceries, and her side employment of crocheting doilies that she has been starting to sell over the Internet, she is better able to provide for the child financially. Much better than the mother who has had no steady career aside from some housecleaning, off the books. My client adds that she hopes to convince her son, as soon as she can establish his whereabouts, to contribute support to Anthony Vincent. She claims his cooperation will be easier once he knows that the child is safe from its mother's bad influence.

"And because I can anticipate opposing counsel's bringing up her DUI record—and even if he doesn't, we have nothing to hide—and her former two-pack-a-day smoking habit, let me stress, with my client's permission, that she has been three months' sober, attends regular meetings of AA at a local church, which, by the way, offers babysitting facilities. And with the help of Smokers Anonymous and the sincere worry about the effects of secondhand smoke on the health of Anthony Vincent, she has been off cigarettes for five weeks. My client reiterates that Darlene Lattanzio is an unfit mother; she, on the other hand, is a mature, stable grandmother, a blood relative who loves her grandchild and can and wants to provide for him."

Finished, he exhales a lungful of air, straightens his

papers, then surveys the table as if he expects a round of applause.

His client obliges by giving him a faux-fingernailed thumbs-up. "Way to go," she adds.

Darlene sits rigid. Her chest rises and falls. Her own fingernails are now dug so deeply into my hand I wouldn't be surprised to see they've drawn blood. But I don't dare pull my hand away; it's all that is keeping her anchored to her chair.

Billy Belcher takes a noisy slurp of coffee from his Styrofoam cup. "There's more," he says.

"More?" Darlene asks. She lets go of me. She grabs the edge of the table. "How could there be more?"

"Believe me, there's plenty. But in the interest of moving things along and not belaboring what must be hurtful facts, I think this will suffice for the start." He turns. "Jack?"

"Point of information, these are not facts, but thank you, Billy," Jack answers.

Thank you for what?

Jack shuffles his papers. He looks up. "In all honesty," he states, "I feel strongly that Mrs. Carlene Lattanzio is to be lauded for stopping smoking and joining AA. These are admirable steps. On the other hand, let me just point out that *my* client has never had the need to seek out such commendable services as AA and Smokers Anonymous. Fortunately, she does not smoke. Luckily, she is a light social drinker."

"A light social drinker who hangs out in bars!" harrumphs Carlene.

Jack holds up a cease-and-desist hand. "Now. Now. Mr. Belcher had *his* chance to speak," he warns. "I will get to all these issues in due course." Once more he runs his fingers through his hair. He pushes an unruly lock off his forehead. "And I believe Mrs. Carlene Lattanzio's love for her grandson is sincere."

Darlene and I spin to face him at the same time, our foreheads creased in the same accusatory you-traitor-to-the-cause astonishment.

"*But,*" he says, ignoring our blatant conjoined disapproval, "nobody loves this child as much as his mother. Nobody is closer or more devoted to this child than his mother. Talk about blood—nobody is closer in blood, nobody bleeds for this child more than his mother." He bangs his hand against his briefcase. "A mother who nourished her child from her own body and who, when her child was cruelly and unfairly taken away—on false accusations—continued to nourish this child despite significant adversity."

For the first time this morning, a partial eclipse of a smile crosses Darlene's face.

"Let me deal with Mr. Belcher's issues one by one." Jack's voice is calm, soothing; it holds a professional solicitousness I have never heard before. He looks up. He smiles. "Karen," he says.

Karen slides the yellow legal pad across the yard of peeling Formica that separates them. I've been so focused on, so riveted by, so *appalled* by Billy Belcher's contentions I didn't notice that her doodles have transformed themselves into bulleted power points. I study the social worker, who seems to have filled pages of her own peace-symboled notebook with a multitude of lists.

Jack checks the legal pad. He smiles again. He is smiling far too much for such a grave situation, I decide. "Fortunately, I have a good memory. I'm afraid Karen's handwriting can't be counted among her many virtues," he chuckles.

Despite the criticism, Karen beams back adoringly.

"First," he goes on, "the breast-feeding." He roots around in his briefcase. "Let me see," he says. He extracts a brittle section of newspaper. "Here's an article from the *New York Times*, dated June 13, 2006." He waves it in front of his face. "May I summarize?"

We all nod.

" '*Not* breast-feeding is dangerous for your baby's health,' " he reads. " 'According to the American Academy of Pediatrics, breast-fed babies are at lower risk for sudden infant death syndrome, asthma, diabetes, leukemia, lymphoma. Breast-feeding protects against respiratory infections, diarrhea, and ear infections, not to mention pneumonia. Those given breast milk scored higher on IQ tests than those who were bottle-fed. Breast-fed children are also at lower risk for obesity.' Permit me to quote from the Health and Human Services Department: 'Our message is that breast milk is the gold standard and anything less than that is inferior.' " He extends the newspaper across the table. "Would you care to take a look for yourselves?" he asks.

"Not necessary," says Billy Belcher.

"It is my client's contention—and the *New York Times* bears this out—that the longer he's breast-fed, the better for her little boy's health," declares Jack.

"But there are social issues to consider. A child who talks, who interacts with other children on playgrounds, who is eating solid food—there is not just inconvenience but social stigma."

"More important than Anthony Vincent's health? Than mother/son bonding?" Jack waits a beat. He signals for

Karen's bottle of water. She passes it. He raises it to his lips, gulps, then hands it back. "But you've had *your* uninterrupted say, Mr. Belcher. Please let me continue."

"Point taken. Do proceed."

"As far as the one incident that led Carlene to call social services and get temporary—let me emphasize *temporary*—custody of Anthony Vincent. My client contends that the child's father was at home asleep on the sofa when, fed up with marital tension and exhausted from sleepless nights and long days of mothering without the father's help, she in all good faith left Anthony Vincent to have a simple drink at a neighborhood bar. There is even a witness to the fact that the father was at home: the neighbor in the next apartment who complained about Joseph Lattanzio's snoring, due to his untreated case of sleep apnea. Unfortunately, the neighbor subsequently moved away with no forwarding address, and attempts so far to locate him have been unsuccessful. And as Carlene well knows, it's been impossible to find her son through normal channels since he's taken off for California and seems to be living out of his pickup truck."

"That bum," Carlene says.

"That good-for-nothing," Darlene echoes.

Jack nods. "Well, at least you agree on the character or lack thereof of Joseph Lattanzio, as well as wanting the best for Anthony Vincent. That's a start."

"Start for what?" Darlene asks.

"Reaching some kind of agreement."

"I will never agree to giving up my grandchild," Carlene begins.

"And she will never again get her hands on my Anthony Vincent," Darlene spits out.

Jack ignores them. He goes on. "With the mention of

Joseph Lattanzio's general irresponsibility, this leads me to my next point. My client admits freely that due to the tensions in her marriage, the volatile nature of her husband, his temper—"

"From the time he was a little boy . . . ," his mother supplies. "The neighbors were pounding their broomsticks from the minute he was born until the day he left home."

"Tell me about it," groans her daughter-in-law.

"Yes," Jack continues, "well, because of these tensions and Joseph Lattanzio's dire need of anger management, Darlene, this emotionally battered wife, admits that she did seek affection from someone else at the bar. One instance only and with a person who is now completely out of her life."

Carlene sighs. Her eyes take on a far-off, dreamy haze. "Been there, done that," she says. Then stops herself. She slaps her own hand. The studded bracelets vibrate alarmingly. "Not that there's any excuse."

"Let me add," Jack says, "that Darlene now has a full-fledged job; she's earning a steady income; her employer is paying Social Security; for the first time she will be filing a tax return; I've been assured that in the future she'll be accruing health benefits. Her employer, Miss Maisie Grey, has come to testify on her behalf." He points at me. "Ms. Grey?"

I stand up. Lacking a Bible, I place my hand on my heart. "Darlene Lattanzio is the best employee I've ever had," I swear. I do not confess she's the only one. "She is essential to the smooth running of Factotum, Inc. She's hardworking, reliable, uncomplaining. She shows initiative. Our clients are extremely appreciative of her. I award her the highest ratings and can see her going far in my—uh—my company." I turn to Jack. "Should I add more? I mean, I can give specific examples of all the ways she's helped."

"This is perfect," says Jack. "If Billy requires more explanation, I'm sure you can provide it. Thank you, Ms. Grey."

I sit down. Darlene leans in toward my ear. "That was great, Maisie," she lauds.

"I have many letters from people of substance and high position in this commonwealth testifying to Darlene's good qualities . . . ," Jack adds. He looks at his watch. "But in the interest of time, I will read only one and pass around the others if any of you want to see them. With Karen's assistance, I can certainly provide copies. Is this agreeable to everyone?"

A unanimous "aye" makes its way around the table.

Jack holds up a fax with a lot of single-spaced typing. The Harvard seal, its bold-printed *Veritas* prominent, can be seen from all angles. "This letter is from Professor Seamus O'Toole, the renowned Joyce scholar."

Darlene nudges me.

"To whom it may concern," Jack reads. "Permit me to sing the wondrous praises of Miss Darlene Lattanzio, housecleaner, organizer, hand-holder, cook, student, adviser, listener, general factotum, miraculous human being *sans pareil*. Since Darlene has been practicing her magic on me, my household has improved, my teaching has improved, my scholarship has improved, my students are happier, the birds sing in the trees outside, and all is much better with the world than it was before Factotum, Inc., produced this domestic genius to help with my onerous chores. Given her charm, her empathy, her industry, her warmth, her intelligence—she's become quite the appreciator of Joyce, by the way—I harbor not a single doubt that she is as brilliant and devoted a mother as she is an employee. Without her cheerful, helpful attendance, my life would be sorely diminished. I can only imagine how diminished her beloved son's life would be without her constant, reassuring presence. Mere words committed to these pages are insufficient to describe her many attributes. She is a miracle worker indeed. And a nurturer in every sense of the word. I heartily entreat you to return this child to his rightful place, in his mother's loving arms." Jack pauses. "Signed 'Seamus O'Toole, C. J. Moynihan Professor of Joyce Studies, Harvard Faculty of Arts and Sciences, Sever Hall, Cambridge, Massachusetts.'"

"How about that," marvels Carlene. "I bought Anthony Vincent one of those little Harvard sweatshirts. With a hood and everything. He's precious in it. That's where I want my Anthony Vincent to go."

"Me, too," Darlene choruses. "I want Anthony Vincent to go to Harvard. That's my goal."

Carlene nods. "He's very smart, you know."

"I'm his mother, of course I know that."

"The way he's learned all his letters . . ."

"He's far ahead for his age. It's probably got something to do with the breast milk. It helps, as that newspaper said, with the IQ."

"Whatever . . ." Carlene examines a fingernail tipped with a gold star. "You should see him at the library hour."

"The library hour?"

"I don't want him to be like me or you. Or my good-for-nothing son. I want him to have one of them careers rather than a job. No grocery store cashier for my grandchild. No shoveling someone's walk or sliding under somebody's ratty pickup." Her voice softens. "Though it sounds like you've got yourself a decent job at last."

"Thanks to Maisie. Though not the kind of job you'd have if you had a real education." She stops. "But Maisie is a graduate of one of the Seven Sisters."

"If you ask me, those sisters are almost as bad as those priests. Those nuns can be twisted. I don't believe in Catholic school. Ever since Joseph went to Saint Michael's . . . well, a lot of good that did him. All that stuff going on. No, it's only Harvard."

"You'll hear no argument from me."

"You have to get an early start to get into there. Each time we go to the library, Anthony Vincent takes out four books. He picks them himself. I read them to him. Then next time he chooses four more."

"Hey," says Darlene. "That's great. I mean, that's really nice of you."

"Thanks." Carlene waits. She picks at her nail. "It sounds like you do okay, too. What that professor said in the letter. He seems to like you. He seems to think you're smart."

"He's helping me with my self-esteem." Darlene pushes a clump of hair behind her ears. "I'm not so smart with men, though."

"Tell me about it," her mother-in-law sighs.

By tacit mutual agreement, the rest of us observe this exchange in silence. As far as we're all concerned, right now we're so much additional furniture, unremarkable, receding into the scratched green walls and torn linoleum. The lawyers nod imperceptibly, the way coaches at the sidelines give their team coded signals of a winning strategy. The social worker's face is a mask of therapeutic neutrality. When I look toward Karen's notebook, I can see an outline of a baby stretched across two laps. Anthony Vincent has two mommies.

"Did you throw away my breast milk?" Darlene now asks Carlene.

"No way. I would never do that."

"Then it's still in your freezer? I've stored bags and jars of it in so many places I can't keep track. Though I know Maisie has a couple. And Seamus O'Toole . . ."

Carlene leans forward. "You have your milk in that professor's freezer?" There's a curious eagerness in her voice. Does she think Seamus's Westinghouse will impart Harvard matriculation prospects to Darlene's milk?

"Only temporarily. Just until I get my baby back. Just in case you need more. Or if Anthony Vincent hasn't been getting the benefits from the milk I was able to get to you . . ."

"Oh, he has."

"How come? Your lawyer said you started him on store-bought."

"Which doesn't mean I would throw away something perfectly good. I defrosted the last of it, and used it in cupcake batter. And I took the cupcakes to story hour last week."

"You *what?*"

"I didn't want it to go to waste. Especially since it was his mother's, *your*, milk."

"You've got to be joking," Darlene exclaims. "You can't be serious."

I think of contamination, of infections, of hepatitis, of AIDS. Maybe Darlene is having such thoughts, too, because, after a few seconds, she asks, "And everyone is all right? No one got sick?"

"They *loved* it. One of the mothers of Anthony Vincent's little friends said it was the best cupcake her kid ever ate."

Is revenge a dish best served in cupcakes from another mother's milk? I wonder, or has Carlene been making imaginative and recycled use of something that she easily might have thrown out in the trash?

The silence persists. The fluorescent lights buzz. The air conditioner chugs. Footsteps pound along an outside corridor. We all wait. Breath held. Pencils poised. Coffee cups aloft.

And then it happens. Darlene laughs. Triggering our collective sigh of relief.

"That's a pretty smart thing," she announces. "To bake the milk into cupcakes."

Carlene laughs, too. "Sure is, if I do say so myself." She pauses. "Can I ask you something?"

"Go ahead," Darlene says.

"What are you planning to do with the baby when you're at work?" Carlene stops. "*If* you get him back, I mean," she corrects herself.

"I've already thought about it. Some places I can take him with me. I don't think the clients will mind. A lot of them aren't home. I bet most of the ones who are would just love to have Anthony Vincent around. Maisie's going to help me look into day care. I hope to find a good sitter. One who doesn't cost too much."

"There's no good sitter like a relative. Like family." She pauses. She fingers a sequined *M*. "No good sitter like a grandmother who loves him. One who wouldn't charge a cent to look after her little boy."

Darlene's mouth falls open. "Are you saying . . . ?"

"Yup."

"You mean . . . ?"

Carlene nods. "I've made mistakes myself. I think you should have your kid with you. I'm not getting any younger.

And I've raised my own no-good son. I sure learned a few lessons along the way. Maybe if I'd taken Joseph to the library instead of the liquor store. In AA we learn to admit our mistakes and move on. Anthony Vincent is going to go to Harvard. He'll get a real chance to make it in this world. He can stay with me when you work. And he'll have the love of both of us."

I shake my head in wonder. People surprise you. Just when you think you've figured someone out . . . I smile. You've got to hand it to her, HOT MAMMA! tank top and all. If only you could seat Darlene and Carlene at the negotiating table and leave them alone to go at it, there'd be peace in the Middle East. The instant I think this, I have another, more pessimistic thought: In my own particular dispute, no matter how high the level of diplomacy, I can't imagine that anyone could bridge the gap between me and my former mother-in-law. But, then, this morning in the Walgreens parking lot, could I ever have predicted that such a solution could be reached before noon around this cheap, peeling Formica conference table in the sad, dusty offices of Somerville Legal Services?

Jack jumps up and grabs his jacket. Billy Belcher puts his spectacles away. "This is what I mean about working things out," Jack marvels. *Yet still making room for plenty of billable hours*, he is wise enough not to express.

He checks his watch again. "And just in time for lunch."

A lunch that I predict will not include his client or his client's boss, yours truly: that former brief, now totally extinguished flame.

"I need to get downtown ASAP," he adds, pushing one arm through a sleeve and with the other sorting papers into files.

Fern Ross-Gratowski shuts her notebook; she adjusts her chain of cats. "Social Services will have to check to make sure everything is all right."

"Natch." Jack smiles. "I'll have Karen write up—no, *type* up—an informal agreement that will set out all the details. And we'll be in touch." He waggles a come-with-me finger at the intern. "All's well that ends well," he nearly sings. He heads for the door; Karen, two Prince Philip steps behind, follows him.

Darlene huddles in a corner; she arranges with her mother-in-law to fetch Anthony Vincent together after they have lunch. "Pizza," I hear. "Pepperoni. Hot-fudge sundae to celebrate."

She walks over to me. "Do you mind . . . ?"

"Take the afternoon off," I order.

She flings her arms around me. She squeezes tight. She pats my back. She squishes a noisy kiss against my cheek. "Thanks, Maisie."

"Got to be in court," Billy Belcher announces. "Days like this make the ambulance chasing all worthwhile." He chuckles at his own joke. "People surprise you every single time."

Everyone's rushing away, abandoning me. Me, who is now left alone. Yet again, junior high revives its ancient taunts: *Wallflower. Nerd. Last one picked for the team. Cum no laude.*

Billy Belcher stops. He turns on his heel. He waves. "Seven Sisters, huh? Kind of makes sense."

SIXTEEN

On the way to Gabriel's house, I stop at the liquor store. First I reach for the beer. I change my mind and seek out the Chianti. Just as I near the cashier, I change my mind again and head for the champagne. I've got a lot of reasons to celebrate. I tick them off: Darlene is getting custody of her child and avoiding court; September is going back to school and saving me from fighting with my son; and with Shakespearean swiftness, the funeral baked meats of my breakup with Jack have furnished forth the pizza party with Gabriel Doyle. I choose a bottle of Veuve Clicquot. I check to make sure it's brut. "Ah, the widow," extols the clerk who takes my credit card and wraps the bottle in gold foil festooned with a large bow.

The widow, indeed. If you think of men and their widowed mothers: Hamlet and Gertrude, Rex and Ina, Gabe clad in the departed Mrs. Doyle's London Fog, then nothing could be more appropriate.

The clerk hands me my package. "You've got good taste," he grants.

"In *some* things," I reply.

* * *

Gabriel Doyle, considerate in *every*thing, has given me precise directions. I make no wrong turns and thus don't need the extra quarter hour's margin of error I always allow for getting lost. Though I pull up in front of his house ten minutes early, he is waiting on the porch. He waves. He rushes down the walk. He is opening my car door even before I've turned the engine off.

"Maisie!" he marvels as if he hasn't had dinner with me just two days ago. "You're here."

It's a long time since someone has been that delighted to see me. I stop. Has someone *ever* been that delighted to see me?

There's not much opportunity to parse degrees of delight in my presence because right away Gabe takes my elbow. He steers me toward the house. It's a small neat bungalow on a tidy handkerchief of mowed lawn, one corner of which is marked by a plaster statue of Madonna and Child. The blue paint has faded; the plaster is crumbled; the child seems to be missing a foot and half its nose.

Gabe follows my gaze. "Oh, that," he dismisses. "It's an eyesore, I know. I keep meaning to do something about it. But my mother loved it so much." He rubs his chin. "It's amazing how you don't notice things, how you can block everything out."

"Maybe because you're the kind to give even an eyesore the benefit of the doubt."

"And you're the kind to overlook my cluelessness."

He holds open the door. I step inside. I turn my head and stare, studying Gabriel Doyle's deceased mother's interior.

If anything shrieks old people's home, old lady's home with a pinch of Miss Havisham thrown in, this is it. A statement I can make with authority since, given Factotum, Inc., I am a bit of an expert on other people's living quarters. My first impression is *What is Gabriel Doyle doing here?* My second impression is *Gabriel Doyle is everywhere here.*

Smiling down from the walls, the mantels, the shelves are photographs of Gabriel in anthropologically improbable multiples of the seven stages of man. Gabriel bare-bottomed on shag carpeting (nicely dimpled buttocks, by the way), Gabriel in spiffy Sunday school short pants and cockeyed bow tie, in red-and-white altar-boy regalia, Gabriel in glasses, in braces, without braces, on bicycle, on circus pony. Short hair, long hair, sideburns, mustache, beard, clean-shaven. Almost as rare as hen's teeth (a fact any ex-Pollock would know) is the scant display of photographs of the five sisters, smaller, less elaborately framed, their sororal black-and-white snapshots tucked behind those of their brother, five daughters almost totally eclipsed by one son.

"You clearly are—were—the favorite," I say.

"Nonsense."

I wave my arm. "Here's the evidence."

He stares at the walls as if he's never noticed those photographs before. "I think the technology got better by the time I came along," he protests.

"I had a friend in college who was convinced her sister was the pet. Every time she went home for vacation, she used to sort the family photographs into two piles. If there was just one more of her sister than of her, she'd make such a fuss her parents would have to bring out the Polaroid."

"I'd say there's some clear pathology involved," Gabriel diagnoses.

"Well, she did become a psychologist." I look at him. "Quite a famous one," I add.

"That's no surprise." He clasps my shoulder. "Come into the living room and we'll have a drink. I've already called the pizza place. They'll deliver in half an hour."

The old-people's-home decoration theme persists into the living room: antimacassars, figurines of shepherds and shepherdesses, religious statuary, overlapping hooked rugs, overstuffed velvet-upholstered furniture, lamps with frilled shades, faded silk flowers in cut-glass vases. On the walls hang more portraits of the only son of Mrs. Doyle along with a few landscapes of moonlit country cottages.

I compare Seamus O'Toole's piles of papers and books—the digs whose exponentially increasing messiness charted the vanishing woman's touch of Georgette. I add to this image my hoarder of a client, the lawyer who stockpiles paper bags, plastic bags, and jelly jars. These are challenges, however daunting, that Factotum, Inc., has tackled with gratifying success. I examine the cloying shepherdesses and fringed lamps. Even Factotum, Inc., I fear, wouldn't be up to the task of Gabriel Doyle's mother's house without my hiring extra staff to supplement Darlene.

Not that Gabriel is about to engage Factotum, Inc.'s services. Not that he even seems to notice the antediluvian clutter. Not that I would work for him anyway. Housecleaners, like shrinks, need to keep their distance. It would be a folly and unprofessional to agree to treat the down-in-the-dumps dump of a friend or relative, let alone a lover. Not that, mind you, I am about to cast Gabriel Doyle in that role.

Now he points to a chair obliterated by a dozen crocheted pillows. "Grab a seat," he says. "Just throw that stuff on the floor."

I pull the gold-wrapped bottle of Veuve Clicquot out of my WGBH tote.

"Is that what I think it is?" Gabriel asks.

I nod.

"Shall I chill it? We can have it with pizza. Or with dessert. I bought a quart of ice cream from Toscanini's. Vanilla."

I hand him the bottle. "Great," I say.

"If I can remember right, my mother kept a couple of champagne flutes somewhere in a kitchen cabinet. She got them for my Communion." He stops. "What are we celebrating?" he asks. "Besides our second date, which is actually our third if you count our coffee in the corridor of Mount Auburn Hospital. Certainly a second, or third, or second and a half date, don't get me wrong, is reason enough to celebrate."

Though I'm happy to count two or three dates as a great excuse to hoist a flute of champagne, I decide not to toast a burgeoning relationship whose newness makes me wary, understandable if you consider my former experience with burgeoning relationships.

I toss the pillows out of the way. I sit down. "Two things to celebrate," I explain. "I took your advice and told September she could stay in my apartment only if she went back to school. To my profound astonishment, she agreed right away. She said she only wanted a mother to tell her what to do."

He claps his hands. "How wonderful. I'm thrilled for you."

I notice that he doesn't add, *See, I told you so*. Or, *I'm glad you listened to me*. Or, *I knew this would happen if you followed my instructions*, the way other men in my life, other more narcissistic men, couldn't resist putting in a claim for credit due. With each passing "date," I am starting to find Gabriel Doyle more and more agreeable.

"And the second reason to celebrate?" he asks.

I tell him about my morning at Somerville Legal Services. I give him the kind of blow-by-blow that might be read back by a professional court stenographer. I describe the people around the table, their various note-taking skills, their wardrobes, their coffee-drinking, gum-chewing, water-swigging habits. I repeat the arguments pro and con, the cupcake revelation, the library story-hour surprise.

Gabriel balances on the edge of his own crocheted-pillow seat, a twin to the one I'm sitting on. Though he has not tossed his pillows to the floor (maybe his photographically archived, adorable posterior is smaller than mine), I assume he's perched that way not because he doesn't have room but because he is so intent on every word I say. You've got to hand it to him. His eyes never leave my face; all his body language indicates total absorption in the person across from him.

I wait a beat. I take a breath.

"You'd make a great police witness," he offers. "You don't miss a single detail."

"Am I boring you? Telling you more than you want to know?"

"On the contrary. Go ahead. Don't leave anything out."

I continue my recitation. When I get to its Solomonic resolution, however, I am so overcome by the dramatic tension I have to stop.

Gabriel pulls a Kleenex from a china box painted with shamrocks and barley sheaves.

I wipe my eyes. "It seemed to come from out of nowhere," I go on. "None of us could ever have predicted it, they were so angry with each other. We nearly had to yank them apart. *Physically.* Talk about happy endings. Perfect endings. They're not going to cut that baby in two. They'll share. Darlene will have custody, but Carlene will babysit her grandchild while Darlene is at work."

Gabriel's laugh holds wonder and delight. "The wise lady from Philadelphia couldn't have found a better solution."

I nod. "What's so great is that they both wanted the best for the child."

"And even more amazing is that they both realized each had the best interests of the child at heart. It's my experience that in the heat of argument it's very easy to lose sight of the truth." He leans back as far as his overpillowed chair will permit. "When I hear a story like this, all I can think is, 'Isn't life great!' "

"In your line of work, you must hear plenty that makes you feel the opposite."

"Sometimes," he grants. "I know it sounds sappy, but I believe, like Anne Frank, that people are really good at heart. I'm a pretty optimistic fellow when it comes to the human race. You'll find this out when you get to know me better."

I smile at a potential truth about to be universally acknowledged, at least in the universe of this room, that I'm going to get to know him better.

"And no time like the present," he adds. He reaches over. He touches my arm. "Maisie," he says. His hand moves to mine.

We sit there for a while, no doubt looking, amid such surroundings, like two old codgers who belong in a pair of matching rocking chairs. But there's nothing old about the feelings the touch of his fingers stirs. When he stands up to pull me onto the sofa with him, I could be a teenager back in my New Hampshire living room inching toward her pre-Electrolux high school crush, her single goal to bang thighs together in the middle of the couch. "Maisie," Gabe says again. And then he kisses me.

Okay, dear reader, I take back all my doubts, all my negative suppositions about his womanless life, his annulled marriage, his adult years sharing his mother's roof, his presumed lack of experience. I state a mea culpa for any preconceived notions about looks, lifestyle, maternal fixations, past sexual history. Did I show favoritism toward hard-driven lawyers and chicken-potpie kings as opposed to members of the gentler, helping professions whose qualities I might have—formerly—consigned to a wimp category? I plead innocence about this kind of guy. I cite inexperience. Oh, what have I been missing? I need to ask myself.

I find out. Gabriel Doyle is a major kisser, a king of kissers. Right now he is doing remarkable things with his tongue; right now his hands, his *healer's* hands, move all over my body. Which has become an instrument of pure sensation, a human tuning fork. "Mmmm," I hum. "There. Higher. Mmmm."

"Mmmm," he choruses. "This way? Like that?"

I could sit here forever, I decide, among the pillows and antimacassars and a small marble saint—who couldn't possibly disapprove of such physical communion, which now is so clearly reaching a spiritual plane. Who, when I peek over Gabriel's shoulder, is, in fact, starting to look as if he's casting a special blessing on the two of us. "That," I command. "Yes. That."

Such caresses should be a basic human right. Although I know touch is essential to the well-being of a child—look at breast-feeding mothers, beatific Madonnas—could I ever have imagined how a nonparental laying on of hands could catapult a middle-aged, formerly touch-deprived adult beyond mere well-being to astonishing levels of ecstasy? Gabriel's mouth finds my ear. "Maisie," he cries.

Just then, in the timeworn not-quite-coitus-interruptus tradition of a drawing room farce, the doorbell rings. Gabriel pulls his tongue away. He yanks his hand from my breast. "Damn," he says.

"Damn," I repeat.

"Pizza," he groans.

"Pizza," I echo.

We could go on like this forever, point and counterpoint, but the bell chimes again, longer and more insistently.

Let me ask you, has any delivery boy ever been greeted with less enthusiasm in his whole career with Pizza by Mamma Mia than the teenager now at Gabriel's front stoop? Gabriel rubs his swollen lips; he smooths his disheveled hair; he tucks his shirt back into his pants. He empties his pockets of change. He grabs the two pizza boxes and shuts the door before the delivery boy has managed to stammer out the first syllable of his thanks. "I suppose we should eat before this gets cold," Gabriel manages to concede.

"I guess so," I reply with an equal lack of enthusiasm.

We sit down at the dinette in his mother's kitchen. It's the room that time forgot, a place stuck somewhere in the fifties with its avocado appliances and ruffled café curtains and thick-glassed Waring blender. Gabriel passes me napkins and plates. He sets out plastic mats of pink-cheeked milkmaids and grazing cows. "Shall we have the champagne now?" he asks. "Or later?"

"Later," I say. I don't meet his eye, but I'm certain—unless I am so out of practice, unless I'm both brain *and* body dead—that we are in total unspoken agreement on what *later* signifies. And it doesn't include a scoop of vanilla ice cream apiece.

He fills two glasses with ice. He runs water from the tap. He tears open each pizza box.

With what I am now learning to see as typical thoughtfulness, he has ordered me the deluxe: anchovies, mushrooms, onions, eggplant, pepperoni, red peppers and green. His own pizza seems to consist solely of tomato sauce and cheese. I look from one to the other. I compare my cup-runneth-over pie to his minimalist no-frills. "You know me, simple tastes," he excuses.

He serves the pizza, replaces a wayward pepperoni. "So, tell me more about Tommy," Gabriel asks now. "Not just about gumdrops and September, but the kind of kid he is."

I'm off and running. The biography of Thomas Grey Pollock from birth to yesterday. Okay, I'm savvy enough to understand that most people might not want to know everything about a child's first tooth, first word, report card, athletic prowess, acts of kindness, showers of brilliance. I realize that even the most attentive of you, faced with such a litany, might start to yawn, eyes glazed, and turn your focus on your grocery list.

Yet Gabe, on the other hand, never acts bored. Not for

one second does his interest flag through the first slice of pizza to the last, through three refills of water from the tap, through the coffee he percolates for us.

"I can't wait to meet him," he says, sounding suddenly shy. "The biggest regret I ever had," he confesses, "is that I didn't have kids."

I don't answer that there's still time, though this is what I think. Despite a majority of high school classmates who became grandparents at forty, I know that people my age are still having kids. A few of those celebrity bumps in the magazine at Mount Auburn Hospital the day Gabe and I first met represented the extruding wombs of women pushing forty-plus. As you already know, after Tommy, I was unable to conceive another baby no matter how hard Rex and I and reproductive science tried. Perhaps, in my case, there were psychological issues involved. Perhaps my troubles with fertility had something to do with my troubles with Rex.

Gabriel pours more coffee. He passes me the milk. "When my mother died," he confides, "I was utterly distraught. I was all alone, waiting for my sisters, who were due to fly in that night. I couldn't seem to sit still. I kept wandering the corridors of the hospital. I had no idea where I was going. But I ended up on the obstetrics floor. A nurse passed me. She was rolling a baby in one of those little clear-sided bassinets. 'Was he just born?' I remember asking. 'At twelve-fourteen,' she said. I was astonished. My mother had just died at exactly that time, at exactly twelve-fourteen. 'What's his name?' I asked. 'Angel DeJesus,' she replied."

He stops. He stirs sugar into his mug. His hand trembles when he picks it up. "It seemed a miracle. I have never forgotten Angel DeJesus. And the comfort it gave me to know that that child was born the exact second my mother passed."

We sit in silence. A moment of silence to acknowledge the sadness of a mother's death and the joy of Angel DeJesus's birth. After a few minutes, Gabriel's fingers once more find mine. His lips resume the activity so rudely interrupted by the pizza delivery boy.

He pulls away. "Shall we . . . ?" Gabriel asks.

"Yes," I nod.

"Now," he says. It is not a question.

"As soon as possible."

He stands.

"Upstairs?" I point to the front hall.

"Your place?" he counters.

I shake my head. "Not with Tommy, and September already moved in."

"Let's find a motel."

"You don't have a bed here?"

"The only double is in my mother's room."

I don't mention that it's easy enough to squeeze onto a single mattress, a sofa, or even a bunch of pillows on the floor. I don't add that I have done this—in my pre–Gabriel Doyle past—without damage to any appendage. I don't point out that desire doesn't need fifty-three inches, coiled springs, or a high thread count. "Oh," is all I say instead.

He must catch the bewilderment in my voice because he reddens and his own voice hushes. "I have something I need to confess. Something that may shock you."

"Shoot," I order. "I am unshockable."

"If only . . ."

"Try me."

"Well," he starts. "Well . . ."

"Go on."

"Well, not to alarm you or anything. Not to give you any opportunity for second thoughts. And I'm sure there's solid psychology behind this. In fact, I can offer you a whole host of psychological explanations for—"

"For what?" I ask. "Just tell me."

"Well . . . ," he starts. Then stops again.

"Yes?" I urge.

He takes a running breath. "I have never been able to have sex under my mother's roof."

Funny, considering all my past experience, you'd figure a statement like this might put the kibosh on my ardor. Surprising, but no warning bells ring for me. I hear no mama's-boy sirens, no mother-back-from-the-grave-to-haunt-you alarms. "That's okay," I allow, "just as long as we can find another roof to have sex under. *Fast.*"

Within ten minutes we are at the Comfort Inn. We hold in our clasped hands the key to room 241, king-sized bed, air conditioner, coffeemaker, lavender-scented toiletries, complimentary ice bucket in which to place our bottle of Veuve Clicquot. Within two minutes we have stripped off our clothes and kicked the quilted floral bedspread onto the floor. Within seconds Gabriel Doyle's body is joined to mine. And as we move together joyously, ecstatically, triumphantly, I hear him whisper, amid the *mmms* and *ohs* and *ahhs,* the *Maisies* and the *darlings,* and the Molly Bloom *yes, yes, yes,* these words: "I think it may be time for me to sell the house."

SEVENTEEN

Tommy, September, and I are having breakfast together this morning, though you couldn't describe us as actually sharing a meal. September is spooning up flaxseed sprinkled with dried berries and shriveled nuts and swimming in rice milk. Tommy munches yeast-free hemp toast spread with soy butter. He sips a thick sludge from a bottle labeled Lifeway Low-fat Kefir Probiotic Cultured Smoothie. I stare at it. Could this belong to one of the four food groups? Where would you buy it? At a grocery store or in a pharmacy?

He peers longingly at my own plate, bacon and scrambled eggs, a block of cream cheese, a bagel that's neither whole, organic, nor 100 percent anything. I'm ravenous. Lots of great sex will do that to you. Boosts the appetite while at the same time, because of added calisthenics, keeps those inches off your hips. I slide my plate over to Tommy. He shakes his head. September nods with the good-boy approval of a sponsor in a twelve-step group. I hold up a slice of bacon. I wave it in front of his face. I pop it into my mouth.

"What an appetite you've developed, Maisie," observes September, her voice like the big bad wolf.

I cast her a sharp look. Does she suspect anything? But her attention has turned to the list of organic ingredients printed on the recycled cardboard of her cereal box.

"Breakfast is the most important meal of the day," I intone. "Nothing is healthier or more comforting." I do not add that I'm scarfing mine down here because no comparable culinary comfort exists at the Comfort Inn.

Though there are other kinds of comfort. If I can get over my shame at (metaphorically) sneaking into the woods, I'm almost happy when the motel clerk fishes out the key to room 241 before Gabe and I even approach his desk. Last night the clerk told me he'd ordered the maid to put extra body lotion in the bathroom because of the rate at which I was using it up. Still, except for those smirks from the staff or the pitying glances aimed at middle-aged lovers who have nowhere else to go, it's not so bad being a regular.

And having regular sex. A logistically possible luxury since Tommy and September's music-groupie schedule allows me to slink back before they even get home. I've got plenty of time to throw on a nightgown and mess up my bed, thereby maintaining my image of setting a good example and moral high-roadedness. Besides, could I have more fun in a penthouse with a view? In the midst of passion, who would make a distinction between a Motel 6 and the Ritz? Blinded by desire, who would notice Picassos on the wall, Persian carpets, high ceilings, an enfilade of rooms when all any lover needs and wants is one big bed, a door that locks, and a shower with water that's reliably hot.

Speaking of hot . . . I take a deep breath. I fan my face with the Living section of the *Globe.* I try to distract myself from twisted sheets and bodies slippery with sweat. But, let me tell you, regular sex has also been good for my morale, my mood, my current motherly mellowness, my all-accepting attitude. When you're happy, you want the whole world to be happy, too, meaning you don't mind so much the sexual lives of your kids the way you did when you viewed their lust through a veil of celibate misery and deemed such shenanigans age inappropriate.

Which explains why September and I are going shopping today. For a back-to-school wardrobe, though school doesn't start for a month. And despite this week's heat wave, the racks and shelves of stores, in their utter and commercially stupid disregard for weather and season, will be stuffed with thick sweaters, scarves, wool skirts, flannel-lined pants, and snow-repellent fleece. Today we're doing a mother/daughter thing.

The kind of thing her mother never did, I found out, when I broached the subject. "Mall or Harvard Square?" I asked.

Instantaneous elation plummeted to paralytic doubt. "I don't know," she said. "My mother never took me to either place."

I must have appeared surprised even though, in view of my previous conversation with Olidia Silva, such an expression shouldn't have crossed my face.

Immediately she assumed a happy-families-are-all-alike facade. "It's okay, Maisie," she soothed. "I didn't miss anything." She stirred her cereal. "Which reminds me," she began. "Tommy told me that a girl at his school . . . It's a real fancy school . . ."

"His grandmother's choice," I stressed.

"This kid," she continued, "wouldn't go to college anywhere in the countryside because, like, it didn't have a place to shop. Tommy told me she picked a city college next to a mall."

I groan with old-fogy, what-is-this-world-coming-to horror.

"I wouldn't know the difference. I *have* been to Harvard Square," she qualified, "though not to stores. Mostly hanging out at the Pit." She considered. "I went to a mall once to get some gym shorts. But never with, like, a mom. Never with a grown-up to help me actually pick out something to wear for school." Worry lines furrowed her forehead. I assumed she'd never confronted an apples-or-oranges choice. "I just can't decide," she cried.

"I know what," I said, and proposed a resolution worthy of Darlene and Carlene Lattanzio. "We'll go to *both*."

She threw her black-bat-wing-sleeved arms around me; she laid her patchouli-scented cheek next to mine. My earring got caught in her tangle of Rasta curls. "Oh, Maisie," she exclaimed. "You're just the best!"

Now we clear the dishes. We tidy up. "I'm going to make the bed," I underscore. "Then put on my lipstick. Run a comb through my hair."

I survey September's usual black rags. Though she often discusses getting changed for this concert or that poetry slam, I've never been able to distinguish between one outfit and the next. "What about you?" I ask.

"Oh, thanks, I'm all set." She smiles.

A smile so endearing that I stifle the mother's universal refrain of "You're wearing *that*?"

The minute September disappears to fetch her purse, Tommy gives me a conspiratorial wink. "Any bacon left?" he asks.

"On the counter."

"Don't tell."

I place my hand on my maternal co-conspirator's heart. "Scout's honor. Grab it now. It should still be crisp."

There's no crispness this morning out on the sidewalks of Somerville, Massachusetts. Waves of heat ruffle the horizon, just like in those TV news reports from the deserts of Iraq. The *Globe* is full of advice for keeping cool: *Stay inside; drink lots of water; take it easy; wear light, loose clothing and comfortable shoes.*

I look down at September's clodhopper platforms teetering inches off the ground. "Maybe we should use the car," I suggest, the pleasing prospect of air-conditioning trumping the poor prospect of finding a place to park.

"No problem," she says. "I can walk for miles in these."

Within the five minutes it takes us to cross the Cambridge/Somerville line to Mass Ave, I have produced more perspiration than in the whole five hours I've spent locked burning flesh to burning flesh in the arms of Gabriel Doyle. Rivulets pour down my cheeks, between my breasts, at the backs of my knees, from the circle my waistband makes. I huff and puff to keep up with September while she glides on her ridiculous shoes with the delicacy and poise of a high-wire artist. I can read the caption now: *Age trudging after beauty.*

We drop into Brooks Pharmacy where I buy us bottles of water. I encourage September to browse the aisles in search of the exact and only shade of black nail polish she deems worthy enough to paint on her toes. "Take your time," I order, my public magnanimity hiding my private selfish love of an artificially cooled interior.

"They don't have the color I like."

"You could ask the manager," I suggest, trying to barter more minutes in these icy aisles, where right now I find myself face-to-face with the sympathy cards. I notice they are slotted under categories: Loss of a Husband, Loss of a Mother, Loss of a Father, Loss of a Mother-in-Law, Loss of a Pet, Loss of a Son. I hustle my eyes away from that particular offering. I pick up a paperback-sized, violet-flowered model, filed under Loss of a Mother-in-Law. *Condolences* is embossed in silver across the top. In the center a single white candle flames next to a solitary white rose. I open it. I examine an impossibly blue sky, clouds as wispy as lace. A treacly Barbie doll of an angel hovers over pale purple script:

You have been the angel in my life
Heaven's gift for me, your son's wife
You made me pies
You soothed my cries
Your love for me was pure, without a flaw
You loved me as a mother, not as a mother-in-law
When the sun shines bright. When the sparrow sings,
I will sense the summer's breeze and feel your angel's wings.

Oh, *give me a break,* I groan. I am delighted to see that, compared to Loss of a Pet, for instance, this specific card is not a bestseller. Except for my own incriminating fingerprints, its stack of cellophane-wrapped angels appears untouched.

"Ready, Maisie?" September asks. She points to my hand. "Are you going to buy that?"

I put it back, fast, before she notices its content or the category under which it's filed. Too bad I can't use such a condolence card. Too bad I don't have the chance to sing *Ding dong the witch is dead!* I imagine you're shocked at this confession. After all, you might point out, my mother-in-law is an ex.

Not enough of an ex, I counter, when your child is her grandchild, when his tuition and cell phone and college fund and summer job depend on her largesse. Not enough of an ex when there are mandatory lunches, conversations, arguments over the perils of teenagers in the modern world. Not enough of an ex when there are simply endless arrangements to be made about schedules and vacations and proper influences. And especially not enough of an ex when the mother-in-law turns up on your bedroom television set where her alliterative potpie promotions touch off such roiling memories, such nightmares, that sleep becomes impossible.

Far better to be Mrs. Doyle—first name Ethel, I learned last night—buried in a well-tended, granite-headstoned plot on the south-sloping lawn of a verdant cemetery. No calls, no meals, no interference, although I picture a double bed upstairs that probably holds a dented pillow right out of A Rose for Emily.

Now September and I walk along Mass Ave in companionable silence. I am feeling almost affectionate toward her. I am congratulating myself on my philanthropy, my exemplary motherliness, my total anti–Ina Pollockness.

That is, until I notice passersby staring at us. At her. We must make an odd couple, me in my self-effacing khaki pants, white shirt, sensible flats, hair pulled back, and September—well, in her full September getup. Embarrassment sets in. What are you staring at? I want to shout. This is the opposite of the usual state of events, the teenager humiliated by being seen with his parents, the teenager who feels compelled to cross the street in case his classmates frame him in the uncool context of Mom and Dad, the teenager mortified by what a mother wears, her hair, her shoes, her mouth even before a single word comes out of it.

As soon as I have this thought, September opens her own mouth. "So, like, who's your boyfriend, Maisie?" flies out of it.

I stop short. "What?" I exclaim. "What did you say?"

"Your boyfriend," she repeats.

I turn my back to her. I feign interest in the window display of a travel agency: Honeymoon destinations. Romantic barge trips along the canals of France. Wine expeditions to Napa. A lovers' tour of Rome. Moonlight in Vermont. April in Paris. Tea for two in the Lake District. PLEASE GO AWAY, a banner instructs.

I want to go away. I want to get lost. I want to tell September to get lost. But all I can do is sputter wordlessly.

"It's okay, Maisie. You don't have to be ashamed."

That it's this *child*, this black-clad, skull-ringed, rag-clad *child* having the gall to reassure *me* gives me back my voice. "What *are* you talking about?" I ask, incredulous.

"You sing in the shower. 'Love Me Tender.' Tommy says you never used to even hum. You look happy. You wear lipstick. You iron your clothes. You threw away your old underpants. You know, the ones with the elastic all stretched out. I saw them when I was recycling. You don't look so lonely. You've got, like, this big appetite but aren't putting on any weight. When Tommy and I go out, you act kind of cheerful to see us leave."

Could Sherlock Holmes produce any more astonishing observations? "I'm not sure that . . . ," I stammer.

"Another girl can always tell," she declares. "And you seem so much younger. Love will do that."

You ought to know, I think. You who are barely the age of consent. You who at sixteen have probably had more lovers, more experience than your middle-aged sister-in-boyfriendness. About Gabriel Doyle. Do I lie? Do I tell the truth?

I take the moral high ground. "I *have* been seeing someone," I admit.

"I knew it!" she says. She slaps me a high five. She looks me up and down with a who-would-have-thought-it shake of her head. "But you don't have to tell me any more until you're ready."

"Well, that's a relief."

All sarcasm is lost on her. She gives me a just-between-us-women, you-go-girl! wink. "Though I do hope you'll tell us about him soon, Maisie. I do hope Tommy and I get to meet him in the next couple of weeks." She hesitates. "But I, of all people, understand. Tommy and I were way *way* hooked up before he decided even to mention me to you."

We have reached Cambridge Common by now and agree, by mutual heat-exhausted, boyfriend-confessional consent, to grab the nearest bench. We sink down on it. We sweep our arms across our streaming brows. Swig our bottles of water. Shake out our plastered-against-us clothes to get some air between fabric and flesh. "You know," she confides, "Tommy said he was sure I was wrong about the boyfriend. Even in spite of the evidence—you singing Elvis

Presley and all. He thought you were over that stuff. Like, he figured you would never be interested in a man again."

"He did, did he?" I suppose from a teenager's perspective, life below the belt might end at forty, at thirty-nine, hell, at thirty. *Tant pis,* so much the worse, as my high school French teacher used to bemoan.

September pushes a matted clump of hair behind her ear. "But when I pointed out that his father had found himself a girlfriend—'My mom's different,' he said. Tommy can be a bit of a sexist at times. Between you and I."

"Between you and me."

"That's right. We girls know all about men." September unzips her pack. She puts her water bottle into it. She brings out a sheaf of paper. "You know," she says, "falling in love is pretty heavy."

I'm tempted to explain that having a boyfriend is not necessarily coupled with falling in love; the two don't go together like chicken and eggs. Or, given the currently sensible custom of the country, like love and marriage. But I keep my mouth shut.

"Love changes everything. Music and the way you see the sky. Even the taste of food."

I stare at her. I assume, considering her diet, a change in the taste of food might be a real benefit.

She cradles the papers in her hand. She looks away. She seems suddenly shy. "You know I write song lyrics . . ."

"Yes, you told me that."

"And I've started to do, like, these poems, too."

I peek at the paper, half expecting a form of the angel-illustrated mother-in-law verse that provoked recent death-wish thoughts in the aisle of Brooks Pharmacy. I offer a noncommittal, "Oh?"

"I'm going to be published."

"You are?"

"There's this box in Union Square. Right where Somerville Avenue turns. It's like one of those newspaper-vending things, but this one says Poetry Port on it. It has, like, a flyer attached and asks people to leave poems—some are written on napkins and the backs of tickets and concert programs and stuff. Anyway, the flyer promises when the box is full, all the poems will be published in a free magazine."

"What a good idea."

"Isn't it?" She shakes her head in wonder. "And guess what, Maisie. I left one, my poem, there! Yesterday the editor called me and said they now had enough and she was taking all the poems to Kinkos to make the magazine. It's coming out next week."

"Wow," I exclaim. "That's great. *Great!*" I cry.

"Isn't it?" she repeats. "They used to make us go to the library at school. And there wasn't anything to do. I mean, like, we couldn't talk or fool around or stuff, so I got hold of these poetry books. I read them. Some of those poets weren't so bad."

"Libraries are amazing." Especially, I note, when you consider how Carlene's taking Anthony Vincent to the library story hour opened the way to détente. "Do you remember who were your favorites?" I ask.

"How could I forget? My two favorites—I wrote them out. Omar Khayyám." She pronounces it Omer Kay Ham. "Did you ever hear of him?"

" 'A jug of wine, a loaf of bread and thou . . .' " I recite, words so evocative of young love, words that, when you grow up, you recognize as Hallmark mush.

"Wow, Maisie!" she exclaims. "I mean, *wow*! You are so smart. Tommy's right. You know pretty much everything."

"Hardly," I say. If only. "And the other . . . ?"

"Elizabeth Barrett Browning. She's really cool. I picked her book up first because it said Portuguese and that's, like, where my family comes from." She turns to me. "Silva is a Portuguese name."

"Yes, I realize that."

"But there was nothing Portuguese about the poems." She frowns. "Weird."

" 'How do I love thee, let me count the ways,' " I show off.

"You know that, too? I don't believe it! How do you know that?"

"I stayed in school," I warn, never one to miss a pedagogical opportunity.

She lets this pass. She smooths the crumpled paper in her fist. She darts a few speculative glances my way. "Would you like to hear my poem?" she offers. "It's the one that's going to be published. I hope to use it for lyrics, too. Tommy promises to help me with the music part."

"I'd love to hear it." And because she's suddenly silent, a sacred hush due to the solemnity of the moment, I add, "*Really*. It would be an honor."

"You're sure?"

"Absolutely."

"It's about Tommy," she explains, "though you might not be able to tell."

"Poems are often about things other than what they seem to be at first."

She's a quick study. "Like Elizabeth Browning not being about the Portuguese?"

"Exactly."

"That's the best thing about them," she says. She brings the paper up to within two inches of her eyes. Does she need glasses? Has she ever been to an ophthalmologist? Would an Olidia Silva make sure she received all her shots, had regular dental appointments, knew what to do when she got her first period? I examine her. The diagnosis is easy: a serious deficiency of a mother's care.

She clears her throat. "Ready?" she asks.

"I'm all ears."

She lowers her voice an octave. She begins:

Dark night of the ghost soul. Black tunnel of loss and misery.
A road to nowhere. To doom to death to cigarette butts on the floor
And music breaking glass through the icy pitch heart of nothingness
Night closes in and steals me away. My soul is sold, broken, lost.
Reach for me if you can. Catch me if you can. I am your ghost.
Let me count the ways a jug of Dao, a loaf of seeded rye will make me weep
And you, only you, beside me, might crack my shell
Then make me whole. Take me from blackness into the light
The light of white, the light of you, that white white light, the light of love.

When she finishes, she tucks the poem back into the backpack, then looks up at me. "So? What do you think?" she implores with a tentative innocence and sudden embarrassment that melts my heart.

"Well," I say.

Her shoulders sink. "You didn't like it."

I grab her arm. "No, it's not that at all," I rush in. "I like it. I like it a lot. I just need a minute to process the words. It's complicated."

Her hand covers mine. "You like it? Complicated is good?"

"Complicated is good," I state. No Hallmark this. No roses are red, violets are blue. What do I think? Not terrible. Dark, morose teenage poetry. Is there any other? But you've got to give her credit . . .

"Did you get the 'let me count the ways'? 'The jug of Dao'?—Dao is the name of a Portuguese wine. I decided it would be cool to stick it in. Did you get—"

"The references to Omar Khayyám and Elizabeth Barrett Browning, you mean?" I interject. "Very clever. A real homage—"

"Homage?"

"A tribute. A compliment. A way to honor something you respect."

She beams. "Homage," she pronounces.

"I love 'a loaf of seeded rye will make me weep.' "

"Me, too. I'm sort of proud of that line. As an homage to Omar Khayyám." She pronounces the name with an academic precision showing she's not only a quick study but also a good listener. "And more personal stuff."

I don't ask what *more personal stuff*? I assume a dietary reference. Or certain between-the-two-of-them imagery related to my son.

"But you really like it?" she beseeches. "What you say counts since you've read a lot of poetry, since you probably even studied it in that college you went to."

"You do study poetry in college English classes," I

proselytize. "If you work hard in high school, you might want to think of college yourself."

"No one in my family ever went to college."

"That's no reason why you can't."

"No one in my family ever finished high school even."

"But you're going to," I say.

"Because of you."

"Because of *you*. Because you're smart. Because deep down you realize a good education is necessary for anything you want to do in life."

"I guess . . . ," she grants in homage to my mother-knows-best, *stand-in* mother-knows-best, platitudes.

Having planted the seed, I deftly return to the subject under discussion. "And I also especially admire the 'lovely white light of love.' "

" 'White white light, the light of love,' " she corrects.

"I need to read it again. It's hard to remember the exact wording."

"I'll make a copy," she says. "Just for you."

"I'd like that. I'd like that very much."

Renewed by the power of poetry, we make quick work of Harvard Square, which now seems more mall—its Gap, its Urban Outfitters, its Starbucks, its empty storefronts where independent booksellers and local retailers once dwelled—than a capital *M* Mall. And in this baking heat, why not opt for waterfalled, climate-controlled, stores-all-together-on-two-levels interiors.

Before we leave, we stop in the Coop, where I send September to pick out notebooks and pencils. "Most of these say Harvard on them," she points out. "Would it be, like, all right if I get them anyway?"

"Of course," I reply, in the spirit of Darlene and Carlene's shared hopes to send Anthony Vincent to Harvard and my own rarely admitted desire to see Tommy tucked away in ivied Ivy League towers. Not for *my* son the Grey mandate to Wellesley unless the school turns coed in the next couple of years. Thanks to Rex, though, he's a Crimson legacy. "Buy the Harvard version," I insist, so deeply do I trust the power of subliminal and not-so-subliminal advertising

While she's at the cash register, I sneak upstairs and find for her a slim hardbound copy of *Sonnets from the Portuguese.* I pay extra to get it gift wrapped. I choose red-and-white-striped paper and a big, glossy red bow. I hide it inside my pocketbook.

We take the T to Lechmere. We walk the two blocks to the Cambridgeside Galleria Mall. We decide to head first to the food court before we start to shop. On our way, in the middle of the mall, in what they call the atrium, we see a crowd gathered. The all-too-familiar smell of fried chicken saturates the air. September wrinkles her nose. "Yuck," she says.

We move closer. I peek through the crowd and spot a long table with about twenty men and two women seated behind it. They are all wearing egg yolk yellow T-shirts, each printed with a cartoon chicken crossing a vanishing-perspective-point road. In front of them lie trays heaped with enough chicken parts to qualify for one of Pollock's assembly lines. Huge plastic cups of water mark every place. "What's going on?" I ask the man next to me.

"A drumstick-eating contest," he explains.

"But why?"

"For the championship. And the prize."

"What's the prize?" I persist.

"Five thousand bucks," he answers.

"You're kidding!"

"It's a sport," he instructs. "There's actually an International Confederation of Competitive Eating." He pats his semiflat stomach. "You couldn't pay me enough."

A bell rings. People cheer. The T-shirted would-be champions start stuffing food into their mouths. Some stand. Some sit. One has plugged in an iPod and dances to a different drummer, a different *drumstick*. I notice the variety of techniques. A few contestants shove in the whole leg; others rotate it. One woman gulps water after every bite. "Come on, Betty," a tracksuited spectator cries out.

Discarded bones pile up on an empty tray like sifted archaeological remains. I puzzle over how you can't escape the source of the Pollock family fortune. It's on TV, in the kitchens of friends and business acquaintances, in the middle of a mall where you go to buy a new pair of jeans for the first day of school. Maybe September has the right idea; her lacto-vegan-whatever acts as the cross to repel the Pollock-family Dracula. Not that a diet, alas, can protect you from the poultry onslaught everywhere.

A fact made even clearer as September tugs at my elbow. Gagging sounds rise from her throat. "Let's get out of here," she says, "before I throw up."

"Don't you want to wait and see who wins the championship?"

She covers her mouth. "Maisie . . . ," she barely manages.

"Just joking," I excuse. "I'd be happy if I never saw another chicken again in my life."

In the food court, we order salads despite September's failure to extract sufficient historical information about the origin of the peppers and the tomatoes, their possible or improbable organic roots, whether the cucumbers had been sprayed and artificially waxed, whether illegal exploited immigrants had picked the cauliflower, the sort of fertilizer used (and if manure, the diet of the cattle that supplied it), the kind of containers the olives were exported in, the purity of the oil, the lettuce's proximity to the *B* in the makings of the BLT. "Lady, do you want a salad or not?" the exasperated server asks.

"I guess so," September allows. She turns to me. "Sometimes you just have to take what you can get."

"An admirable philosophy."

"Grilled chicken on those?" the server adds.

We find a table. We pick up plastic forks. We tear open packets of salt and pepper. We unfold paper napkins onto our laps. From the distance we can still hear the roar of the chicken-drumstick audience.

"You know," September confides, "I really worry that Tommy has to work in such an unhealthy place."

"You mean Pollock's poultry warehouse?"

"It can't be good. All that animal fat. All that disease. Salmonella. Bird flu. Chicken pox."

"You don't get chicken pox from chickens."

She shrugs.

I continue. "Pollock's doesn't breed the chickens. There are no live ones on the premises. They only process the parts."

"It still sucks."

"I'm sure there are no dangers. I'm sure his grandmother would never subject him to anything that wasn't completely sterile, completely clean. The place is inspected regularly."

"That may be," she says. "But that woman is a nut."

I say nothing. Though I resist going on record as attacking the grandmother of my son, I agree with September's psychological assessment. You have to give her credit for her perspicacity.

"Did he tell you about the time she, like, forced him to visit the supplier?"

I lean forward. "No."

"Well, she sent him to the—whatever it's called—the hatchery, the chicken coop, the breeder's. She made one of the warehouse workers drive him. Because she wanted Tommy to photograph the chickens."

"She *what*?"

"She read in the newspaper that sheep grow more wool and are happier when they have, like, photographs of other sheep around to look at."

"Come on."

"No, really. And she figured if that was true for sheep, it would work for chickens, too." She spears a cucumber slice; she studies it with such suspicion I'm tempted to tell her about the tasters hired by kings afraid of poisoning. Tentatively she brings the fork to her mouth. She chews. She swallows. She lives. "So," she continues, "he goes to this place which he says stinks and is disgusting and like he had to breathe the whole time through his mouth. And he takes the photographs. He brings them back. She gets them developed. And then she makes him go again and tack the photos to the walls where the chickens can look at them."

"I don't believe it."

"Ask him. He was really upset."

"Did she think it made a difference? The photos?"

"Tommy said his grandmother was sure the breasts were more tender, the thighs had more meat." She shakes her head. "The place was so awful. I bet the air was full of germs. I kept taking his temperature afterward to make sure he was, like, okay."

"Granted it may have been disgusting, but Ina would never put Tommy in a situation in which there was any risk."

"I suppose so," she says, unconvinced.

"I *know* so. He's the apple of her eye."

"That's for sure," September groans. "It's always Tommy this. Tommy that. My darling grandson. Mr. Perfect. Which is fine . . ." She rubs her eyes. "But, Maisie, why does she hate *me*?"

"I'm certain she doesn't," I answer, the way you reply *great, thank you,* if someone asks you how you are, even if you're creeping around with walking pneumonia.

"Maisie . . . ?"

"Perhaps you're imagining things."

"I'm not. It's a fact. She hates me." She rips a piece of lettuce. She mashes a cube of avocado. "Why, do you think?"

"Why? It's nothing personal. It's because she's the mother of a son—"

"But *you're* the mother of a son. *You're* not like her."

"I hope not," I concede, humbled by such a compliment.

"It *is* personal. The things she's said to me. To my face. That I'm not pretty. That I'm not worthy of her grandson. That I'm a bad influence on him. That my clothes are all wrong. That my family is trash. That the Portuguese never got along with the Jews. Like I don't have any class. Like . . ." She drops her head to her hands. "*You'd* never say such a thing to me, Maisie," she nearly weeps. "I know you'd never even *think* those things!"

I scrape my chair next to hers. I put my arm around her shoulder. "September, you're not alone. You're not the only one. Believe it or not, Ina Pollock has spoken those very same horrible, hurtful, humiliating words to me."

She turns her face, her tear-streaked face, to mine. I stroke her cheek. I think of how often Ina Pollock has made me cry.

"To *you*?" she exclaims. "She said those same mean things to you?"

I nod. We hold each other, two women, two innocent victims of Ina Pollock's vitriol, who, as a result of mind-boggling malice, are now locked into an indissoluble bond.

September blows her nose on her napkin. "At least Tommy takes my side. He really stands up for me," she says now. "He yelled at her that if he heard one more word against me, he would quit his job, never send her a birthday card, return all her gifts, never eat another chicken at the table in her dining room."

"Good for him!" I cheer.

"Chickens!" she exclaims. "It all comes down to chickens."

We sit there for a while. Over our chicken-less salads, amid the din of chicken-eating champions and their chicken-watching audience. At least Tommy's no chicken, at least Tommy's not the kind of chicken his father was, a chicken who couldn't stand up for the woman he loved. My heart bursts with pride for my son. And I give myself a few proud pats on the back for my own mother-in-law-in-training fortitude. Who better than Ina Pollock to teach me to accept a son's girl into my apartment, put aside personal biases, develop flexibility. Could I have had a better example of how not to cause rebellion, strife, and misery? How could I not feel something close to love for this Ina-scorned child who means so much to my son he'd face down his daunting grandmother? I pull at September's bat-winged sleeve. "Let's get going," I say. "We deserve a little retail therapy."

We clear our table. We stack our plates and utensils. On the way to the trash bin, we stop. A woman sits next to the soft-drinks dispenser. She's cradling a newborn in her arms. His pale blue vest and his tiny Red Sox cap announce he's a boy. She hums a lullaby. *Lay thee down now and rest, may thy slumber be blessed,* she sings. Lovingly she's nursing him. Her shirt slides off one shoulder to reveal an inch of rosy breast. The baby makes soft sucking sounds. The mother coos. The baby's tiny fingers squeeze the mother's larger ones. "Look," I whisper to September.

"Sweet," she murmurs.

As we ooh and ahh over this enchanting vision of mother and child, the ugly chickens, the uglier Ina Pollock, the bad things of the world recede. September and I beam down on ideal motherhood, unswerving devotion, pure love. For an instant the mother looks up. She smiles, woman to woman to woman. Then she turns back to her son.

A man pushes past us. He dumps his leftover French fries into the trash. He slams down his tray. He flings his knife and fork at the dirty-silverware repository. He points to the mother and her little boy. "Disgusting," he sneers.

"Doing this out in the open. Making such a public display."

The retail therapy works. We move from shop to shop. September tries on outfits. I offer fashion advice. We laugh so hard at one frilly dress that half-naked customers sneak a glance from their dressing rooms. I buy her two pairs of jeans. I successfully negotiate the purchase of a red sweater along with a black turtleneck. In the shoe department, we choose a pair of purple sandals dotted with silver stars. "They're you," I declare.

"You think so?" she asks. She sticks out her feet. She wiggles her black-polished toes.

"Definitely. They scream September Silva. I love them."

"You need a pair, too, Maisie," she decides.

I study the purple straps, the shining silver stars, and am filled with desire. "I'm far too old," I protest.

"Never," she reprimands. "Wait until your boyfriend sees how cute you look in them."

"Adorable," decrees the salesman the instant I slide them onto my feet.

"Cool," adds the woman my age trying on sensible lace-ups in the chair next to me. She turns to the salesman. "Do you have another pair in size eight?"

On the T home, we find two seats with an empty one in between for all our packages. September laughs. "I have had the best time," she confides. "Except with Tommy, I don't think I've ever had so much fun in my whole life."

I open my pocketbook. I take out the package wrapped

in red and white stripes. I smooth the shiny red ribbon. I hand it to her.

"For me?" she asks. She turns it first this way, then that. She holds it up to her ear. She gives it a gentle shake.

"For you." I say.

"A present?"

I nod.

"What is it?"

"Open it," I order.

"Here? Like now?"

"Why not."

She slides off the ribbon. She pries up the paper making sure not to tear the edges where it's taped. Her breath stops. "Oh," she exhales. She clasps the book to her heart. "Maisie," she whispers. "Oh, Maisie. Maisie," she starts to shout. "Nobody ever gave me anything so wonderful."

She is almost yelling now, enough so that heads turn, enough so that everyone in the car is looking at us—this odd combination, this black-clad platform-heeled girl next to the conventional middle-aged woman old enough to be her mother but bearing no family resemblance, a pair so dissimilar our fellow passengers would have trouble connecting the two of us.

September throws her arms around me. "Thank you. Thank you, Maisie," she rejoices. "I love you. You are the mother I've waited for my whole entire life."

EIGHTEEN

I've come home early, leaving Darlene in the progressively frailer hands of the Misses Elderberry. "Go, Maisie," she demanded, "Carlene's taking Anthony Vincent to the library story hour this afternoon, then out for dinner. I don't have to pick him up until seven." She went back to sprinkling lavender water on the Elderberrys' ancient Belgian linen sheets, inherited from ancestors who brought them back from the grand tour. She tested the iron, then started pressing a hem-stitched border nubby from frequent mending. Steam rose, the lovely smell of lavender filled the room; she whistled while she worked.

I grabbed my keys and my pocketbook. Darlene looked so happy. She *was* happy. Humming *It's a beautiful day in this neighborhood* from the *Mister Rogers* reruns on public television.

Will it be incurring the wrath of the gods of sorrow, with whom I've developed a far too intimate acquaintance, to admit that, these days, I'm feeling happy, too? If I sound a little tentative, well, you know why. After tough times, any kind of joy seems ephemeral, fragile, and tempts fate. But, knock on wood—I'm banging on my kitchen table right this minute, so hard I could split its butcher-block laminate—for the moment, things are going well. The instant Gabe put his mother's house on the market, it sold—granted, to a developer who is going to tear it down to build a Palladian-windowed, crenellated monstrosity. Within two weeks he'd bought a condo two blocks from mine on the Somerville side of the Cambridge/Somerville line. "Why doesn't he just move in with us?" September asked.

I noted the *us*, its staking-a-claim possessiveness, but it didn't bother me. I explained I wasn't ready. *Yet*. I explained I was being cautious, that a failed marriage, a couple of floundering relationships were a good lesson in not rushing into things.

"But Gabe's awesome," September protested.

I had to agree. However cautiously.

What pleases me, though, is that the kids like Gabe; we've been to the movies together, on a hike, to a covering-all-tastes dinner. They've volunteered to help Gabe pack up his mother's things (*most* of his mothers' things, he qualified) for Catholic Charities. They've cleared their schedules to help him move over Labor Day. "Great kids," Gabe exclaimed.

I'd noted the plural, and that didn't bother me either. I guess I've mellowed. "You've become so cool, Mom," Tommy said to me last week. And though I'm not about to paint my fingernails black, I've certainly relaxed. Can you believe it? Here I am with a son and his in-house lover, my own lover about to take up residence two blocks away, and an insider's view of room 241 at the Comfort Inn, not to mention my privileged, on-a-first-name-basis relationship with Rafael the desk clerk and Marietta the maid.

I fill the pasta pot with water. I dig out the colander. I'm making dinner for Gabe, September, and Tommy tonight, spaghetti, whole-wheat noodles imported from Australia, organic tomatoes from Vermont, a meal as neutral as Switzerland. I have champagne in the refrigerator, one glass each for the underage. We're celebrating the publication of *Poetry Port* magazine.

Yesterday I drove to Union Square and helped myself to fifteen copies from the vending box under the hand-lettered sign HELP YOURSELF. "What's that?" a kid on a bike asked.

"A poetry magazine." I extended my hand. "Want one?"

He flinched. "Nah," he said. He pointed to the stapled, Xeroxed pages. "Don't look like any magazine to me."

"Not everyone can recognize art," I defended. "Historically, most acknowledged geniuses were initially dismissed by ignoramuses." I huffed away.

Now I place a copy of *Poetry Port* above each plate. I insert a silky gold ribbon on page three where September's poem is printed. I checked out the other submissions. Let me assure you that I can state flatly, with no prejudice, that hers is the best. I arrange the sunflowers that Genevieve Rochester told me to pick from her yard this morning. What a contrast to all those lonely years of setting a table just for two, or even for one. There's something so heartwarming about four plates, four sets of silverware. Something so wholesome and normal, especially when you consider the changing nature of a family in the twenty-first century. Here we are: mother, boyfriend, son, girlfriend sitting down together for a meal.

Any combination can make a family; all you need to do is define yourself as one.

I stir the sauce. I chop oregano. I wonder who'll arrive first. September from Central Square where she works at Cheapo's, the used-record store, home of the fast-disappearing 45s? Gabe from Mount Auburn Hospital after eight hours of professional listening? Tommy will probably get here last since he's the farthest away, since he has to take a bus and a train from Pollock's Poultry warehouse, then walk from Davis Square.

I tear lettuce for the salad. I think of all my chickens coming home to roost from their separate occupations and diverse geographies. I think of myself here at home, cooking them a meal, setting out *Poetry Port* at each of their plates. Have I ever been so content?

But, of course, as soon as I think this—why did I think this?—angry footsteps pound on the steps, a key slams into the lock, Tommy stomps inside, bangs his backpack on the floor. "I hate her," he shouts.

I come running into the hall. I'm still holding lettuce, which drips down the front of my skirt and onto my shoes. Tommy's face is as red as a toddler's in full tantrum. His hands are balled into toddler's fists. "I hate her," he repeats.

My breath stops. I can't believe it! Just when she and I are starting to form a bond. *Don't fall in love with your kid's steady,* friends advise, *because when they break up it will be like losing a child.* "Oh, no!" I cry. "September?" I venture.

Tommy looks at me as if I've gone mad. "Not September!" he exclaims. "Never!" He shakes his head. "Ina. Grina. My grandmother."

I heave a sigh of relief, which I try to hide. *So what else is new?* I want to ask. I don't. Far be it from me to turn my son away from a member of his family. Especially since that particular family member is so good at turning people away herself. I wait.

"I quit my job," he states.

"Which makes sense. You've only got two weeks to Labor Day, then school."

"That's not the point."

"What is the point?" I take his arm. Under my fingers, I can feel his muscles ridged with tension. "Let's go into the living room. We'll sit down. And you can tell me everything."

We sink into the sofa, end to end. I wish I had gumdrops to offer, crisp bacon, a Snickers bar. But all I can give him is my undivided attention and my unadulterated mother's love.

He looks around. "September's not here yet?"

"Not yet. It's still early."

"I wanted to get home before her." His eyes scan the walls and floors as if he's checking for hidden cameras or concealed microphones. "Promise you'll never breathe a word of this to her?"

"If that's that you want." I study him. "But, from my own experience, I've learned it's not good to keep things from people who are close to you."

"Except when they'd be really hurt. *Really* hurt," he stresses.

"There's that . . . ," I concede. I lean forward. "But what happened with Ina?"

"She just went nuts. She got mad at me and Dad."

"At your father?"

"Yes, she hates Georgette."

"But she swore she liked her." Though I'm not surprised.

In retrospect, I'm sure Ina's defense of Georgette was just another way of highlighting my own inadequacies.

"Like her? Yeah, right. She thinks she's stuck up. She thinks she's always interfering in Pollock's, advising about bird flu, and poultry disease, and other stuff about biology. She's supposed to be the expert, but Grina says nobody can tell Ina Pollock anything she doesn't already know about chickens, about poultry and potpies."

"But didn't Ina *hire* Georgette as an adviser?"

"Mom." He turns to me. "Do you think Grina would ever take advice from *anyone*?"

"I guess you're right."

"Anyway, she told Dad if he didn't break up with Georgette, she'd disinherit him, and wouldn't make him the Pollock heir, plus she'd take back the condo she bought for him, and the car. She doesn't like that Georgette isn't Jewish and is so independent and smart and kind of young . . ."

"Sounds familiar," I sigh. "Here we go again."

He nods. "So Ina told Dad it was either her or Georgette."

"And Dad? What did he do?"

"Well, Dad let Georgette move in a couple of weeks ago since—duh!—he realized he wasn't going to be a bad influence because I was already living with September. But after Grina's fit, he told her maybe she should get her own place and they'd still see each other on the sly. I heard all of this one day when I was visiting Dad. They were really going at it, Dad trying to be reasonable in that way he has—"

"I know that way. That reasonable Rex way."

"—and Georgette screaming and throwing stuff. I understand I shouldn't have listened, but the condo isn't that big. I couldn't help it . . ."

"Of course you couldn't . . ."

"Then, Georgette said *over her dead body*. And that Dad had to choose between her and his mother."

"And what did Dad do?" I ask, though I can pretty much guess the answer to that.

"What a wuss. What a chicken. He said *why couldn't he have both?*"

"He did, did he?"

"Georgette packed up and left that night. I told Dad to go after her. He seemed so sad. And Georgette is really nice"—he stops—"though not as nice as you," he adds loyally.

"I appreciate the sentiment," I smile. "Go on."

"Dad said I'd understand when I grew up. That I didn't realize how the world worked, how much more complicated it was. I said it didn't sound complicated. He had to choose between Ina and Georgette. How hard could that be? He could always get another job. He said I didn't understand." He stops. He frowns. "Mom. He just let Georgette go. He didn't even put up a fight."

"I'm not surprised." I sigh at the capacity of history to repeat itself, at powerful people and their wrongheadedness. At weak people and skewed values and the twistedness of a particular mother's love. "But how does that affect you?" I ask. "Did you quit because you were mad at the way Ina treated Dad?"

He shakes his head. "No, that's Dad's business. But Grina was like a witch on a broomstick who couldn't get off. Next she lit into me. Said she wouldn't pay my tuition, that she'd take away my cell phone, that she'd never give me another cent if I didn't ditch September." He grabs a pillow. He clutches it against his chest. "She even told me that she wouldn't produce the Tommy Tom potpie she was going to name after me. That was no loss. She was going to put my picture on it. Can you think of anything dorkier?"

"At the moment, no." I lean back against the sofa arm. Not that I hadn't predicted this, not that I hadn't expected that Ina would repeat with Tommy what she'd done to me, but not at his tender age, not at sixteen, when you have a whole future of suitable and unsuitable loves in front of you, not when you're a child, when you're barely formed, when you haven't figured out who you are or who you want to be. I reach for his shoulder. I stroke his hair. I touch the heartbreakingly tender back of his neck. "And what did you do?"

"I told her to shove it. I threw my cell phone at her. Well, not *at* her exactly, on the floor. I told her I hated the school anyway and would be more than happy to go to Somerville High where September and I could be in the same class."

"Good for you!" I exclaim, my pride in him winning out over my doubts about college counseling and SAT prep and Ivy League eligibility at a high school low in the number of college-bound graduates and much lower in the number of tax dollars spent on art and language enrichment. "Good for you," I repeat with even greater emphasis. "And how did Ina reply to that?"

"She said horrible things about September. She always says horrible things about her, and I always tell her to shut up, that I won't listen to another word. I either yell at her or walk away. But this time she went too far. She said September was stupid. That she—you are not going to believe this—that she didn't love me, but was only after a piece of the Pollock's Potpie pie. She actually used those words."

"I believe it. I've heard the identical phrase directed at me. It all comes down to chickens," I say. "She equates chickens with money and money with love."

"She knows nothing about love."

"You're absolutely right. I'm glad you realize that."

"Chickens," he spits out. "I should have stuck those photos of chickens all over Grina's house. Maybe she'd start growing feathers like those sheep grew more wool." He searches my face. "Promise you won't tell September. Her feelings would be so hurt. It's just unfair. I am ashamed to have such a prejudiced, materialistic, mean grandmother."

I take him in my arms. Under the scratchy cheek, the gangly teenager's knobs and angles, the adolescent smell of sneakers and sweat, I feel his essential babyness, the sweet soft flesh, the body that could curl so perfectly, fit so effortlessly on a mother's lap, in a mother's arms, against a mother's breast.

"I'm going to take a shower," he says. He pulls away. He stands up. "When September comes, you promise you won't tell her anything?"

"I swear. Not a single word."

He grabs a towel from the linen closet and heads toward the bathroom. I try to process what I've just heard. I compare Rex's shameful, cowardly behavior to the standing-up-for-principles action of my son. It will take longer than the length of a shower for me to begin to figure this out. I push myself up from the sofa.

No sooner have I gone back into the kitchen to check my sauce, to put the lettuce in the crisper than I hear another key turn in the lock. This time footsteps don't stomp, but drag. Maybe someone should do a study of footsteps, the way that sociologist mapped facial expressions as clues to people's innermost personality. I go back into the hall to find September slumped against the wall, every inch of her throwing off vibes of dejection and despair. My first thought is that somehow she found out about Ina's latest attack on her. But how could that be possible?

"September?" I cry. "What's wrong?"

She notices Tommy's backpack on the floor. She points. "Where's Tommy?" she asks.

"In the shower. He just got home."

"Oh, Maisie." She starts to weep.

I take her into my recently vacated arms. I hold her against my recently vacated breast. I pat her tangled hair. I put my cheek against her patchouli-scented one. "What's the matter?"

"Don't tell Tommy," she orders. "It will make him so sad."

"Tell him what?" Gently I lead her to the living room, to the recently vacated confessional couch where the outline of Tommy's body is still visible in the unplumped upholstery. "It's my mother," she wails.

"What about her?" I ask.

"I sent her a copy of *Poetry Port*. I attached a little note explaining my poem was inside. I added my number at work. And the hours when she could reach me there. She never phoned. So today, right after closing, I called her up . . ." She emits a series of hiccuping sobs.

"And . . . ?"

"She said she threw the magazine in the trash. I asked her if she read my poem. *No*, she said, she didn't have the time. She told me not to send her anything else. That she'd just put it in the garbage, as she already gets too much junk mail and can't be bothered to sort through it. And besides, she hates poetry."

"Oh, honey," I say. "Oh, sweetheart." I stroke her hair. I choose my words. "Sometimes people, because of their own lives, because of their own personal difficulties and problems, just can't be there for their children."

"Why not?"

"Because they don't have anything left over to give to somebody else, not even their own daughter, their own deserving, very lovable daughter."

"Mothers shouldn't act like that."

"Of course they shouldn't. But sometimes they just can't help it."

"It's not fair."

"Life is not fair."

"I know that, Maisie." She squeezes my hand. "But it's still hard."

"It *is* hard." I take her in my arms again. I hold her until she calms down. When the hiccups subside, when her breathing slows, I lead her into the dining room. I show her the table set with *Poetry Port* at every place, the gold ribbons marking page three.

"Thank you," she whispers. "At least *you're* on my side." She starts to weep again.

"How about a shower? Or a nice hot bath?" I suggest. "As soon as Tommy's out."

"No, thank you," she says. "I'll be fine. If you don't mind, maybe I'll go have a little rest." She kisses me, then heads toward Tommy's—correction, Tommy and September's—room.

I lower the flames on the burners. I put the salad in the refrigerator. I cut the bread, spread butter and garlic between each slice. What was to be a celebratory dinner is starting to turn into some kind of wake. I am counting on Gabriel Doyle, on his charm, his humor, his ability to make the best of everything. But when he rings the buzzer and trudges upstairs, when I open the door, I abandon all hope. His skin is ashen; the flesh under his eyes is the color of a fresh bruise; his shoulders stoop. He looks exhausted. Though not so tired, I'm relieved to note, that he skimps on his usual Comfort Inn kiss. He pulls me to him. I open my mouth.

"Hey," he says.

"Hey," I say.

He looks around, checks that the coast is clear of teenagers, jams his lips against mine a second time. "What a day I've had," he sighs. "If you give me a quick Scotch, I might just summon up the strength to tell you all about it."

Wary of the three-on-a-match curse, I sit him in the kitchen rather than on the couch. I take out a glass. I add ice. I pour the Scotch. "A couple more fingers, please," he begs.

"That bad?"

"That bad."

I pull up a chair next to him. I wait for him to drink one finger's worth. "What happened?" A question I seem to be posing for the third time this evening. "Why is this night different from any other night?" I ask.

He shoots me a triumphant grin. "And don't you for one minute entertain the thought that I might not know that phrase is from the Passover seder, from the Haggadah."

"Extra points," I award. "Though I don't think you'll be invited to the Pollock family seder anytime soon."

"Families," he groans.

"Families," I groan.

Before we move on to Easter and Christmas, and St. Patrick's Day and Bloody Sunday and Black Monday and Hanukkah, I home in on the current event. "So why such a tough day?"

He gulps more Scotch. He wipes his hand across his mouth. "A real brouhaha," he begins. "Two sisters-in-law gave birth within hours of each other. They opted to share a room. One had a boy; the other a girl. Pink hat. Blue hat."

"So far so good . . ."

"Just you wait. The mother who had the boy—a long labor; he was turned toward the back, and a big baby, eight pounds plus, and ultimately a cesarean—was justifiably exhausted and fast asleep. Her sister-in-law, the mother of the girl, who, incidentally, slid right out, a dainty six pounds, after an hour, with no anesthesia . . ." He looks at me. "Is there a lesson here?"

"That girls are easier than boys?" I shake my head. "I wouldn't know."

"Nor I." He takes another sip. "At any rate, the mother of the girl picked up the fussing hungry boy and nursed him at her own breast so his mother could get some sleep."

"Oh, dear." I assume Carlene's controversial act of baking her daughter-in-law's breast milk into cupcakes and serving them to the children at the library's story hour might fit into a similar category, depending on whether or not blood ties make a case for mitigating circumstances. "What happened next?"

"There was so much ruckus in that room that the staff and other patients started to complain. All the babies began howling. I was called up to obstetrics. I hadn't been in the room two seconds before the mother-in-law showed up."

"I gather from your tone that the mother-in-law wasn't much help?"

"*Help?*" he exclaims. "The exact opposite." His voice softens. His face takes on a faraway look. "The last time I was in that ward was when little Angel DeJesus was born. At the very minute my mother passed."

We pause for a few moments of silence out of respect for Ethel Doyle. Gabriel wipes an eye on his sleeve. I lower my voice to funeral-home solicitousness. "And then?" I press.

"All hell broke loose. The mother-in-law, who, I gather, approves of neither wife her sons picked, threw a fit. It seems the daughters-in-law were best friends, the mutual dislike of their mother-in-law cementing their bond. So of course the mother-in-law jumped right in, protesting her horror and disgust."

"Divide and conquer."

"Exactly. And soon enough she had the two mothers screaming at each other, which was not good for the two babies, who naturally started to wail. Then each mother demanded her own room. The hospital wasn't able to comply since every bed was filled. One of the nurses said she'd try to poll the other new mothers to see if anyone would be willing to swap, but she couldn't promise anything what with the logistics of moving plants and toys and charts and phones and babies. Not to mention the folding beds for those fathers who chose to spend the night."

"What a mess."

"It gets worse. The mother-in-law then brought up

medical issues, viruses, the transmission of disease, lack of immunity, the possibility of contamination due to the breast milk of the one who didn't give birth, the risk that a baby, once having sampled another's milk, might turn away from his or her rightful source of nourishment. The mother-in-law went on to quote the horrifying rates of infant mortality in bygone times. Causing panic in both beds on both sides of the room." He finishes his drink.

I point to the bottle. "Another?" I ask.

"I'm sorely tempted, but I don't want to be sloshed for the celebration."

Celebration. I wince. Wait till he hears about all the spanners thrown into the celebration works. "So what did you do?" I push. "So what was your role in all of this?"

"I tried to calm them down. I tried to reassure them that if each mother was healthy—and their doctors confirmed this, thank God—there would be no medical consequences. I tried to listen to their fears. Tried to explain to the one who nursed the child not her own about boundaries. I tried to explain to the other about forgiveness and good intentions and the fortunate result of no harm done. The nurses were worried about the stitches from her cesarean, so I attempted, unsuccessfully, to teach her the relaxation response. When everything failed, I decided to get the mother in-law out of there."

"Any luck?"

"None. She wouldn't budge. Finally two nurses literally dragged her away, said the warring mothers needed their rest and if she didn't move they would have to notify security. They pulled the curtain between the two beds. Inadequate but the best they could do. It's now like the Berlin Wall in there. The mother-in-law set up a chair in the corridor outside the room 'in case her grandchildren needed her.' The final ironic twist, there she remains, like Madame Defarge, knitting booties, alternating between pink yarn and blue."

By the time we all sit down to dinner, no one's hungry. The sauce is overcooked; the salad's wilted from its hour spent on the counter before I put it back into the fridge. And there's something about whole-wheat noodles, their brownish color, their fiberish taste, that can dim both the healthy and health-minded appetite.

Though I must say, September and Tommy are each looking a lot better. They've lost their pallid faces, their doleful slumps. Their complexions are rosy; their eyes bright; their glances at each other seem knowing and a little smug. The restorative waters of a quick shower, a long hot bath? I don't think so. It just occurs to me that while Gabe and I were in the kitchen examining the fall-out from crossover breast milk, my son and his girlfriend were having crossover sex.

I yearn for room 241. I study Gabe, whose face, unlike the revived ones of Tommy and September, still bears the signs of exhaustion from counseling the uncounselable. I doubt I'll be seeing Rafael the desk clerk and Marietta the maid tonight.

Still, in the way that actors internalize their roles, our initial false cheer leads to real cheer. Gabe sympathizes with September's mother problems. He supports Tommy's stand in relation to his grandmother problems. We all agree that these are nothing compared to the problems of the world—a conclusion that paradoxically inches us up on the happiness scale. We ooh and ahh over page three in

Poetry Port. We insist September stand and read the poem to us. We applaud and whistle and stomp our feet when she finishes. By the time dessert is served—ice cream for me and Gabriel, Tofutti for Tommy and September—we've turned into the kind of raucous high-spirited family that could serve as a model of the functional and the harmonious.

We raise our flutes of champagne. "To the poet in our midst," we toast.

As further proof of our model familyness, everyone pitches in to clear the table, scrape the dishes, put them in the dishwasher, store the leftovers. September and Tommy are off to yet another dank, dark venue to see yet another local cutting-edge music group.

Ten minutes after they leave, Gabriel grabs his briefcase. His eyes are sorrowful. "Do you mind?" he entreats. "I've got to go home and write up my notes for the sister-in-law debacle. I have to sort my books, my mother's clothes."

I don't ask why his mother's clothes are still sitting in her drawers. I don't ask if his mother's London Fog is still entwined with his on the coat rack in the hall. We all have our mother issues, or our mother-in-law issues, I decide. The point is, he's getting rid of his mother's clothes, his mother's house. He's moving out. He's moving close to me.

He moves close to me. He takes me in his arms. "You really don't mind?" he whispers in my ear.

Room 241 will still be there tomorrow. The day after. The day after that. In two weeks, he'll have his own king-sized bed in his own space. We bought the mattress together; we tried it out lying side by side in the furniture store. We stretched our legs across and giggled like little kids. "This model's the most popular," the salesman said, "for your husbands and their wives. For your newlyweds."

"I don't mind at all," I now console. I see him to the door. "Considering the day I've had, considering the day *you've* had, it's probably better to be alone."

I fill my glass with the rest of the champagne. I put my feet up on the coffee table. I contemplate finding a movie to watch on TV. I contemplate checking my shelves for a fat novel to devour. I do nothing. I just sit. Through the window, I watch the darkening sky that signals the end of summer. I observe the lights coming on in the rooms of houses across the street. I marvel at how things can change, the difference from last August to this. A new assistant, an accidental meeting in a hospital corridor, a bad first impression transformed by a shopping trip to a mall, a lousy day soothed by a family meal. So much change.

And yet *plus ça change* . . . I shut my eyes. I fall asleep.

Have hours passed? Or only minutes when the phone rings?

"We need to meet," Ina Pollock demands.

"I don't think so," I reply.

"How about Ben's Deli in Newton Center where we had our last lunch?"

Last supper is more like it. With the chopped-liver sandwich which, after that notorious meal, has joined my own personal do-not-resuscitate menu list. "I don't think so," I repeat.

"We need to talk."

"There's nothing to talk about."

"Oh, yes there is."

"So talk. No time like the present. Right now while you've got me on the line." I could hang up on her—a gesture guaranteed to supply me with the fleeting pleasure of making her mad. But I am curious.

"What I have to tell you would be better face-to-face."

"Then I'll say good-bye."

"Don't hang up!" she orders. Do I sense an undertone of panic in that tyrannical voice?

"You've got my full attention. For the moment at least."

"It's about Tommy, my grandson."

"*My* son," I correct. "I heard what happened."

"Whatever you may or may not have heard, I know I'm in the right."

"Tommy made it very clear about how utterly misguided you are," I counter. "And have always been."

"I will swear on the Bible, on the heads of my children and grandchildren that I have never made a single mistake as far as they are concerned. I have no regrets. I have done nothing wrong."

"In that case, this conversation is beyond useless. We haven't a thing to say to each other."

"Wait," she orders. "Just listen to me," she huffs.

"Why should I?"

"As a courtesy."

"If the situations were reversed," I begin, then take the high road. "Okay, I'm listening."

"Though I've done nothing wrong," she goes on, " I realize the world has changed."

"Oh, really? It's the world's fault now?" I pause. "Changed in what way?"

"I've had second thoughts."

"I see. About September? Georgette? About me?"

"No, of course not. Not them. Not you. That trashy

girl. That know-it-all Georgette. And you, let's be honest, you were my son's first bad choice."

"I don't need to hear this. I am hanging up right now."

"Wait! It's not about you. It's about Tommy. My darling boy."

"Mrs. Pollock, you ruined my marriage. You destroyed Rex's happiness. From what I'm told, you caused him to lose Georgette. You are not going to ruin Tommy, too. Haven't you learned by now that saying nasty words about a girlfriend is a surefire way to send your darling boy right into that girl's arms?"

"It didn't happen with Rex."

"Rex," I scorn. "Frankly," I go on, "your making Tommy's job intolerable, disinheriting him, taking away his tuition and cell phone is no doubt the best thing you could have done for him."

"Baloney," she spits out. She takes a deep, hacking breath. "Whatever animosity between the two of us, we both want the best for him."

"In *that* we are agreed," I concede, Darlene to her Carlene.

She lowers her voice. "And, okay okay, I have to give you this, you've raised one really outstanding son. You brought him up great."

So stunned am I by this admission—Ina Pollock gives Maisie Grey a *compliment*!!—that I'm tempted to print it out and drop it in the *Poetry Port* vending box. For a couple of seconds I savor her words, then ask, "And what do you plan to do?"

"Go back to the way things were. I was angry. Everything I said, I didn't mean."

"*Everything?*"

"Not *everything*."

"Well, you'll have to talk to Tommy. See how he feels. I can't speak for him."

"Why not? You're his mother."

"His mother, not his dictator, not his jailer, not his ventriloquist, not his puppeteer." I pause. "Not his utterly misguided grandmother."

This hardly implicit criticism falls on deaf ears. "To show you how I changed my mind, right before supper I sent in the tuition for his first term."

"He may not want to go. Currently he has his heart set on Somerville High."

"With that girl?"

"That girl has a name. She's an important part of his life."

She sighs the quintessential oh-what-have-I-done-to-deserve-this mother's sigh.

"He doesn't approve of the elite nature of private school," I continue.

"I've discussed this issue with Rex. He agrees that Tommy's school offers not just a better education, but will get him into Harvard."

"He may not want to go to Harvard."

"Nonsense. Everyone wants to go to Harvard. Rex plans to talk to him; he's promised to convince him that it's the smartest choice."

"It's Tommy's decision," I reiterate. "It's totally up to him. These days, I wouldn't count too much on Rex's influence. And as far as I, his mother, am concerned, I'm starting to lean toward Somerville High. Years of private school did nothing to put a backbone in *your* son. I believe in public education, in a diverse student body. In democratic principles. It worked out just fine for me."

"Oh, yeah?"

"*Yes.*"

"We'll see," she says.

"And the fact that September's enrolled there will be a real drawing card."

"Ha!" she chokes out. She switches subjects. "You know I never liked you, Maisie," she says now.

"I never liked you either, Mrs. Pollock."

"But I respect you."

"I wish I could say the same."

I hear only her hypertensive breathing and the tap of a pencil against the phone.

"What about Georgette?" I ask.

"I don't like her *and* I don't respect her." She stops. "And Rex holds the identical opinion now that he's finally got rid of her."

"Though she's the one who left."

"It's the end result that counts."

"That must please you."

"*Some* people listen to their mothers. Some people realize their mothers know best." Her voice softens. Is that muted cackle an actual laugh? "Though, between you and me, I never did."

"Excuse me?"

"My mother quite disapproved of Arnie. Didn't like his appearance. Said he was a greenhorn. Found his manners terrible. Looked down on his family. Though all of us were poor back then, my mother was convinced he never had a chance of making a blessed cent. She threatened so many terrible things. She wouldn't come to our wedding. We had to elope."

I sit back, stunned. She herself suffered from a mother's prejudice against her true love. Imagine! She herself lived through the nightmare of such a tragedy, and then she turns around and does the same thing to her son? And turns around a second time and inflicts this exact sin on the grandchild she claims to adore? Gabe must have a word for this kind of blindness; it must be a syndrome of some sort, a disease to be found in the *Diagnostic and Statistical Manual of Mental Disorders*. "Does Rex know this story?" I ask.

"No, Arnie never wanted me to tell anyone. He made me promise. He was so ashamed of how my family treated him."

"You can hardly blame him. Such rejection hurts." I clarify, "As I know from personal experience."

"Compared to me, you've had it soft."

"Not from you."

"I was only sticking up for my son. For my principles."

I ignore this. It's hopeless. I'll never get through to her. "Why tell me now?" I ask.

"I was always loyal to my Arnie. But things change. Now that he's been gone so long—may he rest in peace—I don't have to keep secrets anymore, now that I've found someone else."

I clutch the receiver. "*What* did you just say?" I nearly yell. I must be hallucinating. There must be static on the line. I must be going deaf from turning my sofa into a confessional box.

"You heard me right. I'm seeing someone," she confides. "A nice gentleman, an educated, cultured man. A retired manufacturer." Her voice rises. "Oh, dear, it's already eight o'clock. I have to go. I have to pack up some of our deluxe potpies to bring to him. That man has nothing in his refrigerator. He needs a woman to take care of him." She chuckles, then adds, "We're going to Wellesley Center for dessert."

"Make sure you divide the bill down to the last penny."

"Even *you* should know it's the person who invites you who is supposed to pay. Which, in any case, is always the duty of the man." She pauses. "Maybe, someday, Maisie, you'll find somebody, too. Maybe if you put on a little weight. Maybe if you do more with your hair. Maybe if you learn how to flatter a member of the opposite sex."

"I give up!" I shout. "'Bye, Mrs. Pollock," I grunt. "Good-*bye*."

NINETEEN

It's two weeks after Labor Day. Tommy and September are back in school, back in their *separate* schools. Still, I promised Tommy if he wasn't happy at the end of fall term, he could switch to Somerville High, a step I think will be good for him. I'm afraid Rex did a first-rate job of lobbying Tommy to stay where he was. I suspect bribery was involved, driving lessons, for example, the possibility of his own car one day if he kept up his grades, two prized concert tickets for the Radiohead tour. But it's Tommy's decision. His father and I have agreed on that.

Let me get you up to date. Gabe's moved into his condo. He saved only one of his mother's shepherdess figurines, which stands in such a discreet spot on the bookcase you hardly notice it. An antimacassar, which she is reputed to have tatted herself, now lies thrown over the back of a bedroom chair. Frankly, I never catch a glimpse of it; that chair is always covered with both Gabe's and my tossed clothes, my bra tangled lasciviously with his shirt, the legs of my jeans wrapped sweetly around the legs of his.

Room 241 at the Comfort Inn will be taken over by someone else. I like to imagine another pair of middle-aged lovers clutching that cherished key, another pair who found lust late in life, who are too enthralled with each other to mind the view of the back parking lot, another couple similarly thrilled by the body lotion and the sewing kits and the recognition as regulars in the eyes of Marietta and Rafael.

Do I miss room 241? Perhaps. I miss the sense of adventure and raffishness, the sneaking around—though two nonadulterous adults hardly needed to sneak. But when you marry so young and suffer from mother-in-law-induced guilt like me, when you've had a failed engagement and an annulled marriage and mother-induced guilt like Gabe, the clandestine nature of motel sex carries the forbidden appeal of a deadly sin.

Nevertheless, I much prefer the king-sized bed we chose, the high-thread-count Egyptian cotton sheets we picked out at Bloomingdale's. Sometimes I iron them, sprinkling them with lavender water the way Darlene treats the Elderberrys' inherited hemstitched bedding and lace-bordered pillowcases. They smell so great and glide against our naked flesh like silk.

My life is full of pleasure these days. Just know I'm yet again knocking on wood as I utter such words. Tommy and September act even more in love than when she first moved in with us. She's become not only a regular contributor to *Poetry Port* but also the poet in residence at Somerville High. On Tuesday and Thursday afternoons, she's volunteered to help me and Darlene at Factotum, Inc.

I need her help. Can you believe that my business has taken off, thanks to word of mouth and the letters of recommendation from my satisfied clientele? I'm going to be on the cover of the November issue of *Boston Entrepreneurial Woman*. "Why not the centerfold?" Tommy joked, then added, "I'm so proud of you." He even told Rex, who called me up with no agenda other than to offer his congratulations.

I've heard from Tommy that his grandmother and "the gentleman she's seeing" are still, as she phrases it, "keeping company." Tommy's met him, Sam's his name; he bears an uncanny resemblance to the photos of the late and lately not-so-heavily lamented Arnie, photos that are now confined solely to one table in the den of the Wellesley house. Though I realize I will never win over the MIL—and no longer want to or care—I try not to taint Tommy's relationship with her while, at the same time, I encourage him to ask her to stop paying his way.

Last week, at the take-out counter at Redbones, I bumped into Jack. He was with the intern from that life-changing, mind-blowing meeting at Legal Services. He looked embarrassed. "Hi, Maisie," he said, his eyes focused on my toes. "Do you remember Karen?"

We shook hands. We talked about the merits of the jerk chicken as opposed to the ribs. "Everything okay?" he asked.

"Great," I said. "*Really* great." And, for once, I meant each word.

If this were a Shakespeare play—a comedy, not one of his tragedies, which might cast Ina as Lady Macbeth—everybody would have been matched up by the final act. Georgette would have returned to Seamus or to Rex. Seamus would have crossed class lines to woo Darlene. Anthony Vincent would have ended up with the daughter of one of the battling breast-feeding sisters-in-law.

But life, unlike fiction, unlike a dramatic construction,

leaves loose ends. Some of the players in my own world remain uncoupled. Others, the spear-carriers, the secondary characters, have simply walked offstage. Olidia Silva renounced her maternal rights, leaving me *in loco parentis* as far as September is concerned. It's a role I've taken to more than I would ever have thought. There's no woman sharing General Gau's Chicken with Rex, though he's had a few dates, Tommy reports. Georgette has accepted a research position on the West Coast. "Why don't you plan a trip to California," I suggested to Rex when we were on the phone scheduling a parent-teacher conference at Tommy's school.

"You think?" he asked.

"You're a grown-up," I reminded him. "You don't need a permission slip from your mom."

Seamus's sans-Georgette loneliness seems eased by the adoring academic acolytes who, with their gleaming hair and lip-glossed lips, sit in his living room copying his pearls of wisdom into notebooks marked, like September's, with the Harvard seal. When I was there last week, he asked me to clear out his freezer and donate the Pollock potpies to the soup kitchen at the church in Porter Square. "Unless you want them for yourself," he added.

"I hate them," I replied.

He smiled his sad Irish-poet smile. "So do I, my dear," he declaimed. "So do I."

Darlene remains the best worker I ever had. Anthony Vincent is thriving under her and Carlene's joint care. He already knows his numbers and his alphabet and all the words to *Goodnight Moon*. "He's so smart," I observed.

"He sure is," she marveled. "It's going to be hard to keep up with him." She is thinking of taking a course in child development at Cambridge Community College this spring. Despite this, she promises me that, after Anthony Vincent, Factotum, Inc., is—and will always be—her first priority.

She's on call for me this weekend. Gabriel and I are going to his sister Sheila's wedding in Vermont. Along with the invitation, the bride and groom have sent a list of recommended B and Bs in the vicinity. Gabriel and I went onto the Web and chose one famous for its charm, its blueberry muffins, its pancake breakfast and afternoon teas. Its rooms are decorated with local antiques and flower arrangements replenished daily by the ladies of the garden club. It's also the inn the farthest away from the festivities. "To protect you from a total and sudden onslaught of the Doyle clan, the sisters, their spouses, the nephews and nieces, my aunts, my uncles, my cousins," he explained.

"Is there something I should worry about?"

"Not in the least," he reassured. "My sisters can be a bit overwhelming is all."

"I'm a little nervous," I confessed. In fact, I was a *lot* nervous about coming up against a five-person-strong phalanx of the daughters of Ethel Doyle.

"Nothing to be nervous about," Gabriel insisted. "And besides, after the wedding you'll hardly see them, since none of them lives nearby. All that matters is you and me. But they are going to love you. I guarantee it." He took my hand. "Though no one could ever love you as much as I do."

If you discount the strong pull of nostalgia, of habit, and the stronger pull of first-place-we-made-love geography, our room at the Sugar House Bed and Breakfast has much to recommend it over number 241 of the Comfort Inn: views of mountains and trees, a welcoming basket of fruit on the table between two wing chairs, samplers on the wall stitched by the hands of children in the eighteenth and nineteenth centuries. There are recent copies of the *New Yorker, Yankee,* the *Atlantic, Vermont Life* stacked in a brass coal shuttle, chocolate mints overflowing a china candy dish, hooked rugs with rustic scenes of cows and geese. And the bed. Four posters support a net canopy, through which we can peek up at a ceiling of painted stars, wispy clouds, the arc of a rainbow, a small fat cherub.

Immediately we try out the bed. In fact, we test its glorious properties so thoroughly we miss the get-acquainted tea with our hosts and innkeepers, Janie and Jimmy Jacobson, formerly of Scarsdale, New York. What's more, we have just enough time to take showers, get dressed, and drive to the church.

Jimmy Jacobson is at the reception desk when we go downstairs. "Missed you at the tea," he says.

"Sorry," we both apologize.

"Nice group of people. Lovely class of guests. Janie made her famous maple syrup cookies. And her lemon pound cake. Served with a blueberry sauce from berries that grow right out back." He gestures toward the rear of the house. He smacks his lips. "Afraid there's not a morsel left."

"That's too bad," I say. "I'm sure it was delicious."

"You were probably tired from your trip up this morning."

I grab the excuse. "Yes," I agree.

"We were really exhausted," Gabe seconds. "We needed a bit of a rest."

He studies our rested selves. He adjusts a blotter. He straightens a bird-watching brochure. "So you know where you're going?" he asks.

Gabe nods. "I MapQuested the place for the reception—the Leaf Peepers Club? Have you heard of it?"

"Lovely venue. They just hired a new chef. Getting a lot of local attention up this way. Though I'm sure he can't make a cake like my Janie's lemon pound," he adds with a tone of uxorious loyalty that warms my heart.

"We'll have to take a rain check on that cake," Gabe promises. He picks up the bird-watchers brochure. He examines a pileated woodpecker. "Could you give us directions to the church?" He turns to me. "What's its name? Maisie, have you got the invitation in your purse?"

"I left it in our room. On the night table, I think. I'll run upstairs."

"Don't bother," says Jimmy Jacobson. He reaches under the desk. "The bride and groom dropped off a pile of directions to the church just this morning. I've got one right here." He hands us a sheet of paper rolled up with a raffia bow. "Nice touch, that," he acknowledges.

Despite the directions, we get lost on the winding roads and arrive at the church with only minutes to spare. It's a picture-postcard setting, a classic white New England church, columned, bell-towered, on a quaint and immaculate town green.

"I'm glad Sheila's marrying a Congregationalist," Gabe notes. "Better architecture."

Hand in hand, we hurry up the church steps. A white-haired couple make room for us on a bench in the last row. We squeeze together into a space meant for one.

Gabe cranes his neck looking for other Doyles. I try to discern, from the backs of a sea of heads, the formidable sisters. I don't think I've spent enough time studying the back of Gabriel's head to make genetic comparisons. I admire the flowers. The polished wooden beams. The stained-glass windows. The tall ivory tapers.

"Funny," Gabe says. "Hmmm," he muses. Jammed against my thigh, his body twists and turns. "Oh, dear," he sighs. "Oh, no," he groans.

"Is something the matter?" I ask. "Maybe the people next to us can move another inch and give you more room."

"It's not that," he says. Quietly he starts to laugh.

"Shhh," a woman reprimands from across the aisle. "They're about to start."

The string quartet at the side of the church moves forward. The musicians, in silver robes, lift their instruments. The first strains of Pachelbel's *Canon* ring out. Everybody jumps up.

Gabe puts his mouth on my ear. He's breathing fast. "It's not Sheila," he whispers.

"What?"

"I'm the only Doyle on these premises."

"What?" I repeat.

The cello strums. The violin joins in. He raises his voice. "Maisie, we're at the wrong church. The innkeeper gave us directions to the wrong wedding."

Just then the wrong bride appears on the arm of the wrong escort—not Gabriel's uncle Brian, brother of his dead father, making the trip from Phoenix to assume the paternal mantle—no, the man wearing the tuxedo, a white orchid in his satin lapel, is an utter stranger. The music swells. Gabriel takes my hand. My eyes fill. He looks at me. His own eyes, too, brim with tears.

Together we turn and watch the bride, *a* bride, march down the aisle.

I squeeze Gabriel's hand. I interlace my fingers with his.

She may be the wrong bride, I think, but she, like all brides, like all daring women about to take a leap, like all brave wives-to-be on the threshold of a new life, is beautiful.

Later we will make our way to the right reception. Later we will meet all the Doyles. Later we will eat a cake—perhaps, or perhaps not—inferior to Janie Jacobson's lemon pound. Later we will return to the four-poster canopied bed.

And later, years later, we will laugh about this.

But now, right now, in this candlelit, flower-filled graceful church on a town green in picturesque Vermont, Gabriel and I stand together, hand in hand, hip to hip, and watch a beautiful bride surrounded by friends and family, by people who wish her well, walk toward hope, possibility, happiness. Right here, right now, we watch her walk toward love.

Acknowledgments

Deepest thanks to my adored and incomparable agent, Lisa Bankoff; my delightful editor, Lucia Macro; her terrific assistant, Esi Sogah; and the fabulous head of publicity, Dee Dee DeBartlo. Their hard work and enthusiasm have made all the difference.

My first reader and dearest of friends, Elinor Lipman, has the toughest eye and the softest heart, and I owe her a huge debt on both accounts. Sara Lewis held my hand across the telephone wires, always hitting just the right note of encouragement. Though John Aherne has a cameo in most of my books, he's got a starring role in everything else. I am grateful for so many kindnesses and so many laughs.

Bonnie and Neil Moynihan's refrigerator gave me the idea. Lisa Cukier provided insight into custody hearings. Gregory Gauvin, M.D., offered a tour of the pathology lab at Mount Auburn Hospital. My friends and family, my community of fellow writers, and all my wonderful neighbors on the Ave offered support at every turn. Thanks also to the divine Sharissa Jones and Marnie Davidoff. And the heartiest welcome to Mili Medwed, born February 12, 2007.

Last, once more and forever, thanks to Howard.

A+

AUTHOR INSIGHTS, EXTRAS, & MORE...

FROM

MAMEVE MEDWED

AND

AVON A

If comedians joke about the shackles that bind men to their wives—balls and chains, apron strings—I can only praise the wires, cables, and cell towers that keep me and my mate connected in ways we never could have imagined in our youth. Driving home from work, my husband rings me up; "Do we need milk?" he asks. Despite the three floors that might separate us in a department store, sporting goods is only a phone call away from women's shoes. My husband and I have been together since I was 18 and he was 20. Still, considering that we met in nursery school, we could now be blowing out a huddled mass of candles on a multi-tiered, skyscraper-high anniversary cake. Though I don't remember him when I was a toddler, he swears he remembers me. "I fell in love with you right then and there," he lies. "You were wearing that white dress with the frilly collar." "Ruffles," I supply.

Such fashion intelligence is hardly the norm for a husband who, if asked what I had on today five minutes after I've taken it off, will panic like a student who has crammed for the wrong exam in the wrong lecture hall.

No, he remembers the white dress with the ruffle—a pinafore, I inform him—because we have a blown-up photo of the two of us at a long-ago nursery school birthday party, sitting directly across from each other. "I arranged it that way," he'll boast about this totally coincidental seating plan. He's wearing short pants and a wide tie.

I must not have held this outfit against him because when we met again, by telephone, I jumped to accept the date. I was home in Bangor, Maine, the summer after my freshman year of college in Boston and taking inventory for an auto parts store. I had flunked my driving test—parallel parking—and was bored and stuck. No guys—cute or plain—were hankering to take me to Miller's for a hamburger or to the drive-in double feature across the Penobscot River Bridge. Neither spark plugs nor my summer reading list—Kafka, Camus, Dostoyevsky—sufficed for the faux-sophisticate me who had just spent an academic year in the Athens of America parsing Kierkegaard and dancing a mean twist at mixers at Harvard and MIT.

That summer evening, my sister answered the phone. "It's a boy!" she shouted, her ability to humiliate undiminished since my jump from high school to higher ed. The boy was in Skowhegan, Maine, also home from college, working in a shoe factory and as bored as I. He'd run into my cousin at an amateur car race. They'd gone to summer camp together as kids. "Know any girls?" he asked. We set up the date. He'd drive to Bangor, sixty miles west, and take me out to Miller's for that hamburger. I started to ask him the usual questions, his major, how he liked school, what did he think of Kafka? He cut me short. "I'd better go," he said, then paused. "This *is* a long distance call."

Should I have heeded cheapskate warnings? Should I have been insulted that a long distance of sixty miles and a few extra nickels canceled the equal opportunity to describe *my* major? Not at all. In my family, too, "long distance" denoted as much portentous profligacy as "private jet" or "designer handbag." We called our grandparents in New York and my mother's sister in Arizona at odd hours and only on days when the rates were lowest. We, like my husband, were parsimonious citizens of Maine. Though bighearted and generous to a fault—he sent flowers, reached for restaurant checks—he was careful about the small economies: you'd go five miles out of your way to avoid a toll, you'd wait forever in a line at the post office rather than pay the UPS surcharge on a roll of stamps.

Though our phones now offer more minutes than we can use, though every baseboard in our house sports a stapled tangle of wires and cables that keep us in touch 24/7, it wasn't like that in the beginning of our courtship. Most weekends my husband would hitchhike from New Jersey to Boston where we'd do our homework in the beau parlors my college supplied—both feet on the floor, doors open—for the chaste entertainment of members of the opposite sex. Away from each other, we wrote every day, letters on one single sheet of paper stamped with our respective, single gender college seals. We declared our love in unoriginal roses-are-red-violets-are-blue prose. It was hard to be creative on a daily basis, especially when you had a paper due.

Our daily love letters, our constant communication, our strong connection infuriated his mother and caused, alternately, tirades or terrible silences. She didn't like me, forbid him to see me. On vacation at home, he snuck out to phone booths or called from his job. Was it because we were serious at such a young age? I wondered. Maybe it was Oedipal, I deduced, after a year of intro to psychology. After all, he was the only son born after three much older sisters. I couldn't understand it. I was popular, kind, from a "good" family, a family who adored her son. I tried to win her over. I cooked Julia Child dinners. She didn't show up. "I won't eat under your roof," she scorned. I wasn't pretty enough, she complained. "But you're beautiful," my husband said. I wasn't rich enough, she stated. "She has rotten values," my husband said. When he called to tell her he'd proposed, she slammed down the phone. When my mother dialed long distance from Bangor to Skowhegan to express congratulations and delight, she hung up on her, too.

She scowled through our wedding of five invited guests. "Poor you," whispered my maid of honor. "What a battle-ax." At the tense lunch afterwards, my mother sat at her side and buttered her up. "I can understand how hard it is to marry off your adored only son," my mother confided traitorously. My husband's mother turned to me. "Maybe if you're anything like your mother, I'll start to like you," she allowed. I guess I never measured up, no matter how hard I tried. She took away our car, threatened to withhold my husband's law school tuition. My husband's father would call us from phone booths to apologize for his passive role as accomplice in her irrational acts. " I can't help it," he'd excuse. "She's making my life a living hell."

She died two years after our wedding. At the funeral, her eulogy was minimal: she had four children, she kept a tidy house, she read the newspaper every day.

Though long dead, she hasn't disappeared. The fallout takes us by surprise. My husband, a lawyer, advises his clients never to say a word of criticism about the significant others of their children. Never ever, he emphasizes. Sometimes when we have a fight, his jaw takes on an intimidating jut. *You look just like your mother* pops out of my mouth. Cruel, uncalled for and below the belt. If only she could see us now: our strong longtime marriage, our terrific kids, our good citizenship. But when we look back on our early courtship and marriage, we do some editing, deleting her like the excised black sheep in the family album. We pick up the phone and call our kids. These days we never hesitate—whether they're in Japan, England, Utah, New York, or a half-mile away in Harvard Square. And then we laugh. Remember when we were in college, we prompt each other.

Back then, we devised what we thought were ingenious ways to fool Ma Bell. Because my husband's college quarters were a way station for roommates, visitors, and friends,

I'd call person-to-person. If he answered, he'd still reply that the party in question was not in. Then I'd know to dial right back at the house-to-house rates. For a semi-emergency—he was my precomputer Google on matters of geography or politics—I'd phone collect. He'd refuse the call, then within seconds get back to me. Smitten by subterfuge, we developed more elaborate ruses. Here's my excuse: I was a college English major newly sprung from Maine into a world of Bohemian black stockings, a beret whose jaunty angle I now cringe to remember, and a bunch of quotes cribbed from the Cavalier poets. Our preordained signals became our personal Enigma machine. I called collect from Richard Lovelace. He called person-to-person for Woodrow Wilson. We were insufferable. When his thesis on India won honors, it was Pulitzer Nehru on the end of the line. When I got an A- in my Shakespeare course, Anne Marie Hathaway waited for the "not there" response. Those telephone operators, actual living breathing people, let all our coded calls fly across the wires with nary a gulp of suspicion in their modulated, professionally helpful voices.

Until one day, unrepentant of my felonious conduct but feeling flush and in need of instant gratification, I dialed person-to-person for Howard Medwed. The operator hesitated. I repeated both names, enunciated carefully. I spelled Medwed, sounding out each letter of its two syllables. "Med. Wed." "Please wait," I was told. After a burst of static and some whispering, I heard the operator announce to her colleague. "It's a trick. I know it's a trick." "What do you mean?" the other voice asked. "Howard Medwed," she repeated. "Get it? Meet you Wednesday."

I wish I could say, to come full circle, that two of our favorite phone calls happened on a Wednesday. Alas, I don't remember the date, only the joy of each call. "She said yes," announced our older boy. Four years later, our younger repeated the same words. We clutched the phone. We waltzed it, cordless, around our living room. Two lovely sons. Two beloved daughters-in-law. Not Anne Marie Hathaway, but Anne Pauline Hathaway. A+.

Mameve Medwed

Photo by Debi Milligan

MAMEVE MEDWED is the author of *Mail*, *Host Family*, *The End of an Error*, *How Elizabeth Barrett Browning Saved My Life*, and *Of Men and Their Mothers*. Her stories, essays, and reviews have appeared in many publications including the *Missouri Review*, *Redbook*, the *Boston Globe*, *Yankee*, *Playgirl*, the *Washington Post*, and *Newsday*. Born in Maine, she and her husband have two sons and live in Cambridge, Massachusetts.